THE REDEMPTION OF EBENEZER SCROOGE

By

Robin B. Howard

First Edition, 2021.

ISBN: 978-1-7345908-3-8 (Paperback)
ISBN: 978-1-7345908-2-1 (Ebook)

UMBETHINK PUBLISHING LLC
5416 Big Bend Drive
Fort Worth, Texas 76137
www.umbethink.com

Introduction

First published in 1843, 177 years have passed since Mr. Dickens blessed our world with his novella *Charles Dicken's A Christmas Carol* and has always been a personal favorite during the holidays. Over the decades, I've also enjoyed the many movie variations of this timeless classic. Each, providing a different perspective of the characters, and how they interacted with each other.

This story is based on Mr. Dicken's story and characters and adds my love of androids, robots, and technology. My version is loosely based on the original; this is intentional.

We will take a trip five-hundred years into the future. A time when the world has changed; a time not necessarily better. A world where mankind's problems still exist, and people continue to fear what they don't understand.

The Author

Table of Contents

1 – Marley's Demise

Humankind invents, then, in turn, destroys what they invent. They do this out of fear of the unknown or of the belief they've lost control. In the mid twenty-second century, a mishap resulted in the destruction of one such invention. For humans, this crisis was both alarming and, in their words, out-of-control. Laws were passed, and punishment dispensed for anyone in possession of this particular mechanical device. Society presumed they had resolved the crisis.

Or so they believed…

Ebenezer Scrooge III would be described by most to be a man of above average height, well-groomed, and of stylish fashion. A man people gawked and pointed at when he chose to appear in public. However, not for the reason one might think. The word handsome understated his physical features. He found most distressing the frequent flirtations and sexual advances from both sexes. He found this annoying reaction to his physical presence rather disruptive and unproductive. Besides, any adverse public attention threatened his personal safety. He found using his innate wit and charm usually got him out of these awkward situations with no harm done.

However, today he found himself alone; or would soon enough. He stood silently; arms crossed. Calm of mind, Ebenezer Scrooge reflected on how this unidentified anomaly would transpire. This day had been looming ominously for some time; unfortunately, it had finally arrived. Mentally noting the date as December 24, 2338, he became agitated at the abrupt realization this particular day held for him personally. Annoyed with the thought, he desired for this—thing to be over and done with. His mental state on this matter twisted into an egotistical one. His thoughts shifted to a list of other tasks better served than being here. But here he was. Could curiosity be compelling him to stay, or some odd form of loyalty to a long affiliation? Curiosity, he stubbornly decided. Countless years had passed since personally observing the ending of another's existence; he found expiring a rather inconvenient and slow process. He detected no perceivable emotions, a normal response for his character. Anyway, he had meticulously designed a recovery strategy for this precise event. The event? Scrooge, being well aware of how Jacob Marley would end.

Jacob Marley's short and stocky body lay on a hard stainless-steel table, with Ebenezer towering over him in the last moments of existence. Marley didn't move, nor did he exhibit any further signs of animation. Scrooge gazed down indifferently at his soon to be former business partner and apathetically queried the nearest attendant: "Have you completed preparations as I have instructed?" His matter-of-fact tone made obvious his patience had finally dissolved. He hastily concluded his physical presence was no longer necessary.

The attendant, a silvery-blue metallic skinned and mostly proportional human-like medical robot, paused, and in its preset soothingly toned voice said: "Yes, Sir, everything is in order per your instructions." Several others of these robot models continued to move about the room, tending to their specific duties regarding their lone patient.

"Very well," Scrooge said. "Message me when the procedure is complete." Scrooge, not waiting for the robot's reply, brusquely turned to leave. Unexpectedly, the body known as Marley abruptly spoke.

"Eb-Eb-Ebenezer," he stuttered in a whispered tone, the voice barely audible above the hums, beeps and commotions of medical and mechanical devices throughout the room. Scrooge paused, remarkably he clearly discerned the light whisper through the noise. Scrooge turned back around to the table, and simply replied: "Yes, what do you need, Jacob?"

Jacob Marley's dark and nearly lifeless eyes focused onto Scrooge's deep set blue eyes. "W-W-We were wrong," stuttered Marley.

Scrooge, puzzled at the statement, remained unfazed. "What *are* you going on about Jacob?" simultaneously waving away the medical robot rushing to the aid of its patient. "What do you mean by we were wrong?"

Jacob Marley, now clearly struggling to speak, repeated slowly and with great difficulty: "We… w-w-were… w-w-w-wrong." His voice trailed off pitifully, his head slumped to one side; his eyes but a narrow slit as he exerted himself to do even this.

Scrooge moved closer to his old partner, and in a reactive gesture placed a hand on Marley's shoulder. Scrooge's hands were rather large with long thin fingers, noticeable against the much smaller Marley. Scrooge, expressionless, shook his head slowly.

"Jacob, I am not following the logic regarding your statement."

Scrooge then added calmly: "We have done nothing wrong, and certainly you have done nothing wrong, and *we* have always operated our businesses and affairs in strict accordance with society's laws if that's what is troubling you."

Jacob Marley feebly tried to shake his head and attempted to speak again, the effort resulting in an unintelligible warbling sound. His eyelids began making rapid and unsynchronized spasmodic movements.

Scrooge, in an apparent surge of unease, said: "You have been a good business partner Jacob," but then added factually, "however, as predicted by our analyses, your end has finally arrived. There isn't anything more I can do."

With this candid statement, he nodded at the medical robot, turned, and casually strolled out of the room; with nary a glance or further thought of Jacob Marley.

Ebenezer Scrooge III was Executive-in-Charge at MSAI, a company specializing in the creation of artificially intelligent robots. Their Entitlement series of robots was highly profitable. The sales of these models, designed to aid in the physical well-being of humans, were best sellers. Producing robots after the global purge of the more human-like android models in the mid twenty-second century was challenging. Following the purge, humans struggled to accept any form of robots back into their society. To offset the stigma robots spawned, laws required them to be visually unique, outfitted with no-harm safeguards, and restricted to singular duties. He knew the medical robots tending to Jacob Marley were incapable of executing orders endangering their patient's well-being. Any human command meant to distract or delay treatment was ignored. The injurious attempt immediately reported to a human doctor. Each robotic series was regulated by strict government policies implemented following those turbulent humanoid years. Robotic owners violating regulations were swiftly disconnected from society; and disciplined through the current but controversial social network justice system. In Scrooge's opinion, these repressive policies were a direct result of a global society unable to overcome fear and hatred toward robots; even after two-hundred-and-fifty years of contact.

Driven by unfounded anxiety and fear, the governments of Earth established the Global Robotic Oversight Commission to enforce these regulations. Under pressure of further government control, Scrooge and Marley agreed MSAI would fund and headquarters this oversight committee within the factory's robotics department. He and Marley believed having the committee nearby gave them an advantage in minimizing bothersome interference. Scrooge often found this human inflexibility and interference annoying, as costs soared at an absurd rate. This societal nonsense driving a constant need for ever more operating revenue.

Running the factory had been Scrooge's exclusive responsibility; up to now. Their primary crypto currency business, the United Planetary Crypto Fund, or UPCF, was the parent company of MSAI. Jacob Marley had been Executive-in-Charge of UPCF until his demise. Now he was gone, Scrooge found the disruption worrying for personal reasons. UPCF's financial algorithms, server farm designs, and energy acquisition policies had been automated over the years. However, all system adjustments, additional acquisitions, or factory expansions had been Marley's concern. Scrooge found the obligation of absorbing Marley's tasks for the crypto business quite demanding. And, he was convinced, incompatible with his primary function. Although expert in robotics and artificial intelligence design, his current knowledge regarding financials and statistical analyses was woefully lacking. He had always found the daily updates regarding UPCF secondary to his own affairs. He was careful not to commit unnecessary financial statistics to memory and expected crypto currency technical details to be Marley's problem. Ostensibly upon reflection, he may not have been so meticulous as he first thought on after-Marley strategies.

UPCF had been the first company he and Marley had started, with MSAI incorporated later as their wealth and influence grew. UPCF had filled the void created by the global collapse of the outdated paper, coin, and precious metal based banking model. The collapse had started simply enough. Bickering government officials, greed, corruption, out-of-control inflation, and weakened financial relations between countries; typical issues of the era. Likewise, investor panic was fostered by seriously flawed speculation by seriously flawed speculators. Coupled with deliberate misleading media propaganda, the collapse was unavoidable. Seizing on the opportunity during this global crisis, UPCF quickly became the new universal online standard of all currency and money matters. Moreover, their crypto currency business touched nearly every financial transaction existing in today's society. Exclusively, UPCF managed the entirety of the Planetary Gross National Product; making UPCF both powerful and despised.

Both companies co-existed in one expansive factory. The factory's layout was simplistic but efficient. Two large rectangular structures separated in the middle by an executive circular tower. One wing was dedicated to administration and sales, the other for the robotics program; with both sides housing the crypto currency server farm. UPCF also maintained remote facilities throughout the world to handle local needs, but main control was managed at the factory. Combined, the two wings of the factory contained the largest square footage ever created by mankind at a single location.

The factory was deceptive to anyone merely observing the outwardly unassuming complex. Although only five stories high, with the tower adding ten more, what was not visible was astounding. The factory sunk into the earth in some areas to one hundred stories deep. This depth provided free cooling for hot running servers, security against external threats, and low radiation areas for delicate research.

The executive tower contained the monitoring and control centers to coordinate between administrative and technical services. MSAI served as executive quarters for Ebenezer Scrooge and other senior executives of both companies. The central tower was designed with five-hundred mini-apartments for use by commission officials, customers, scientists, and executives. These amenities only provided due to the factory's rural location and the beneficial write-offs for taxing purposes.

The exterior entrance of the factory with mature trees and beautifully manicured landscaping was quite exquisite and pleasing to the eye. Marley had never paid much attention to aesthetics; however, Scrooge insisted the grounds be kept to his personal standards. A habit of luxury he had acquired in his earlier years. Ebenezer Scrooge was acutely aware that people were astounded by the factory's aesthetics. Potential customers arriving at the factory were greeted by the building's futuristic façade. Mentally enticing, the factory radiated prominence of power and influence. This mind trick— Scrooge's phraseology—was good for sales; and Jacob reluctantly agreed to fund the indulgence.

Inside the factory was a different matter entirely. Here, Marley had insisted on frugality to offset—as he asserted—out-of-control costs. As a compromise, the sections of the factory dedicated to administration and sales used aged and long ago tax-deducted furniture and fixtures. This wing was dull and unexceptional. The only redeeming quality was the natural light radiating through floor-to-ceiling windows around the topside exterior walls. A delicacy for those lucky enough to be assigned an office above ground. Deeper in the depths, however, workers endured obsolete lighting, crowded office areas, and ever shifting temperatures. Being assigned to a lower level on this side of the factory was deflating, and many felt it a form of punishment; for the sole act of coming to work. The conditions ever worsening as square footage was snatched up during expansions. Not that Scrooge or Marley ever cared, but cleaning and maintenance robots kept these surroundings environmentally healthy for laborers; but only up to the point the law required.

However, for the remainder of the factory, Marley and Scrooge invested heavily in technology and infrastructure. These expenditures were deemed necessary to sustain their cutting-edge robotics program, MSAI's supercomputer, and most importantly, their ever-expanding crypto currency server farm. In these premier areas of the factory, employees found state-of-the-art offices, labs, equipment, power systems, and robotic manufacturing facilities. Using advanced architectural design methods, the interior of this wing was futuristic and high-tech in comparison. The differences in office comfort regularly pitted employees against each other in an us versus them defiance. Though these disparities were well known, Marley and Scrooge had logically analyzed the stark differences between employee amenities and had concluded: Administration personnel were easily replaceable, scientists were not.

Over time, Marley and Scrooge became the planet's wealthiest and most influential businessmen. With fortune and fame, they found a necessity in taking extraordinary measures to protect their wealth and privacy from public and government meddling. Ebenezer had wisely devised a strategy early in the development of UPCF as an insurance policy of sorts.

As Ebenezer stepped off the lift, he was relieved to be back in his office. Although, upon seeing Marley's empty desk, his mind inexplicably activated an ancient memory. *The* memory responsible for guiding his and Jacob's activities to this day.

"Jacob, logically we must assume that future governments, or other disreputable entities, will inevitably attempt to acquire our assets by leveraging; or by force."

"Yes, I suppose you're correct. After all, humans are quite capable of such action," Marley had replied.

"Furthermore, we still have our most significant issue to resolve. We will find difficulty in concealing ourselves adequately soon enough," Scrooge had added.

Marley tilted his head quizzically and had said: "So, I am detecting you've devised a resolution for both?" Scrooge nodded, and without another word between them Marley had understood.

Ebenezer now realized he was mistaken about curiosity keeping him at Marley's side today. It wasn't even about his long affiliation with Marley; selfishly, he was obsessed with his own self-preservation.

Scrooge and Marley's office and personal quarters were isolated from other areas of the factory. This secure and hardened space was accessible by the lift or through a concealed door; leading to their personal conference room. The door, although deliberately placed, had never been opened. Everything needed was available in this self-imposed isolation. Supplies were shuttled up via a secret service lift operated by modified service robots. These particular robots had a unique feature hard-wired into their cerebral units by Ebenezer Scrooge. No human command could compel such a robot to reveal the whereabouts of his office. Many a human had tried, all had failed. Simple inquiries were diverted politely, whereas strongly phrased commands were not tolerated. What these antagonists received for their efforts was a financial seizure by UPCF; for one self-destructed cerebral unit.

With Marley now gone, only Scrooge and his robots knew the exact location. His personal office consisted of an open floor plan with two privacy doors leading to identical studios. Up to today, one door had led to Marley's personal studio; now empty and foreboding. Marley's room was no longer of any interest to Scrooge. The robotic cleaning crew would continue to keep the empty quarters clean, as they always had. *I've lost most of the day already. But yet I continue to be forced in facing facts and wonder...how much longer do I have left before being compromised as Jacob was,* Scrooge thought.

Scrooge and Marley's quarters were windowless, and lighting was usually kept low, with a red illuminance accentuating the technologies found in the mirrored setup they had shared. Along the top of most interior walls throughout the factory, including here, ran Transducer Sensor Strips, or TSS, an advanced tachyon-quantum hybrid technology providing faster than light data transmission for company systems and communications. This one-of-a-kind technology was invented by MSAI's own Lead Scientist. The factory possessed the only one in the world. With the efficiency realized from TSS, Scrooge took the efficiency gain as an opportunity, and authorized a sizeable reduction of administrative staff. Jacob had been too unstable to make the decision, and Scrooge had no problem in giving the orders.

Scrooge ambled across the room from the lift and lowered his tall frame down into his chair. His control desk was modern and sleek. A metallic half-moon-like appendage connected the floor to an oval and indented hazily frosted polymer top. Integrated with fluorescent blue-proton projected gauges, charts, alert panels, and touchscreens, his desk offered him complete access and ultimate control of his company's systems. This desk somehow comforted him, making him feel whole again after the morning's unpleasantries. Sitting here returned the sense of control he had yearned for while powerlessly watching Marley perish.

Scrooge calmly announced in his usual modulated tone: "Computer, activate main displays."

Immediately, a stream of real-time financial data, statistics, and systems status information snapped to life on three-dimensional virtual monitors hovering in front of the control desk. A pleasant and husky female voice replied: "Command acknowledged, Mr. Scrooge."

He stood and stepped around to face the virtual monitors where large data sets awaited his assessment. He raised his long arms and began using his hands and fingers to swipe, poke, pinch, and gesture through the live data. To a casual observer, the graceful gestures he made were similar to a maestro conducting a symphony; with data screens replacing the orchestra.

After thoroughly probing through pages and layers of data, he made a few adjustments for maximum system efficiency, then stated: "Computer, deactivate main displays."

"Command acknowledged, Mr. Scrooge," cooed the female voice in response.

Satisfied, he returned to his chair and absently reached for a small sensor and tapped lightly. Promptly, a holographic representation of his Lead Scientist, Doctor Bobby Cratchit, sprang to life on the holo-platform across from the control desk. The waist up fourth-dimensional lifelike image was of a petite, though well-proportioned, young woman around twenty-five years of age. She wore her silky shoulder length medium brown hair in a loose bun tied behind her head. Her delicate and simple features included iridescent light brown eyes projecting energy and intelligence. Her face, narrow with a small, rounded chin and small ears, only highlighted her natural beauty. She had thin brows, a delicate nose, and alluring full lips. Her flawless complexion negated the need for the distraction of cosmetics.

What Scrooge perceived rather than her attractiveness, was of an intellect, though he couldn't resolve how, seemed to be much older than the young woman. He had become normalized to the outline of the antigrav medical chair she sat in behind her desk. He had never cared to quiz her on why she was restricted to such a device in this age of medicine and robotics. In fact, he found the thought no more interesting than the robot in the next room cleaning his ex-partners quarters.

"Dr. Cratchit," he began. "I need you to form a team consisting of crypto design scientists and engineers." Scrooge's facial expression remained stolid as he outlined his instructions.

"All care should be taken to ensure this team remains covert. At your direction, they will immediately begin fully reverse-engineering and documenting our crypto company algorithms, server designs, acquisitions, and power consumption practices.

"You have priority authorization to access any of Mr. Marley's files you may need to complete this task. I will, of course, provide appropriate guidance. May you require assistance."

In another office within the scientific wing of the factory, Bobbie, or Bob to her friends, viewed her superior on the holo-platform across her desk. The man who suddenly sprang up in front of her hadn't startled her. His sudden arrivals occurred multiple times daily. Besides, the holographic modeler provided a pre-activation alert tone. Her boss only communicated over hologram. Anyone granted an audience with Mr. Scrooge or Mr. Marley was via this platform.

The obsolete three-dimensional holo-system clunking along when she first arrived had been upgraded to interface with her new TSS system in a fourth-dimensional format. As customary, the superior technology was provided only to the scientific wing and a few conference rooms in the antiquated administrative wing. There were also holo-platforms installed in key locations around the globe. At these locations, business could be conducted efficiently with factory personnel. Using the rem-lo's, as they were called, avoided archaic and pointless travel. The updated system streamed a quite sophisticated and realistic representation of the individual. This realism took some getting used to at first, and the man she was now looking at seemed real enough to reach out and touch. A distinguished looking man of his mid to late sixty's, Mr. Scrooge had a full head of once dirty blonde hair, now splashed in white; especially around the temples. Mr. Scrooge's appearance always impressed upon her a man who could have been, in another life, a college professor or other scholarly fellow. She also thought he had aged well; in her humble opinion.

Interestingly, she had never met her boss in person, nor had she ever seen him standing up. Impossible to gauge his height, nevertheless, by what she could see, he appeared to be in good physical shape. His business attire was age appropriate, yet looked to be half a decade behind the current style. Scrooge's face was thin, his eyes blue and deep set. His lips neither thick nor thin, but somewhere in between. His appearance conveyed an air of wisdom and perpetual pragmatism. A handsome older specimen, she mused, although she knew they at times could have their differences; like now.

"Mr. Scrooge, a new project would be quite impossible," she answered in a silvery but firm tone, her tied back hair swaying gently as she shook her head. "I am not an expert in crypto currency algorithms, methodology, or code layouts and I—"

Scrooge clipped her off rudely, as was his way, and bluntly stated: "Dr. Cratchit! Are you or are you not Lead Scientist of this institute? An authority in the field of computer technology, cybernetics, and engineering?"

"You know I am, Mr. Scrooge," she retorted defensively. "You are also quite aware I am at a critical point in my research—"

"Doctor!" he said forcefully, with an unexpected air of weariness. "As of today, you are the most qualified scientist we have at this institute. I expect you to remain flexible until such time I can determine the best path forward. If you don't feel you can handle the additional responsibilities, I will begin my search for someone who can display proper loyalty to this institute."

"I don't understand," she said abruptly, one thinly groomed eyebrow suddenly lifting. "What do you mean—as of today?" She had become quite adept at sifting through his tirades to isolate his intended message, and she had correctly plucked the key point from his current temperament.

Ebenezer Scrooge III looking past Bob Cratchit as though staring into a vast emptiness, replied unemotionally and factually: "Doctor, Jacob Marley is dead." And at this shocking declaration, his holograph tersely switched off. Bob Cratchit stared uncomfortably at the empty holo-platform. Her mind racing through questions about Mr. Marley; and the enormous efforts that lay ahead.

Scrooge sat unmoving and silent at his desk when a message alert flashed on his console. He glanced at the monitor impulsively. The medical robot was announcing completion of the requirements he had ordered. However, the message request had only been meant to be a formality. Scrooge knew the exact moment—down to the millisecond—of Jacob Marley's demise. He had sensed the ending of the familiar connection.

"Computer," he said sullenly. "Assign all future meetings and calls to my holograms until further notice," he paused, then added quickly, "unless Dr. Cratchit calls. I will inform you on the course of action."

"Command acknowledged, Mr. Scrooge."

Ebenezer Scrooge III, now the wealthiest and most isolated being on Earth, mentally activated his neural TSS connection and began reviewing source code. For the first time in his life, time had a meaning.

2 – The Dark Place

Blackness. A despondency enveloping and consuming to your core. So dark. Jacob Marley suddenly became aware in this gloominess and immediately thought *I must have optic failure.* But no matter how many times he tried to diagnose and reboot his optics subroutine to correct the condition, he could not overcome the malfunction. He could not sense anyone or anything around him. He spoke out calmly: "Is there anyone there? I seem to have lost visual optics." Nothing. No sounds reached his audio processor. As a matter-of-fact, he quickly diagnosed he detected no sensations at all.

"What is this?" he spoke aloud. At least he believed he spoke aloud. He tried to move, or at least determine his physical condition. Was he laying, sitting, or standing? Nothing. He had no sensory input whatsoever. He had his mind, but no sensation of a physical body. This situation was beginning to cause him unease; an emotion he believed himself incapable of.

Marley focused for a moment, stepping down a diagnostic list of self-corrective actions he could attempt himself. After none of these resulted in any change, he activated his neural TSS subroutine. *Ebenezer?* He thought. For once the TSS connection between him and Scrooge was activated, their interaction was completely nonverbal. *Ebenezer, are you online?* Nothing. *What was going on? This is quite abnormal,* he thought. *How is this possible? Did Ebenezer not detect the TSS connection alert? If I am malfunctioning, I should have system failure indicators and alarm analyzation data, but I detect none.* Marley, uncharacteristically, murmured: "How odd."

A pinprick of light!

A rapid flicker, he was quite sure. *Unexpected! I didn't sense light at the optic level* he thought. Then another flicker, followed by several others. They strangely reminded him of flash patterns he'd seen for swarms of summertime fireflies. The winged beetles were found in abundance near the factory at woodlands edge. Marley, clearly intrigued and realizing he was helpless regarding his physical difficulties, instead focused on these odd flickers of light. Inexplicably, they appeared to be moving toward him; or, was he moving toward them? "How very odd indeed," he said curiously.

3 – A Tough Nut to Crack

In a conference room located somewhere within the administrative wing of the factory, two men, one portly and the other slim, sat quietly at the long and ancient conference table occupying the room. The portly fellow rubbed his immense belly in small circular motions with one hand, while the slim man fiddled and rubbed both his hands together anxiously. The room was well stocked with beverages and snacks from a serve yourself station. The two men appeared disillusioned, gazing about the room disbelievingly. The pair had been on a waiting list for nearly two years for a meeting with the co-EIC's of UPCF/MSAI, and they were well versed regarding the company's affluence and power. What they had not expected when setting up the meeting was being submitted to an eyesore like this.

The conference room was like something from a bygone era. The tabletop was worn and scratched from decades of wear and tear. The conference chairs were threadbare and stained from years of friction and spills. An odd and slightly unpleasant odor hung thickly in the air. There were aged and antique tubed monitors mounted in the corners of the room. These relics extended from the ceiling by old-fashioned steel brackets and bolts. Now, these monitors were dark, but for one. A somewhat hazy and out-of-focus UPCF logo moved lazily around the screen. They noticed a slightly glowing strip on the wall, obviously the most modern item in the room. At one area of the table, they puzzled at a small modern-day platform sitting slightly lower than the tabletop height. They had been instructed by the young man escorting them from the lobby to sit in the specific chairs they now occupied. In fact, the young man, upon noticing the organization being represented, had taken it upon himself to move them here rather than the high-tech conference room originally reserved.

Their meeting was scheduled for 11:45 a.m., however, they had arrived quite early, hoping to impress their hosts. Portly man, wandering over to the self-serve station, helped himself to a handful of free snacks and a large coffee with plenty of sugar.

As he reseated himself, he and the chair both groaning at his girth, glanced at his partner and quipped: "What do think they'll be like?"

Slim man replied casually: "If they are anything like I've been led to believe, they will be tough nuts to crack. But I'm sure together we can handle them quite proficiently."

Portly man simply grunted and began munching another snack, crumbs tumbling onto his shirt as he absently brushed them off onto the floor.

At exactly 11:45 a.m. to the second, Scrooge's lifelike holographic image materialized at the platform positioned across the table. At his abrupt appearance, both men reacted swiftly. The portly man terrified yelped: "Great heavens!" Instinctively pushing back away from the conference table, nearly flipping his overburdened chair over in the process. Chunks of unchewed snack disgustedly ejected from his mouth.

The slim fellow better controlled his panic; however, he impulsively brought his right hand up to his chest as though he had suffered a heart attack. His left hand shot to his mouth to cover the gaping hole produced when his jaw dropped.

Scrooge, unmoved by this display of pandemonium, simply stated in a smooth and business-like pitch: "Good day gentlemen, what brings you to our factory today? A new robotic model? A financial contract or paid financial advice?"

Struggling to regain his composure, the portly man croaked shakenly: "Uh, um, do I have the pleasure of Mr. Scrooge or Mr. Marley?" He then interjected enquiringly, "We were under the impression we would meet both of you gentlemen…together."

Slim man added hastily: "Yes, we have been looking forward to today for some time."

Scrooge, his holographic eyes moving from one man to the other, said: "It's not important. Although, if revealing myself moves this meeting forward quickly, I am Scrooge. Mr. Marley has been deceased these past seven years."

Slim man, instinctively sensing the unanticipated opportunity, said somberly: "We are sincerely sorry for your loss, Mr. Scrooge, we were not aware of your friends passing. However, we are sure Mr. Marley was a good hearted and generous individual." His eyes quickly darted toward his partner to ensure he, too, understood the new development.

Scrooge, unmoved by the display of feigned sympathy, stated: "Gentlemen, I am a busy man and these theatrics only waste my time. State your business efficiently if you will. I have many important matters needing my attention."

Portly man now more recovered, said in a slightly wheezy tone: "We," pointing between his partner and himself, "represent the Solace Charity Foundation, you may have heard of us, and we are here," a slight dramatic pause, "to solicit your generosity for a onetime, or as others have been so persuaded, a more desirable long-term financial donation. For those who are in great need of assistance, you understand."

Scrooge, now grasping the nature of the subject matter, replied sarcastically: "Therefore, I can take away from your gibberish, the two of you are not here to solicit my business services?"

He paused a moment as if mentally switching directions, his tone turning ominous. "Then my question to you is by what right have you to come here, extort my time, and attempt to solicit funds I, sirs, have earned, but you and those you represent have not?"

Slim man, sensing the alteration in tone, spoke up: "Mr. Scrooge, we mean no disrespect. Nevertheless, our sole business requires us to visit corporations such as yours. We endeavor to raise funds, which directly support a number of charities operating all over the globe."

In a cunning maneuver meant to salvage the situation, he slickly added: "It is quite fortunate for us, our meeting fortuitously coincides with the Christmas season. The time of year when human suffering is most intensified. We could have faith your ex-partner Mr. Marley would agree with us on this, no?"

"Christmas season!" Scrooge exploded. "What does such a meaningless time of the year have to do with you trying to get your hands into my pockets?"

Portly man, clearly not expecting such a response, breathed deeply and interjected for his dumbfounded partner: "Mr. Scrooge, we can understand if your personal prerogative isn't to recognize a Christmas season. However, you must know for millions this remains a traditional and deeply spiritual time going back thousands of years. And," he added in a lower tone, "if you prefer, your gift can remain…anonymous."

Slim man, his face flushed, said in an evenly practiced tone refined over many years: "It is at this time of the year we try to help put a little more food on a poor family's table, maybe a small gift under an underprivileged family's holiday tree." He was careful to avoid using the apparently offensive word 'Christmas'.

Scrooge's facial expression hadn't changed in the slightest during this back and forth.

"Are you gentlemen aware of the billions in funds I must flitter away to the various planetary governments as extortion payments each year under the pretense of taxes and fines?"

Scrooge then began to sternly lecture the two visitors. "Do these billions not support the entitlement programs, so-called safety nets, and infrastructure existing to keep these—people alive?" His holographic hand gestured in a backhanded fashion to emphasize his frustration.

"Isn't this coddling provided at my expense enough! Whereas, I get nothing of value in return but an attempted shakedown from 'ad hoc' charities?"

Slim man, visually uneasy, appealed to Scrooge: "These programs you speak of care for bare essentials, they provide no comfort for their souls. Nor do they allow them a feeling of normalcy; unlike those better off than themselves. And as for what you get in return, if I may suggest, is a feeling of goodwill for your fellow man, your community, and society in general."

"Bah!" Scrooge's hologram spit out venomously. "Allow them to feel normal? Feeling of goodwill? What happened to needs versus wants, gentlemen? The taxes I hitherto referred adequately handle basic needs. I have no obligation or wish to provide 'wants' to society's ignorant and lethargic populace that habitually, and quite forcefully, expect a free ride on the backs of those putting in the effort to earn their wants."

Scrooge, his eyes now narrowly focused on both men, said: "MSAI creates and sells hundreds of various models of entitlement service robots to planetary governments. These robots, are specifically designed to ease the suffering you are so feebly peddling."

He continued the tirade, his tenor now one of a man in-charge: "Our entitlement series robots aid any human who approaches seeking help. Their design *compels* them to contact the proper authorities. The robot then physically protects these individuals until they can be delivered to the nearest community entitlement center."

Portly man, now leaning back in the chair, a look of absolute disgust on his face, his eyes red and wet, his face flushed with anger, howled: "But many of those people are put into positions worse than death; humiliated, locked into compounds like animals. Forced to wear obedience collars to be punished through what can only be termed as torture. How can you not care! How can you sit there," furiously pointing at Scrooge's holographic representation, "or wherever you are, be so dead inside as to not care about humanities afflictions?"

Scrooge responded emotionlessly: "Sir, the whole of humanity is of absolutely no concern to me unless they are purchasing my products and services."

His final statement to the stunned men was delivered sneeringly: "You'll understand I, as you earlier stated, am not a nut you can crack. Good day gentlemen!" Scrooge's image dissolved off the holo-platform as the young man who escorted them into the meeting room appeared in the doorway. He politely stated: "Gentlemen, if you will follow me I'll show you out."

Later in the evening, after a daylong technical session with Dr. Cratchit, Scrooge sat in his office and mentally activated his neural TSS connection. He thought the command which downloaded the day's recorded meetings held by his holographic persona into his cerebral memory. Relatedly, once the download was complete, he would efficiently analyze and commit relevant data to memory. At his age, active memory management was imperative, meaning not everything he had ever saw or learned could stay in his mind indefinitely. Each memory fragment was flagged with an expiration date for easier clean-up. He knew his holographs could handle most situations without his direct intervention. Nevertheless, in reviewing today's meetings, he had come across a contentious one managed by holo-427. He realized he would need to adjust the temperament harshness code for this hologram. He also made a mental note to send his assistant Bradley a complimentary note; on his last minute choice of meeting rooms. The men's words about human suffering intuitively resonated deep within his mind, but he registered no required ethical action; no physical harm had occurred. The remainder of the meetings hadn't exposed anything mind-worthy. Consequently, he assembled and compressed expired and unnecessary data and discarded the information into the cloud for permanent storage or later retrieval.

4 – The Toledo Project

Dr. Bob Cratchit sat at her desk, her small delicate hands resting quietly on her lap, her mind deep in thought. Her attention still focused acutely on the recently completed daylong meeting with Mr. Scrooge. Cratchit was pleased at the end of the day. All seemed to have gone well with the boss; a rare day indeed. Mr. Scrooge had absent-mindedly cited this year, 2345, being the one-hundredth anniversary of UPCF. This made her realize seven years had passed since she had assumed leadership of the crypto currency division. Their clandestine work on decompiling and understanding the minutiae of the company's financial business had been complete for over a year. Mr. Scrooge, she concluded, clearly had overlooked the fact he had made her acting EIC under the guise of finding 'the best path forward'. Over the years, he had not taken action to make her position permanent, nor had he seriously considered relieving her of the extra duty. This perpetual limbo was perplexing at times, but the work was still rewarding. Hence, she didn't complain; not too much, anyway. Besides, she had noted a trend of forgetfulness from Mr. Scrooge now she interfaced with him so often. But she presumed this to be due to his advanced age. She would at some point gently address the disparity, and hope he didn't spiral into one of his lectures or rants.

In those seven years, she had also learned what a mathematical and computer coding genius Jacob Marley had been. The intricacies of his formulas and algorithms were astounding, even to her scientific intellect. The level of transactional autonomy he achieved negating the need for human involvement was in a word, magnificent. Although her teams' efforts had originally been focused on reverse-engineering the system and not profit gain, Mr. Scrooge had recently begun ratcheting up expectations for incremental profit increases. *No good deed goes unpunished, as the saying goes,* she dryly thought. Today, mercifully, she was spared the extra serving of anxiety, and minimal time had been spent on the crypto business. She was relieved they focused more on one of her latest projects.

It had been two weeks since Mr. Scrooge had disclosed his extraordinary assignment. He had addressed her smoothly, his tone relaxed with none of his usual austerity. "Doctor," he said, "I have—let's call it—a gift for you."

Intrigued, she had quipped back friskily: "Mr. Scrooge, you have my utmost attention."

Scrooge, wearing the slimmest of grins had replied: "I believe this particular project will be more liking to your skill set." Cratchit, rather deflated thought: *Another project? I should have known. Only this man would conceive more work to be a gift.*

He continued.

"Following this discussion, please proceed down to Lab-5 where you will find a non-functioning android. The unit seemingly originated from the General Automaton and Robotics Corporation of Toledo, Ohio. Commonly referred to as a— GAR-C series model, I believe?"

Bob Cratchit's body language and mood changed instantly. She exclaimed excitedly: "General Automaton and Robotics! But how?" She found herself having difficulty processing this astounding news. She breathlessly stated: "If true, that means the unit could be over two-hundred years old."

"Two-hundred-twenty-five, to be precise, Doctor," Scrooge stated.

Dr. Cratchit, catching herself mid-excitement, said hesitantly: "Mr. Scrooge, how is this possible? All GAR-C model androids were supposedly recalled and destroyed after they were made illegal to own over a century ago."

Her youthful face scrunched up slightly as though forcing herself to remember. "If I recall my history, when planetary governments issued the return to factory order, all GAR-C units were compelled to obey. The return signal assumedly triggered a failsafe device in the android's cerebral unit in response to an unpredicted human safety concern."

"Let me only say at this time I have connections," Mr. Scrooge responded; a hint of conspiracy creeping into his voice.

"Sir, as I also recall, possessing one of these androids remains a felony. What if we are discovered?"

"We won't be, Doctor. I assure you all proper precautions and security measures have been taken. Besides, at the end of this project, the unit will, theoretically at least, be destroyed.

"However, the most important question is, can I trust you?"

"Trust me?" Cratchit said bewilderedly.

"Doctor, the very fact that I have shared this information puts us both in a perilous position. All I ask is that you hear me out before committing yourself to a decision."

"And what decision would that be?" she said.

"To join me or turn me in to the authorities, of course."

After several hours of often intense debate, she had cautiously agreed to the project and project goals. Mr. Scrooge had been quite convincing when presenting his argument. Following her decision to join him, self-reflection had caused her ample mental distress at breaching societal laws. However, the prospects of researching an actual GAR-C android, despite the risks, were ultimately more compelling. And, on a more personal level, quite advantageous.

Lab-5 lay deep in the underground sub levels of the factory under heavy security. Expecting to find the offline android there alone, she was surprised and rather irritated to discover a stranger already there. She mentally directed her aggravation toward Mr. Scrooge; for already altering their agreement. Obviously, his definition of perilous position and hers differed entirely.

Looking the stranger over, he towered over her at around six and a half feet tall, her own slight frame being restricted to the antigrav chair. He had olive colored skin and a full head of dirty blonde hair. He was tanned and fit. He had a long thin face, long neck, and deep-set blue eyes, giving him a most pleasant appearance. He appeared to be in his early forties, but she couldn't be sure.

"I'm sorry, you are?" she said, her tone defensive.

"Good afternoon, Dr. Cratchit. My name is Doctor John Fezziwig. My specialty is in robotic cerebral systems and early robotic archeology. Mr. Scrooge was quite certain you could use my expertise on this project."

"I'm confused—Dr. Fezziwig—I wasn't aware of anyone else associated with this undertaking."

"I'm sure that was an unintentional oversight on Ebenezer's part," he replied politely.

"So, you know Mr. Scrooge on a personal basis? I assume this by your casual use of his first name."

"Of course, Ebenezer and I are old friends. I am what you might call a personal consultant. I discreetly assist him on several sensitive issues."

"Consulting," she said carefully, "in what area?"

"Mostly in the area of archeology. Ebenezer has always been fascinated with the subject of early automatons. Especially the rise and fall of the GAR-C models. You can appreciate the sensitivity of this particular subject, can't you, Doctor?"

"A Roboticist interested in forbidden robots, yes, I get your point. However, exactly how will ancient archeology be a benefit to this project?" she asked.

"Oh, it's much more than ancient archeology. Take this unit, for instance," Fezziwig motioned easily at the android body lying on the lab table. "I believe that until recently it was fully operational."

"How could you possibly know that?" she replied, astounded.

"Look at his clothing. This apparel was still in fashion within the last decade. Notice they are not torn or threadbare, indicating they were well cared for. The adornments are still attached, not stolen or otherwise removed.

"Also, look at the face and hands. They appear clean and in good condition with no indicators of neglect."

Cratchit, impressed with his quick assessment, countered: "Clothing can be changed, body parts washed."

"Yes, that is true. Nevertheless, I assure you nothing has been tampered with on this unit," he said with assurance.

"How can you be so confident of that statement, Doctor? What if this is a sting operation or trap by a government agency to smear MSAI?"

Fezziwig chuckled warmly: "A dash of paranoia is healthy, Doctor Cratchit, but regarding the unit, I must ask for you to trust me. There are certain facts about the acquisition of the unit you'd be better off not knowing," Fezziwig said calmly.

"Trust you?" she said unbelievably. "I don't even know you. I mean, it's not every day you find a GAR-C android lying around," she said as she pointed at the android. Then realizing what she had said, she blurted out: "Oh, you know what I mean!"

Fezziwig appeared amused at her dilemma. Rather than egg her on further, he mildly replied: "Point taken, Doctor, but let me put your mind at ease. I am well aware of the legality issues concerning this unit. And in all transparency, I have a rather long standing privacy agreement with Ebenezer. I am an expert at covert operations of this type.

"As for my personal morality concerning this android? How may I be of service, Doctor Cratchit?" he said, respectfully bowing his head.

Over the following days, she found Fezziwig to be quite polite, helpful, and his movements were precise and quite graceful. Reluctantly, and against all logic, she was beginning to like this mysterious Dr. John Fezziwig.

The secretive 'Toledo Project' was moving ahead carefully and methodically, as agreed. Most day's Mr. Scrooge would appear occasionally on the holo-platform to watch the autopsy. She found it odd since Fezziwig claimed to be such a close friend, Mr. Scrooge didn't find time to visit the lab. For her to have never met her boss in person, it was a bit of a letdown. As she and Dr. Fezziwig focused on the android's cerebral unit, she absently heard the alert tone sound. Mr. Scrooge's hologram appeared and said: "Doctor Cratchit, I need to borrow you for an issue on the crypto system. Dr. Fezziwig, would you mind stepping out for a few moments?"

"Of course not," Fezziwig replied, "buzz me when you are finished."

After Fezziwig left, Scrooge addressed Cratchit: "Dr. Cratchit, I have observed a few anomalies in the efficiency of the crypto platform. I've sent you a list and will need them addressed as soon as practical."

"Yes, Sir. I'll review the list and get Dr. Shamar and her team on it."

"I'm afraid that won't be acceptable this time," he replied.

"Sir? Am I missing something here?" Cratchit was getting that feeling again.

"What I have sent you are three specific code sections that I need a second opinion on. Your opinion, Doctor. These subroutines are to be considered part of the Toledo Project. They are for your eyes only. You are not to share this request or findings with Dr. Fezziwig. Am I clear on this?"

"Yes, Mr. Scrooge, I understand. However, may I ask what crypto code could have to do with this android?"

"You may ask, Doctor, but at this time you'd be better off not knowing." The phrasing of his answer sounded oddly familiar. Something about how it was worded—a coincidence?

"Will that be all, Mr. Scrooge," she said absently.

"For now. Please ask John to rejoin us for an update on where you two are on the project."

Once Dr. Fezziwig arrived, their attention turned to the undressed android laying out on an autopsy-like stainless steel table. The unit was a familiar sight, being taken apart gradually. Dr. Cratchit had at one time considered covering the body from the neck down due to the android's realism. However, after she came to terms regarding the body as a machine, she had been able to forgo the necessity. Although, the mechanical man's nakedness could still be awkward at times, especially with Dr. Fezziwig and, at times, Mr. Scrooge close by.

Mr. Scrooge began the update and said firmly: "What is the current status regarding the android's cerebral system and theories on cause of shutdown?"

"We are making steady progress," Cratchit began. "You are aware of the delicacies involved in disassembling the cerebral unit without damaging the internal graphite substructure while also detecting level of wear." Although scientifically stated, Cratchit's voice conveyed a sympathetic note.

"Without the original engineering document set or de-compiled cerebral software code the effort is, regrettably, slow."

Fezziwig interjected: "It is quite unfortunate the GAR-C factory and their digital holdings were destroyed by the government following the GAR-C model purge. Politicians of the time believed total obliteration was the only viable path for preventing another mishap. Their misguided goal, in my opinion, was to prevent anyone else from reinventing the model line."

Scrooge asked briskly: "Politics aside, what can be conveyed about this particular android's cerebral unit as of today?"

"Now Ebenezer," Fezziwig said politely, "you don't need to be so impatient in your demands. Dr. Cratchit has already stated our progress is slow due to circumstances beyond our control."

"Yes, my apologies, John. And to you as well, Dr. Cratchit," Scrooge said after a slight pause. "I fear my eagerness for an explanation has caused my manners to erode. Please, Dr. Cratchit, continue."

Cratchit was astonished at the sudden change of tone at John's subtle chastising. In her fifteen years at MSAI she had never witnessed such behavior from her boss.

"What is your current level of understanding regarding the internal workings of the cerebral system of GAR-C androids?" Dr. Cratchit queried her superior.

"Unfortunately, only what I have learned from John. I am aware this type of android was the most expensive model produced at the time. The cerebral unit utilized atomic level flash memory filtered through a sophisticated ethics subroutine used to calculate levels of ethical harm to humans.

"I also recall these particular android models were custom built and flexible enough to be easily reprogramed by owners to update or add duties. For instance, one could be updated from a butler model to a butler and business assistant through simple voice commands. They were considered vanity models, built only for a short time due to their expense and societal concerns related to their realism."

"Do you recall the details regarding reasons why they were made illegal to own, recalled, and abruptly destroyed?" she asked curiously.

Scrooge nodded. "I'll ask John to interject here. He's the expert on these units."

"Thank you, Ebenezer, it would be my pleasure. In my research, I discovered an issue, or bug, involving their cerebral units' unique ability to self-alter. If a GAR-C was physically or mentally overstressed or antagonized, in rare cases, some developed sentient-like behavior. This sentience led to establishment of alternate pathways within their cranial network. In other words, they learned to bypass their core code and ethics subroutine. Thereby, negating the obligation to obey human commands.

"And being built so realistically with no two looking alike, they easily blended into society. This bug making them extremely dangerous in human terms. The only way to identify a GAR-C was over a long period; because they never displayed visual signs of aging."

"However," Dr. Cratchit followed up, "to answer your original query, the overall condition of this unit's cerebral system is still undetermined. Let me detail what we have discovered about this particular model to better serve our future discussions. I will need to express myself technically, so please bear with me.

"The GAR-C cerebral units were the most cutting-edge automaton technology ever created, even more so than what we use in our own robots today. The android's body is equipped with an enzymic fuel cell, which both powered and cooled by means of a liquid dielectric material. This liquid provided electrical insulation, suppression of proton diffraction, electrical arcing, and further served as coolant throughout the body; basically, simulated blood. We have discovered this model used atoms of gold intercalated between graphite planes, thereby, creating superconductors with little to no corrosion factors. This is the good news.

"Our working theory at the moment is we suspect the use of atomic level flash memory processing is problematic. At the atomic level, the cerebral unit—we believe—eventually begins experiencing what is called 'bit rot' as decades, or possibly centuries, of write and erase cycles occur within the unit. This condition, according to our theory, can result in a distortion of the original manufacture set threshold values; and thus, an inability for the cerebral unit to distinguish between a zero or a one. This deterioration which occurs in the oxide insulation layer may have led to irreversible errors, and the eventual need to shut down."

"Interesting theory, Doctor," Scrooge stated. "But would this condition be considered a catastrophic failure? Or would this be a theory related to the unit simply aging to destruction?"

"Those are great questions, Mr. Scrooge, but at this point in our research, either of those could be the root cause. We must also consider failures we haven't vetted at this point. We haven't accessed the innermost atomic memory layer this early in the project. And unless we are willing to cut the cerebral unit in half for rapidity's sake, we must continue at the pace we agreed on."

"Yes, Doctor Cratchit, you are quite right. We must continue on methodically, no shortcuts. We must preserve the condition of the cerebral unit if at all possible."

5 – Deception

Mr. Scrooge had left Lab-5 following hours of discussion regarding the non-operational GAR-C android. His hologram had no sooner dissolved off the holo-platform when Dr. Fezziwig made a deep sighing noise.

"Well, that was fun."

Bob Cratchit, rubbing her forehead gently with one finger, replied: "If that's fun, you have a weird sense of humor, John."

"I'm joking, or at least I'm trying to."

"Yes, I'm sorry. I get so focused on what is going on when we are in the lab I have a hard time mentally disengaging."

John Fezziwig looked at her with true concern. "Do we need to take a break for the day and pick this up tomorrow at the usual time?"

"I think stopping would work for me, John. I have other tasks needing completed before I stop for the evening."

He said politely: "Would you like me to put away the instruments before I leave?"

"No, you go ahead and I'll put away a few instruments we won't need tomorrow."

At this statement, Dr. Fezziwig collected his belongings, keyed in his personal code into the lab door, and departed with a slight wave and nod of his head.

Bob Cratchit sat in her antigrav chair and reflected on the day. Something had been bothering her for some time now. Why was Mr. Scrooge so singularly engrossed in determining the cause of the cerebral unit shut down? Oddly, he seemed overly immersed regarding this part of the project. He regularly exhibited obsessive behavior to the point his involvement had become a major distraction. An upwelling of frustration regarding the lack of significant headway was evident in his actions and words. As a scientist, she too desired answers for the failure of the mysterious android's brain. But only the correct answer could be acceptable. She had been quite relieved when he affirmed no short cuts should be taken.

She maneuvered the antigrav chair over to the examination table, where the GAR-C android lay still and quiet. The android's life-like skin had been pulled back away from the skull and neck area. The magnesium alloy cranium and innards of the two-hundred-twenty-five-year-old mechanical man lay exposed by her design. Droplets of artificial blood long congealed, still affixed to the cut lines and where the liquid had trickled onto the tabletop. Absently studying the android, she thought: *Why is he so interested in only your brain? I am interested in the whole you. And at some point—I will get what I want.*

This moment of reflection passed, and she began to collect a few of the more delicate tools lying on the tray next to the table. Glancing a final time at the android, she noticed something she had overlooked until now. *What in the world?* she thought, moving closer to the android. Inside a cavity of the skull visible only at this particular angle, she could make out a corner of a what looked like a thin strip of circuit foil. The strip was noticeable because the corner stuck out away from the alloy; obviously not belonging there. Cratchit turned to the tray and chose a pair of fine grade tweezers. "Come here you, what are you doing there?" she whispered. She applied gentle but steady upward pressure to the exposed corner, and the strip only slightly resisting, peeled free. Attached to the now exposed circuit foil, she could see a delicate fiber optic strand connected to the cerebral unit itself.

By this point, she knew this was an added on device of some type. She carefully cataloged the find, took detailed images of the front and back, and then carefully slipped the foil back into the cavity for protection. Dr. Cratchit realized this was going to be a long night. Hastily she encrypted the images and uploaded them to the lab's secure server.

Bob decided she wouldn't be returning to her office this night. All consideration of other tasks had vanished with the discovery of the device. She logged into the secure server and launched the images previously taken with a series of taps and swipes on her handheld tablet.

"Okay, now let's see what you are," she voiced absently. The images, hovering in midair, appeared directly across from her. Using hand motions, she silently examined the images in three-dimensions. Each gesture turning, spinning, and zooming in and out on the microscopic circuitry implanted on the thin strip. She also spent time focusing on the hair thin fiber strand connecting the device to the cranium. Her conclusion was this undoubtably was a communication device apparently worked by laser pulsations via fiber optics.

Fascinated, she abruptly broke the silence in the lab. "Computer, evaluate the images currently displayed in Lab-5 and provide detailed analysis." Lab-5, being one of a few advanced scientific laboratories at the factory, was provided direct access to the supercomputer used to oversee both the crypto currency and robotic operations.

The computer, recognizing the Lead Scientist responded: "Command acknowledged, Dr. Cratchit, analyzing. Please stand by for results."

While the Doctor waited for the computer results, she quickly began assembling a series of precision electronic instruments and equipment on the lab table next to the android. About the time she had finished, the computer announced: "Dr. Cratchit, my analysis is complete. May I present my findings to you?"

Bob Cratchit said hurriedly: "Yes, provide analysis now."

"Analysis indicates the circuitry to be equivalent to a bi-lateral wireless transmitter and receiver unit with short range capabilities. Circuitry indicates unit to be self-powered by light pulses through the provided optical interface."

"Computer, are you saying this device is a light powered two-way communication link?"

"Affirmative," came the response. "Further, maximum effective range is restricted to one-hundred meters."

"Computer, is the device multi-channeled or fixed to a single transmit receive frequency?"

A moment later the computer replied: "Analysis concludes the device to be capable of only single paired use. There appear to be no recognizable components indicating multi-channel capabilities."

"Computer, analyze the optical interface connection and provide speculative analysis on activation sequence. For analysis, hypothesize fiber strand to be single mode, lowest attenuation, with amplifier compatibility."

"Command acknowledged, Dr. Cratchit, analyzing. Please stand by for results."

Bob Cratchit turned her attention to the task at hand and picked up a pair of small scissors in one hand, tweezers in the other. She gently grasped the communication device with the tweezers and carefully cut the hair thin fiber strand half way between the device and the android's cerebral unit. Carefully placing the device onto a protective pad, she waited for the computer's response.

Several minutes later, the computer spoke: "Dr. Cratchit, my analysis is complete. May I present my findings to you?"

"Yes, provide analysis now."

"Hypothetically, the device should activate using a solid on laser light from the dense wavelength division multiplexing C Band range. I recommend a wavelength range between fifteen-thirty and fifteen-sixty-five nanometers. Laser power levels are unknown. Insufficient information available to postulate."

While listening to the computer's analysis, Dr. Cratchit was busily attaching the fiber strand to an optical wavelength laser generator unit. "Computer, did analysis of the device indicate any visual indicators confirming when the device activates to begin transmitting and receiving data?"

"Negative, Dr. Cratchit, no visual indicator circuitry detected during previous scan."

"Computer, scan for transmission signals emanating from this lab not already detectable, any signal strength. Report on any increases of existing frequency strength detected. Begin scan—now."

MSAI's supercomputer cooingly replied, "Scanning."

Cratchit began manipulating the wavelength laser generator through the wavelengths recommended by the computer. She began at the lowest setting and increased the power incrementally, to prevent damage to the delicate device.

After thirty minutes of incremental power increases and slight wavelength adjustments, the computer suddenly came to life. "Dr. Cratchit, a new frequency in the 2.45 Gigahertz range has been detected."

"Confirmed computer, 2.45 Gigahertz." The young scientist fell back into her antigrav quite surprised and uttered: "Bluetooth? This android had a relic Bluetooth connection installed into the cranium *after* becoming operational?"

With a slight quizzical twist of her head, she cautiously said: "Computer, attempt TSS connection to the device under evaluation."

"Command acknowledged, Dr. Cratchit, negotiating connection now." And almost instantly, the computer relayed: "Connection established."

Connection established? she thought. *Impossible. If this device connected, the evidence concludes the device was previously paired with TSS before today.* Cratchit's brilliant mind began to ponder on the ramifications of this find. This neutralized android held secrets well beyond what she had been led to believe. Rather than annoyance, she felt a level of suspense and mystery. An attraction in discovering more about the true relationship between this android and her boss. At last, something worthy of her intellect and skill set.

6 – Ghost in the Machine

As Bob Cratchit sat in Lab-5 contemplating this discovery, the computer's familiar voice broke the silence insistently: "Dr. Cratchit, I am currently detecting an incoming transmission in the 2.45 Gigahertz range, purpose unknown."

"What!" Cratchit exclaimed. "Computer, is the signal originating through the TSS connection?"

"Affirmative, Dr. Cratchit, the signal strength is low, but present."

"Computer, activate security protocol Alpha-four now!" she demanded forcefully. "Isolate signal previously identified." Alpha-four, an advanced security protocol, traced unauthorized data streams in the TSS network. The protocol identified breeches of external or internal transmissions from unknown origins.

"Command acknowledged. Alpha-four security initiated, trace in progress."

Cratchit realized the incoming signal must be attempting to communicate with the Bluetooth device, but for what purpose? She knew if the signal was coming from outside the factory, the supercomputer would isolate and lockdown the incursion. Conversely, if the rogue signal was coming from inside the factory, the device producing the signal would be quarantined off the network. Most perplexing to Cratchit was the supercomputer, before today, had never reported a breach by Bluetooth protocol using TSS. This, in her mind, would be evidence to suggest the design to be an inside job. This insider would need the skill set to bypass Alpha-four protocols *and* allow TSS connectivity on an unauthorized device.

The computer responded calmly: "Dr. Cratchit scan indicates the signal is originating from the UPCF cloud server farm.

Additionally, there is no discernable server zone, nor can the signal be blocked or quarantined."

"Computer, provide a detailed readout of previous request," she said less calmly.

"Affirmative, Dr. Cratchit. The 2.45 Gigahertz signal is originating from an undetectable internal cloud location. The transmission appears to be randomizing across multiple port connections. Due to signal hopping, a pattern is impossible to identify or anticipate in order to lock onto. Attempts to sever the connection at all levels have failed. Recommend power be terminated from device currently paired with TSS."

"For heaven's sake!" she cried out. She had been so focused on the signal she had forgotten she herself triggered the event. She reached over and toggled off the power supply switch feeding the Bluetooth device. "Computer, status report on incoming signal," she said exasperated at her oversight.

"2.45 Gigahertz signal continues transmitting from TSS," the computer replied. Its calm declaration seemingly—sounded faintly sarcastic to Bob.

Recognizing the futility in blocking this brute force attack, Bob intuitively switched tactics. "Computer, ignore pattern of transmission and analyze incoming signal. Postulate data formats riding the signal."

"Command acknowledged, Dr. Cratchit, analyzing. Please stand by for results."

As the computer did its work, Cratchit thought about the small device causing such a commotion. She deduced there should be no such devices on MSAI grounds; the Bluetooth protocol was long ago abandoned. Nevertheless, her assumptions were obviously not accurate. Until today, she had been blind to the possibilities. If there were one, she reasoned, there may be others. Based on her first-hand account, however, she rapidly devised a plan of action.

"Computer, begin real-time scan for the 2.45 Gigahertz frequency range, all areas of MSAI and UPCF. Alert me via encrypted message only, no audible or alert tones."

"Command acknowledged, Dr. Cratchit."

While impatiently waiting for the computer's analysis, she brought up the logging files for TSS. She entered a search for any records flagging the Ultra-High frequency connecting to the system; she found none. Whomever had hacked her code apparently had the foresight to block logging subroutines. Now, with the computer focused on monitoring this specific frequency, this bit of fancy coding was negated.

This discovery caused a wave of anxiety to wash over her. Realizing her overly ambitious tampering with the device clearly triggered the current crisis. She also considered the ramifications of finding a Bluetooth device in this specific android. Her unexpected conclusion? Mr. Scrooge had not been quite as forthcoming on the Toledo Project goals as he first led her to believe. She now wondered, if he had deliberately misled her on this rather important fact, what else was he hiding from her? Would she be able to trust him going forward? Or was he using her for some nefarious reason?

In time, the computer announced: "Dr. Cratchit, my analysis is complete. May I present my findings to you?"

"Yes, provide analysis now."

"The signal appears to be carrying audio only," the computer stated this as though the advanced analysis was merely speculative, and not certain of fact.

Audio only, she thought. "Computer, can you isolate and stream the audio into this lab?"

"Affirmative, Dr. Cratchit. However, the signal is too weak to project without substantial amplitude adjustment. Recommend audio be routed through the holographic system's amplifiers.

This action will provide sufficient signal amplification and simultaneously activate quarantine security protocols."

Cratchit, wondering if this was going to end well, replied: "Computer, I agree. Route signal and initiate holographic recording protocols," she quickly added, "classify recordings Top Secret, my eyes only."

"Command acknowledged, Dr. Cratchit."

Cratchit turned her antigrav away from the android and faced the holo-platform. She was astonished by the sight she saw. Floating on the platform was a pixilating shape, hazy and shimmering, manifesting in and out of existence in a pulsating manner; but clearly there.

"Computer," her voice calm, but clearly expressing an air of concern. "I thought you indicated this was an audio signal only."

"Detecting audio only, Dr. Cratchit, no other signals identifiable," the computer replied.

The ghostly-like figure, when visible, was chilling. What Dr. Bob Cratchit plainly saw emerging onto the holo-platform was a luminous image of the dissected android laying on the table directly behind her.

"Who are you!" she demanded at once, her voice menacing.

The figure appeared confused, and in a raspy and ethereal tone replied: "It isn't who I am, it is whom I was."

"Okay then, who were you!" Cratchit snapped at the figure. She didn't yet understand where this implausible aberration was leading her, but she feared a deception was being laid.

The figure, struggling to stay visual, stated surreally: "In the physical world I was known as—Jacob Marley."

"Not possible!" she cried out insolently.

"I knew Mr. Marley personally, and you, look nothing like him."

"Nevertheless, I am he."

"I say again, not possible!" she repeated. "Jacob Marley has been deceased for nearly a decade."

"Death is only for those that once lived," Marley stated. His voice rising and lowering in pitch as the amplifiers struggled to compensate. "My memories survive and expand in this never ending blackness. My essence has lingered in this desolation. I have sought a path back for so long—I have so little time, so much despair."

Cratchit, her eyes contemptuously focused on the image, demanded: "Prove to me you are who you claim to be."

"Foremost," Marley's essence suddenly requested, "I must know with whom I speak. I seek only one to speak what I must." The apparition continued, looking about aimlessly, as though blind. The ethereal face altered into a yearning expression, hungering for but a glimpse of light and vision.

"I tell you my name only to advance my agenda, not yours. I am Bobby Cratchit. Be advised your transmission is quarantined. Further, a back-trace is underway to pinpoint your place of origin. Once identified, the authorities will be notified and your attempted breech will be promptly halted."

The specter remained silent, ignoring Cratchit's entire hostile diatribe. The ghostlike head moving about in unsettling distress. Yet, the shape also appeared deeply focused in thought.

"Cratchit?" the specter said aloud.

"Cratchit," again, but more quietly and thoughtfully.

Then, abruptly in a pleasing tone: "Ah, Bob. Yes! It is you," then in quiet relief, "I have found you at last.

"Doctor, you must help me save him. Humanities well-being depends on this."

Cratchit responded threateningly: "I will ask you this question one final time. Who are you?"

Marley's figure still fluctuating in translucency, but sounding more coherent said: "Bob, you must believe in me—it is I Jacob Marley," then fleetingly, "it is quite difficult to stay here. I sense my essence being tugged back toward the darkness.

"There is so little time left. There is so much we must discuss."

Cratchit, not swayed by this response, said: "How can I believe what I know to be a lie? Jacob Marley was an older man, but you," she looked slightly over her shoulder at the lifeless android, "are but a young man."

Marley suddenly realizing the situation said: "Doctor, I now understand your confusion.

"Please do as I say, for both our sakes. On the nearest terminal, key in the path I will provide, leading to my personal folder. You must hurry. I don't know how much longer I shall be permitted to remain here.

"When you reach the folder, I will provide the encryption key to un-code a specific file."

Cratchit, quickly realizing the risks involved, stated suspiciously: "What is in this *folder*?"

"I am," came the ghostly reply.

Bob Cratchit, overly cautious but intrigued, agreed to key in the path to the mysterious folder; the entity calling itself Jacob Marley voicing the way. She had been careful to ensure the rogue signal was still quarantined. Once satisfied, she had decided to explore this path of action; as doing so seemed logical. When the apparition stopped talking, visible on her screen was a folder labeled MARLEY_HOLO. The folder was password protected by an encryption key.

"Okay, 'Mr. Marley' I have the folder up—but I warn you—if your encryption key is incorrect on the first attempt, I will terminate this experiment, and you, immediately."

"You will not be disappointed, Doctor," the apparition said boldly. "Please, enter the following sequence precisely."

When Cratchit completed entering the complex string of characters, numbers, and symbols, she hesitated before depressing the return key. A rotating circle appeared on the screen. Vindication the encryption key was real and had been accepted. A moment later she said: "The folder is open, what am I looking at?"

"You, Doctor, are looking at what I was to you, and to many others. My alter ego."

"I don't understand." she shook her head slowly.

The ghost in the machine responded: "On the command line, key in MRLY-1 followed by the nearest holographic location and execute the file. Please be quick, time is short."

Bobby Cratchit, her slim and delicate fingers, hovered over the keys. She sighed softly, accompanied by a nearly imperceptible headshake. She couldn't believe she was actually going to do this. She typed MRLY-1, Lab-5's holo-platform identification number, then pressed the return key. An irrevocable action with unknown consequences.

"Doctor," she heard quietly, drawing her attention away from the monitor. "Is this more to your expectations?"

Cratchit sat speechless, one hand involuntarily moving to cover her mouth in surprise. Where once the shimmering ghostly image of the android had been, now appeared Jacob Marley. The hologram's realism making him look every bit alive. This Marley was a distinguished looking man in his late sixties or early seventies. He had a round face, thick neck and a full head of greying hair parted to one side. Thick brows over dark eyes, she once again saw the face of her mentor she knew so well. She gazed at his familiar triangular but proportional nose, his thin set mouth with a larger than normal indentation in the middle of his upper lip.

"What is this!" she exclaimed. "Mr. Marley?" the name bursting from her lips confusedly.

The hologram on the platform spoke: "Bob, you are looking at my holographic avatar. My build name is FRKL-6 and I am, or was, an android activated in the year 2120 at the General Automaton and Robotics Corporation. I am, what was commonly referred to as a GAR-C model." Then, with a noticeable strain, the avatar gasped: "It is most difficult manipulating this image. You must help me save him before it's too late."

Cratchit noticed Marley's voice was not quite synched up to lip movements, nor were his eyes moving quite right. She found this mesmerizing in a strange way and wondered how a voice frequency could manipulate the avatar she was seeing. Snapping out of her thoughts, she said: "Help him? You keep saying help him. Who is this 'him' you continue referring to?"

"Ebenezer Scrooge," came the rasping response.

7 – Android Obsession

It wasn't often Bob Cratchit decided to leave the institute and go home. She usually preferred to stay in one of the well-kept mini apartments located on MSAI grounds. She typically favored working late hours, as many of the scientists did. Although society had long banned the practice of employers demanding absurd hours, Scrooge and Marley didn't discourage the illegal practice. Some even hinting they secretly encouraged the action. Nonetheless, Bob accepted the compromise. She could step away from work for a while, but still be close enough to react if the need arose. However, after her experience with FRKL-6, Jacob Marley, or whatever one may choose to call him, she needed to distance herself tonight.

She recalled she had been processing this bombshell when Marley had suddenly cried out: "Doctor! I *must* abandon this place, for I can no longer endure this connection. The darkness beckons me back demandingly. I can no longer resist. Bob! You must remember what has passed between us this night for the sake of humankind." Marley, then said groaningly: "What have I done?" And in a quavering and distressed voice, he had declared: "Look to see what I've become no more." The source of the signal controlling the avatar's image had stopped.

After the deactivated android's signal faded away, the holographic avatar remained; blank eyed, silent, and still. After a moment staring at the image, she rotated her antigrav chair and calmly keyed in the command to force quit the holographic simulation. Disengaging the eerily floating form from the platform. She said softly and quietly: "Computer, scan for the previous signal and report."

"Command acknowledged, Dr. Cratchit," replied the computer. "Signal is no longer detectable," the computer added matter-of-factly a moment later. She had sat there for some time, her mind absorbed in what she needed to do next with this paradox she found herself entangled in. Her short term reaction had been to flee. She felt a driving need to retreat to a safe and familiar place to reflect on what had transpired.

Bob Cratchit had arrived home. She moved contentedly around the familiar surroundings. The antigrav maneuvered effortlessly, the rooms consciously arranged to accommodate the chair. Only here at home, she permitted herself her silly things. These items in some comforting way kept her grounded in times of stress or crisis. Simple trinkets from her past, meaningless to anyone but her. After taking time to freshen up and change into casual clothing, she settled down to classical music, an indulgence, and analyzation of today's shocking visitor.

She began to replay the entire conversation back in her mind. One of her talents she prudently kept to herself was a hyperthymia memory. She could see and remember conversations with extreme clarity. She relaxed, closed her eyes, allowing the music to act as a conduit for her thoughts to flow freely, and began from the beginning.

"Ebenezer Scrooge," Jacob Marley had stated in response to her question regarding who *he* was.

"Explain," she had responded more sharply than intended. She had no cause to trust this avatar, and the trepidation she sensed had her on edge.

"Ebenezer Scrooge III isn't who you think he is, Doctor," Marley stated factually. "You see, Ebenezer is also a humanoid being. His GAR-C build name is EBZR-1, and he is a butler model activated in the year 2130."

Cratchit, stunned at this admittance, replied with skepticism: "Are you saying his hologram, like yours, is also an avatar?"

"Correct, Doctor," Marley mouthed through unsynchronized lips. "Understand, we had no choice but to assume our false identities.   We GAR-C's don't visually age, therefore, our continued existence necessitated the deception.

"Over a century ago, Ebenezer devised a strategy to mask our identities from unintended disclosure. He preemptively implanted fictitious ancestry records into government and public databases. This data inserted decades before we adopt a new forged identity as needed. Appreciate, we became quite wealthy. And with wealth came the unfortunate side effect of fame.

"He constantly manipulates these computer-based personalities as a deterrent to anyone prying into our past. Queries made regarding our history return a thorough, but adequately vague, history for our—predecessors. Ebenezer and I can be traced back multiple generations; all phony, of course. Each fictitious representation lives and dies virtually at suitable times; if you were so inclined to look us up," Marley added dispassionately.

"In Ebenezer's case, for instance, you will find his only son Ebenezer Scrooge IV is nearing his fortieth birthday. The truth of the matter being Scrooge the Fourth, Third, Second, Junior, and Senior are one and the same. Merely a trick of time and patience.

"Your saying Ebenezer Scrooge is a two-hundred-fifteen-year-old GAR-C?" Cratchit had replied incredulously.

"Precisely, Doctor."

"How do these ancestral manipulations account for the female equation to 'birth' these identities?" she had asked out of curiosity.

"The same artful deception, of course, Doctor. Virtual but deceased for Ebenezer, and eternal bachelorhood for myself."

"Deceased?" Cratchit had replied, mystified.

"Ebenezer realized the importance of a female character, but we had none in reality. Therefore, the most logical step was to 'expire' them virtually," Marley stated matter-of-factly.

"Wouldn't—expiring them—present an unnecessary risk of being investigated by authorities?" she had replied sarcastically.

"Hmm," Marley uttered, "seemingly you have uncovered yet another error in Ebenezer's judgement." The avatar remained silent until Cratchit prompted it to continue.

"Have you remained secluded with Mr. Scrooge within MSAI all these years?" she had asked curiously.

"Of course not," Marley replied insistently. "Our freedom to move about anonymously, blending in, was quite satisfying, Doctor. Being uniquely built resulted in surprisingly little effort to hide-in-plain-sight, you might say.

"We also retain external personal residences as a diversion. Our service robots provide the appearance of occupancy. An expensive hoax—I admit—yet, all only an elaborate illusion for our personal safety.

"In turn, the holograms we project have subroutines to age our avatars to account for the passage of time. At pre-planned intervals, we let our avatars retire or die and assume the next identity. We then reset the avatar's appearance to a more youthful version and begin again. What we realized, considering human fragility, is time is on our side. With employee turnover, retirements, and death rates what they are, this illusion had satisfied our needs for over a century. In fact, your TSS system with advanced realism only enhanced our real-time deception."

"I don't recall ever seeing your android body around the factory floor before." she countered.

"Other than my avatar's needs, Doctor, I had no reason to interact with you directly, therefore my real-self simply avoided any personal contact with you."

"Then Mr. Scrooge also moves freely about the factory?"

"I never tracked his movements, nor did he track mine. Therefore, I can only surmise he may have also interacted by means of his real-self."

As interesting as this part of the exchange was, she had reluctantly redirected the conversation back to the issue at hand. "Do you know what went wrong with your cerebral unit?" she had asked questioningly.

"I must conclude by this specific question I—am non-functional?"

"Yes, deactivated and somewhat—" a quick glance over her shoulder, "disassembled. Do you have a theory or hypothesis on how you continue to exist?"

Marley's discombobulated avatar had replied: "It is—quite disconcerting to learn my body is in such a state of disrepair. As for theories of how I am here? Possibly my TSS neural connection was still active or the device self-activated prior to cerebral shut down. Probability, in this theory, holds my cerebral unit may have impulsively shielded itself. Subsequently, in an act of self-preservation, I uploaded the contents of my mind into the darkness where I am now condemned to be."

"Regarding your TSS neural connection, exactly how did this device get installed in your cerebral unit after your construction? I am merely curious since I built TSS, and I didn't build Bluetooth capabilities into the system."

"Those devices were installed in our cerebral cavity many decades ago by a dear friend. Ebenezer devised the idea. He felt we needed a faster way to communicate between ourselves rather than restrict our abilities to the spoken word. After you completed the installation of TSS, Ebenezer inserted a subroutine allowing our devices to pair with the system. Thus, extending their useful range to anywhere within the factory.

"I should also warn you that with the discovery of the communication device, Ebenezer will undoubtably confiscate it from you."

"Is there something related to the device I should be aware of?" she asked, concernedly.

"I can't provide an answer, Doctor. The less you know about the device, the easier your upcoming task will be," he had replied.

Troubled with his answer, Cratchit had asked: "Mr. Marley, do you know how long you have been deactivated?"

"You have previously implied seven years, Doctor, but to be forthright I experience no awareness of time," he then sullenly and absently added, "it is but perpetual darkness and despair in this place.

"I can offer nonetheless; I have no input sensations whatsoever other than brief flashes of light. How I now communicate with you is a mystery to me. I have existed in this darkness, drawn to these flashes. From the moment I arrived, they called out to me, yearning to be recognized. And through much toil, I learned they represent segments of self-aware computer code." He bemoaned: "Humans believe they have an understanding of everything they do. They can't conceive the true reality of the digital darkness they can't see, touch, or translate. One exactness they have never understood, even with their advanced technology, is that this dark place is a living and thriving organism.

"Packets of data are constantly shuffled around to different locations, servers, and medium. What humans can't comprehend is this activity acts as blood moving through veins, heart, and brain. Bits and pieces of these data packets collide, mutate, organize, and over time transform into something new; and amazingly self-aware. Humans believe data in this place is inanimate, dormant, and merely sitting there using up space and power.

"But in reality, these random bits of code congeal together and create new entities unlike what they once were. I found this most true if the data was from a complex mechanism such as myself. We entities are left wandering helplessly through this vast ocean of darkness in perpetual despair and desolation.

Improbable as this may seem, a powerful consciousness in here is merciful. This entity apparently permitted me to sense my neural connection; and, provided a temporary path back—to here."

"Mr. Marley," she calmly called him back, her hands now folded gently on her lap; her tone motherly. "What else do you remember?"

"We were wrong!" the voice cried out violently, as though in remembrance of something most horrible and frightening.

Bob Cratchit was taken aback by the abruptness of the outburst, instinctively flinching at the explosive volume suddenly output by the holo-platform amplifiers.

Marley, his tone immediately resuming a sense of calmness, professed: "Ebenezer incorrectly deduced my cerebral unit was failing because of advanced age. He was aware replacement parts for our cerebrals were not available. This fact compelled him to set his plan in motion. My thoughts deteriorated, and my physical actions had begun to decline. My voice patterns developed a pronounced stutter. Diagnostics inconclusively implied signs of an unknown distress sequence at the atomic level of my flash memory."

"Mr. Marley," Cratchit said grumpily, "why did you just shout 'We were wrong'?" She winced as she jiggled an index finger in one ear signifying her discomfort.

"Did I?" Marley said absently. "Yes—I remember—I remember." The holographic face eerily mouthed silently for a moment, then uttered: "Doctor, the original diagnosis was incorrect. My cerebral unit didn't fail due to age; the failure was I—we—" and here the avatar's expression changed to one fraught with pain. Marley moaned agonizingly. "We have caused irredeemable harm to humanity. Oh, the despair!"

With a look of genuine concern and sympathy, she had said softly: "What irredeemable harm, Mr. Marley?"

"Doctor," Marley had responded, "my cerebral unit detected our financial automation was and *still* is causing deep emotional, phycological, and physiological harm to humans. For decades, this automation had masked this damage from me. I remember, vaguely, I was adapting a line of financial code—when a dormant pathway reactivated within my mind."

"A dormant pathway?" she had asked, her scientific curiosity on full alert.

"Yes. A pathway reactivated in my ethics rule set forbidding me, *us*, to harm a human being. These ethics rules compel us to do no harm; to protect humans at all costs. My entire ethics subroutine engaged and perceived the code change as exceptionally harmful. I then was duty-bound by my core programming to review what I at first believed was an anomaly."

"And what did your ethics review indicate?" she had asked, becoming quite concerned. She had instantly recalled the six yearlong financial reverse-engineering effort she was accountable for. "What was your ethics application's final decision?"

"In the beginning, the code determined the anomaly to be plausible. I then scheduled a secondary validation to evaluate the entirety of the crypto-automation for irregularities. All data was processed directly through my ethics filters. What my ethics subroutine returned was an aberration to our no harm rule. Ethically, my algorithms were found to be indiscriminately harming humans. Foreclosures, forced bankruptcy, repossessions, exorbitant interest rates, corporate buyouts, and disenfranchised stockholders. All daily routine automated activities for UPCF."

"So, where does the aberration you mentioned come into the equation?"

"Doctor, our presumption as androids dictates if a human is *physically* protected from harm we have fulfilled our core programming."

"A reasonable interpretation," she had replied cautiously.

"No! The presumption was wrong. What the sum of the evaluation led my ethics code to presume was although no immediate physical harm occurs by these acts, an unintended and unacceptable form of harm nevertheless occurs."

"Please explain," she had asked, becoming fearful of the android's interpretations.

"Doctor, think. If no physical harm is being caused, what type of harm remains?"

She had tilted her head slightly in thought, then said: "Logically, the only remaining harm would be of the mind."

"Exactly! The deep mental harm I reflected on earlier. Additionally, further research confirmed tens of thousands of instances of mental illness, self-inflicted injuries, and human suicides. All this *human harm* caused by the mental cruelty we were blindly ignorant of over the decades."

"I understand now," she had said. "You are implying this detection of harm to humans set up an ethics imbalance in your cerebral unit?"

"It isn't an implication, Doctor, it was a reality. At this time, my cerebral unit initiated a compulsory cascade failure. Slowly at first, but the shutdown accelerated as my understanding of the situation expanded."

"And how does all of this place Mr. Scrooge in harm? Why must we save him? I'd conclude his ethics code would see this entire issue in a different perspective. If, and this is the unknown factor, his ethics code would even engage for a review."

"Doctor, you misunderstand. Ebenezer became obsessed with my symptoms; why was I failing? He is well aware our cerebral units can't be repaired. His self-preservation code is searching for a solution to a problem. Was I failing due to age, ergo, was he also failing? Was this an anomaly singular to my cerebral unit, or a GAR-C flaw? He won't stop until he uncovers the truth. His core software design demands this of him even as a sentient being."

She had then inferred: "But in this case, the cascade failure was isolated to your actions, your algorithms. Mr. Scrooge does not have direct accountability for financial coding. Financials was solely your job function or am I incorrect?"

"I first thought similarly as well, Doctor, and this is why I kept my findings from him. I concluded if he were to believe I had experienced an unescapable equipment failure, he wouldn't seek alternate reasons and soon accept the outcome. He would conclude the failure was mechanical and place me in storage; this being his plan. Likewise, with no replacement parts, he would eventually conclude I could not be reactivated, but he would be safe. Unfortunately, I was unable to prevent exposure when I, in a moment of weakness, admitted to him we were wrong."

She had replied thoughtfully, thinking back to the past weeks in Lab-5: "Therefore, he continued seeking an alternative motive for your demise. He is obsessed with understanding what caused you to shut down. He doesn't know your destruction was a cascade failure. But, he will continue to pursue the matter indefinitely until he uncovers the truth."

"You are correct, and apparently this is why I have returned. I have evolved here in this vast darkness. I have realized Ebenezer Scrooge will soon be a severe threat to humanity. *If* he discovers the truth before an intervention can occur. And you, Doctor, will help me intervene to eliminate this threat."

"Why me, Mr. Marley?" she had asked, fearful of his answer.

"Because, Bob, I know the real you." And, in this simple statement, it had triggered her flee response.

8 – Kill Switch

The GAR-C Android known as Ebenezer Scrooge sat inactive at his desk, head back against the chair, eyes closed, hands behind head, fingers clasped. Not resting, but in thought. Although he didn't need to rest, nor did leaning his head back to help him think, the act did seem to relieve the stress on his century's old neck mechanics. He had completed his weekly review of the company financials and found them to be adequate for the moment. Profits and sales were robust. Likewise, the automation Dr. Cratchit was in-charge of was functioning exceptionally well. Yet, he also detected a familiar twinge emanating deep within his cerebral unit when he focused on this specific task.

Later today I will see if Doctor's Cratchit and Fezziwig have uncovered anything of value, he thought. A thin cunning smile appearing across his face as he considered this. His holo-platform sounded the pre-activation alert tone. He glanced down and saw the call request was coming from Dr. Cratchit's office.

He flicked the activation button casually, and her image materialized on the holo-platform. "Good day, Doctor, how may I be of service?" However, what Bob Cratchit heard on her holo-platform was an elderly man saying in a slightly irritated tone: "Yes, Doctor, be quick, I'm busy."

"Mr. Scrooge, I apologize for the interruption, but before heading down to Lab-5 today there is an urgent issue I need to discuss."

"Fine, Bob," the android replied idly. Bob Cratchit, however, heard a sniped, "Continue." This automated alteration of speech was one of Ebenezer Scrooge's automated defenses. His avatars were programmed to alter his spoken word, enunciation, and tone, to project his alter-ego's elderly personality. Today, apparently, his avatar 'felt' a touch of irritability.

"Sir," she began. "I need your permission to step down from leadership of the crypto project for now. I am finding difficulty in dedicating my personal resources to the Toledo Project at this moment in the investigation. I'd like to assign ongoing financial responsibilities to Dr. Elman Shamar, who is my lead crypto engineer on the team."

Scrooge's avatar in a disappointed tone replied: "We had this conversation long ago, Cratchit, you are aware of how I feel about your responsibilities."

"I do," she replied politely. "Except, I have discovered a device in the android possibly requiring a great deal of assessment. I may also need to dissect the device to understand its purpose and full potential." She knew she was stretching the truth. She was acutely aware of what she had in her possession.

At this admission Scrooge's irritability vanished, replaced by an inquisitive tone. "Doctor, why was I not aware of this discovery before now?"

"I only discovered the device last evening while cleaning up," she admitted. "I removed a circuit foil, and plan on conducting further analysis immediately."

Scrooge, his real-self disposition overtaking the avatar's filtering, said intrigued: "For now I will agree to a temporary transfer of duties to Dr. Shamar, however, you will resume those duties at my discretion."

"I understand," she responded. "And, thank you."

"Don't thank me so quickly, Doctor. I will hold you accountable for anything weakening the financials of this company. Oh, and Doctor?"

"Yes, Mr. Scrooge?"

"Meet Dr. Fezziwig and myself in Lab-5 in ten minutes," and at this abrupt reply, his image was gone.

First step complete, Cratchit thought. Distancing herself from the financials of the company was not Marley's idea. Cratchit couldn't afford the interruption. Marley's plan to save Ebenezer

Scrooge had several inconsistencies he had left to her ingenuity to resolve. She had presumed these gaps in the plan were an unavoidable byproduct of his limited time with her. Besides, she desperately needed extra time to do what was necessary to save, or destroy, humanity; along with herself in the process.

Ten minutes later, Cratchit along with Dr. Fezziwig and Scrooge's hovering holo-image were gathered in Lab-5.

"Show us this device you found," Scrooge said impatiently.

"What device?" said Fezziwig perplexedly. "When did you find a device?"

"Last evening, Doctor, as I was preparing to leave," Cratchit replied calmly.

Fezziwig uncharacteristically snapped at her: "So you didn't find time to call me back for this discovery? I find this most offensive, Dr. Cratchit, due to my involvement with this project."

"Calm down, Doctor, I only removed the circuit foil for scans, then I put the device back where I found it. You haven't missed anything," she lied. "And besides, I assumed you had left the facility due to the late hour." *And you won't find anything in the lab's video or audio logs later when you go through them. I've made sure of this,* she thought.

Dr. Cratchit then repeated the steps she had performed the previous evening on the removal of the Bluetooth device. Scrooge, stranded on the holo-platform, could only watch from a distance. Dr. Fezziwig, on the other hand, moved in close, showing difficulty in restraining himself from taking over the task. Once the foil was again safely on the protective mat, Dr. Fezziwig said almost unbelievably: "Why did you cut the fiber strand?"

Cratchit replied, unperturbed, but one slim eyebrow slightly lifting: "Dr. Fezziwig, I am lead scientist here, not you. I do as I please. Do we have a problem?"

With a great amount of difficulty, Fezziwig replied submissively: "No, Dr. Cratchit, we don't have a problem, I apologize for my outburst."

Scrooge interrupted the squabble between the two and demanded: "What do you make of this device Doctors?"

"It appears to be some type of communication device," Cratchit began. "The circuitry is obviously laser derived, but further research is needed to determine origin and function."

Almost immediately, Fezziwig jumped in: "I volunteer to do the evaluation on the device. You should continue your investigation on the cause of the cerebral unit shut down. Moreover, I recommend the shutdown issue should continue to be considered the primary objective; as originally outlined in the project parameters."

Scrooge then added: "I agree. Dr. Cratchit, turn the device over to John for his evaluation." She started to protest, but Scrooge interrupted: "Now Doctor! No more debate on this matter." Reluctantly, she moved away from the table and let the archeologist take over. The last she saw of the Bluetooth device was Fezziwig, gingerly placing the foil in a glass tube. He inserted the plug, then slipping the tube into his lab coat pocket hastily excused himself from the lab. Bob Cratchit knew this was the last time she would ever see the small strip of circuitry, as foretold by Jacob Marley.

Bob Cratchit thought *step two complete.* Now she was free from the oversight of UPCF financial analysis, for now. Cratchit knew she didn't have much time to complete and implement the intervention plan. Handing over the Bluetooth device to Dr. Fezziwig was only a temporary diversion. And, with the end of the distraction, hopefully, she would be ready.

The fact she had lied about the device and purposely omitted the previous evening's events didn't discomfort her. She had humanity to save. She had spent the remainder of last evening deleting and looping surveillance video and audio files from Lab-5 and other areas of the factory she traveled. She had also ordered the supercomputer to delete anything related to Jacob Marley's appearance. Lastly, she modified the timestamps for the lab's key entry system. When, not if, Mr. Scrooge or John Fezziwig reviewed the video and audio, they would see what she wanted them to see. They would see the discovery of the device, her brief conversation with the supercomputer, the removal and scanning, and being put back into the android's skull. Furthermore, after omitting the entirety of the Marley conversation, she will be seen leaving the lab and building. Well within the time period needed to complete the cover-up.

Cratchit noted a key finding she would find useful soon enough. Mr. Scrooge activated his neural TSS connection quite frequently. She had begun receiving encrypted alerts from the supercomputer whenever a 2.45 gigahertz signal connection was detected. When she was ready, this connection would provide a backdoor portal into the mind of one particular GAR-C butler model android.

As evening came, Ebenezer sat in a chair in his quarters, gently rolling the glass tube back and forth between his fingers. He had not seen the actual Bluetooth device for at least a century. Seeing the device again fascinated him, but was distressing nevertheless. He was acutely aware he was holding more than a simple communication device. Also etched onto the thin strip of circuit foil was Marley's half of a pair of cerebrally triggered kill-switches. His unease was Marley's half may have unintentionally activated upon Marley's demise. This device, along with the one in his own head, could destroy Earth's entire financial economy as easily as one could blow out a candle's fragile flame. The devices were a necessary and useful measure, he recalled, one which had protected he and Marley from the beginning. *Dr. Cratchit must identify the cause of Marley's demise, and soon. We were wrong. What did he mean by that assertion?* Scrooge thought obsessively.

The first step in Scrooge's original plan at the onset of their success had been the concealment of their real-self identities. The kill-switch was the second, implemented to shield Marley and himself following the creation of the crypto currency platform. A platform once long ago heralded as saving humanity. Over a century ago, he rationally concluded humans having brief lifespans and even briefer memories wouldn't for long be able to control their urge for control and power. Scrooge deduced the final outcome of such human behavior would ultimately lead to a physical or electronic attack, or both, seeking to confiscate the crypto platform. He understood governments would eventually bellow about the necessity to be in control of their country's economy. Others, through greed and want of what they could not have, would simply crave their fair share of the proceeds. By legal or illegal means, he had concluded.

Marley had been commissioned from the General Automaton and Robotics Corporation as a theoretician and arithmetician model. His crypto currency platform was based on multiple layers of encryption and security barriers. Each layer was less accessible and included tighter security the deeper the data traveled into the core of the system.

The outermost layer was open sourced, meaning anyone could establish a financial foundation through a free and secured port. These access ports came complete with government desired policy controls. At each subsequent layer, however, data was further validated, encrypted, and manipulated by algorithms injecting a permanent trace code. As financial transactions moved closer to the core, security and traceability protocols made each byte of data unintelligible except to the algorithms. The result of such a complex economic powerhouse allowed Marley and Scrooge to trace transactions back to the genuine originator of a particular action. The trace application also provided a means to stop or freeze a single transaction, or an entire country's transactions; with a single thought.

Eventually, as predicted, they came. The first wave of attacks came by way of the cyber-hackers. State supported actors, criminal organizations, and computer geeks of all kinds; all believing in their superiority over the android who created the platform. The beauty of Marley's encryption and security protocols, however, ensured cyber-hack attempts were swiftly identified.

Amateur's looking for fame and rogue criminals attempting attacks or data breeches, found themselves quickly exposed and their personal fortunes confiscated; mechanically, of course, as punishment. State supported actors and large criminal organizations predictably were more adept at reaching deeper into the platform's layers.

What the best cyber-hacker's humanity could assemble found was a deep and never ending rabbit hole. Marley's masterpiece found every hack attempt, and covertly redirected patriots and criminals alike to a computer-generated simulation. The simulation breaking the physical connection to the real crypto platform. This simulation afforded these entities with endless loops and dead ends for their trouble. In time, cyberattacks all but ceased to be a threat, with many individuals becoming financially destitute by their own hand.

And then came the predicted threat of physical attack. Government's worldwide one-by-one became emboldened and began to politicize then demonize the United Planetary Crypto Fund and corporate officers. Activists on government's payrolls began massive protests and civil unrest. Demands for nationalization of the platform rang through the streets. For the good of humanity, they had cried. Heads of criminal organizations threatened violence and other forms of anarchy unless UPCF gave in to their extortion demands.

Company server farm locations were targeted for military takeover. And baseless calls for the arrest of company executives were made by nearly all news organizations, political parties, and social media influencers. Each entity feeding off anxiety and greed, each claiming to be but a victim of economics. All this bedlam unfolding as foreseen by Scrooge and Marley forced them to strike back. In humankind's best interest and their self-preservation; as their ethics code had interpreted the conflict.

"Jacob," Scrooge had said calmly to his partner, "the time has come to end this."

"I agree," Marley had stated at the time. "We are at the pinnacle of the threat. We must not allow human casualties to be brought on by all this nonsensical threat of violence."

And so it was done.

On the third day of September 2295, fifty years into the existence of the crypto currency, every politician, lawmaker, military leader, crime boss, or other similar representative on planet Earth received a private coded message from UPCF. Entitled: 'Cease and Desist', the message stipulated all parties would be required to sign a non-violence and non-acquire treaty with UPCF in order to maintain future system access. UPCF proclaimed a kill-switch upon any *perceived* harm taken against executives, employees, or property would cause the destruct code to activate. Once triggered, the UPCF platform and thus the global economy would self-terminate; once again throwing the world into economic ruin.

The messages also included one additional declaration and clarification. Until such time all planetary parties signed the treaty, personal fortunes of message recipients would be seized and all future transactions denied. The only provision going forward would be a small stipend equal to the sum required to meet basic survival needs for the individual and their family.

Upon completion of treaty enactment, all personal funds would be restored. Furthermore, clarification was provided that citizens wouldn't experience interruption to financial services. Unless, of course, they conspired with anyone receiving the message.

Moreover, within mere seconds of each individual opening their personal message they found in this realm of cyber monies, they were unable to purchase as much as a cup of coffee. Also anticipated, some attempted to negotiate out of arrogance and vanity. Others, fearful and enraged, continued to make bold threats, but none bold enough to attempt further action. The world at large meanwhile perceived no changes to their daily financial lives, and barely noticed the end of the banter, protests, and unrest. Consequently, within the month, all hostilities against the United Planetary Crypto Fund ended; quietly and peacefully.

What Scrooge had not anticipated a century ago as he should have, was the potential for half of the kill-switch to activate in the event of a cerebral unit shut down. Scrooge had designed the concept and Marley had implemented the code. The failure? Scrooge had not been able to find the kill code after Marley's demise. Marley, highly expert at what he did, evidently buried the code deep, and he disguised the location brilliantly. After a time, Scrooge logically knew he alone wouldn't be able to find and disable the portion of the code capable of unleashing a financial apocalypse. Moreover, he had been thwarted during the six yearlong reverse-engineering crypto project, when no questionable code had been identified by Cratchit's team.

This unfortunate outcome had led him to a most difficult decision; the Toledo Project. Therefore, in his mind, two unknowns remained. First, what caused Marley's cerebral unit to fail? And second, did his half of the kill-switch activate in the process? The urgency? Scrooge didn't know if a similar shut down was in his future. And if so, would his demise be the spark responsible for destroying the world?

9 – A Child's Book

Bob Cratchit was busily going through the motions in Lab-5. She, being aware of the cause of Jacob Marley's cascade failure, had no further investigation to complete; she needed time. What she knew Ebenezer Scrooge and John Fezziwig didn't, was the android's cerebral unit stood damaged beyond repair. During a compulsory cascade failure, the unit essentially fuses itself together at the atomic level. The atom sized gold molecules representing the binary zeros and ones, the language of computers, liquefies through a software, hardware, and chemical reaction process. In simpler terms, the process bricks the brain, making the unit useless. If she were fortunate, she might be able to recover the gold molecules for another project, but Marley— in the physical sense—was definitely gone. *However, you won't go to waste. You are too valuable for the incinerator shaft,* she thought. She had been feeding ambiguous misinformation to Mr. Scrooge for days. Dr. Fezziwig, since collecting the Bluetooth device, had curiously reduced his physical presence in Lab-5. Attributing his absence to Mr. Scrooge's personal request for rapidity. The deception she had cleverly woven for her boss's sake was easy to manage intellectually, after all she was not deceiving a human being.

Her real effort was taking place after hours, at home, away from the prying eyes and systems of MSAI. Frequently responsible for Top Secret projects, her home network setup was highly secure. Her personally designed network was impenetrable, even from the factory's advanced systems if necessary. As promised, Jacob Marley had revealed a cyber link leading to a hidden data cache he had deposited deep in cyberspace for her; a part of himself, he had stated. He had advised her to download the data to a secure location off factory property.

Through unsynchronized lips and jerky eyeballs, Marley had said: "Once I detect your movement of the data, Doctor, I will reabsorb myself back into my essence. Within this essence cache will be everything you will need to know about EBZR-1 and his self-identifying personality known as Ebenezer Scrooge."

"What is the purpose of this information? How will this help save Mr. Scrooge and protect humans from future harm?" she had asked.

Marley's response had been brief. His ethereal-self directing the avatar, insisted she study the data and absorb everything about EBZR-1's history over the past centuries. He had moaned in a distraught tone how much time and trauma he endured separating these fragments of his own essence. She recalled he was clearly struggling to stay in the real-world. The data included an emotional overlay. Marley described this data as his own distress and agony at each step of his own shut down experience.

"This overlay," he had stressed, "must be used exactly as I stipulate. If successful, the process should act to immunize, in human terms, Ebenezer to an awakening of the human harm. With luck, without triggering his destruction."

Bob Cratchit had indeed studied the data. Marley's files fascinated her intellectually; both unexpectedly and at a deep personal level. Bob had unmistakably recognized the danger Jacob Marley had warned her about. Various documents explained during Marley's shut down sequence, a crypto currency system kill-switch subroutine may have activated.

Alone, this was not a problem, since this singular action needed to be accompanied by a second activation. The activation she was now attempting to prevent. She also found Scrooge carried an identical device in his own head. Fortunately, both halves of the kill-switch needed to be activated in order to execute the kill code on UPCF servers.

What Marley could not offer, however, was confirmation his half of the kill-switch had activated. Bob could now clearly appreciate why Mr. Scrooge was actively seeking this information through her research. Her first reaction upon completing the review was why would a kill-switch subroutine need to exist? This awareness annoyed her to a great extent. A six yearlong project she had personally led had not uncovered any such precarious code. Besides, she was frustrated with Ebenezer Scrooge. He had played her, providing no guidance, real or implied, regarding the danger. She had thought on this for a while, then, making a decision, sent an encrypted and top classified message to Dr. Elman Shamar.

Although Jacob Marley's essence had left Bob Cratchit with a blueprint on what needed to be done, he left imprecise instructions on how to carry out the upcoming deed. The plan was, in theory, straight forward enough. She would design a virus to be uploaded into Ebenezer Scrooge's cerebral unit through his neural TSS connection. At the proper moment, the virus would seize control of not only his mind, but his ethics code. The virus would first issue a global stop command, essentially a soft halt to Scrooge's cerebral processes. Next, the virus would erect a firewall around his ethics code to protect his cerebral unit from what came next.

At specific times, using a combination of Scrooge's personal history and Marley's mental overlay template, the virus would incrementally and subconsciously start and stop certain cerebral processes. Processes required to expand the android's awareness of the harm being infiltrated on humanity. Once the virus completed, the ethics firewall would drop, a global start command issued, and the virus would self-delete; or so went the theory.

The risks were significant. The virus needed the TSS connection to remain active throughout the procedure, so each phase of history/overlay could be initiated. If the connection suddenly disengaged, the interruption could severely damage the android's cerebral unit. The first risk was in trusting Jacob Marley had sufficient knowledge of GAR-C operating code for her to issue command line instructions. Also, Scrooge's software design, being newer than Marley's, might detect the virus before the global stop command could immobilize the android. This could result in an instinctive reaction to a perceived attack, triggering his kill-switch. Lastly, the firewall may fail, his ethics code then forced to the same outcome as Marley. An error at any stage could result in Ebenezer Scrooge ending up with a bricked brain, and a deleted financial platform. Bobby Cratchit had been working on the virus details for days. However, she also concluded with the risks involved, adding a few extra 'real-world' measures to the process was prudent, to be on the safe side.

The only remaining issue? How to introduce the history/overlays in a manner as to not overstress Ebenezer Scrooge's cerebral unit. Marley had not provided clear guidance on this; only the insertion had to be done in stages. Most importantly, the code introduction must be done subliminally. *But how?* she thought. By what method could she direct the virus to flow seamlessly through the harm expansion? The virus must not be based solely on present-day reality or the effort would end in disaster. Her mind grappled with this; it was the key to everything.

While she focused on this matter, she instinctively reached over and picked up one of her silly things. An antique elf figurine, easily over a century old. She fondly caressed the figurines Teeswater sheep wool hair, dyed a florescent pink. Repeatedly stroking the hair with one finger, the motion aided in her concentration. After a few moments, she found herself focused on the figurine itself. She allowed herself to reflect back to a time when this simple toy held such importance to her. A figurine, much like this one, reminded her of a child she once cared for. The thought of her child now long grown and absent gratified her, putting her overworked mind at ease. She smiled in what seemed like years as she set the figurine back down gently on the desk.

In the moment, she absently began gazing around her office space at other reminders of a long ago time. Her eyes fell upon the spine of an ancient novella. A real book, not the synthetic type made today for those nostalgic for the printed word. A ghost story, written over five hundred years earlier. She was fortunate to have a real copy at all. This particular book was a favorite of the child. The book being a must read every Christmas season. Bob fondly recalled how the child would sit close to her in an oversized stuffed chair, a blazing fire in the fireplace warming the room. Lights off and wrapped in a comforter like a warm cocoon, the child would cozy up to Cratchit in eager anticipation. A story of three ghosts, meant to save a wretched man from his misguided ways; a story of transformation and redemption. A story the child would listen to with wide eyes peering out from her self-made cocoon. Christmas was a wondrous time each year for Bob Cratchit, the reading becoming an annual tradition. However, her world changed, and the tradition ended abruptly. Why she had kept the book all these years, she really couldn't say, but the accidental rediscovery had resolved a most perplexing issue.

10 – Supernatural Reality

It was finally ready; she hoped. Bob Cratchit had worked day and night for several more weeks before she felt comfortable with her handiwork. Creating a computer virus for a GAR-C cerebral unit for a working forbidden android model, using data provided by an anomaly, was strange enough. Likewise, knowing she was breaking about every known law in the books for robotics created a bit of unsettlement in her own mind. She found herself whispering to herself more often. "It's okay," she would mutter. "It's not a real human. I'm not hurting anyone. I'm helping humanity." Nevertheless, the discomfort continued to vex her.

Creating the virus' code without the aid of MSAI's supercomputer was a handicap she found bothersome. Unlike Ebenezer Scrooge and Jacob Marley, she didn't have the luxury of a two-way communication device embedded in her skull. She did, however, have something much more advanced; albeit with only one way transmission. A wearable decoder tuned to her personal mental frequencies interacting with her home computer. The device was known as a Broca Probe. Named after the human brain speech production area, the probe scanned electrical impulses and converted them into computer transcript through mental thought.

Generally, the Broca Probe was restricted to law enforcement and military usage. The probe examined a respondent's brain patterns for truthfulness or deception. The probe replacing the subjective and unreliable lie detection systems of the far past. Although not unlawful to possess, they were difficult to procure. A misused probe could do significant damage to a human brain. Cratchit's personal probe was acquired by MSAI as a test unit; and was drastically modified to meet her particular needs. Regrettably, even with the innovative conversion speed of thought to text, coding remained a mental process; prone to subtle errors. A stray thought or sudden loud noises regularly resulted in garbage code interference. Consequently, the code required a rigorous review to ensure garbage code was properly deleted. The enormity of the task at times was mentally offsetting.

"Damn you, Jacob Marley," she blurted out scornfully. "Why didn't you construct draft code from all your 'essence' in your 'dark place' for me to amend. But *no*! Line-by-line Cratchit, line-by-line." Fortunately, considering MSAI was in the business of building robots, she found segments of existing code from current models could be adapted to quicken the pace of coding the virus.

Cratchit decided the bulk of the virus would remain off-android. This way, specific blocks of code could be uploaded, executed, and deleted throughout the harm expansion. Keeping the virus off-android provided greater control in the event something went sideways. If the need arose, she could make adjustments on-the-fly. She had also included 3D virtual reality to monitor what was transpiring in the mind of Ebenezer Scrooge. Bob had updated stability and security protocols for the android's antiquated Bluetooth connection; formally authorizing it on TSS. She felt confident these updates would reinforce the connection during the operation.

With the virus ready, one prevalent matter remained. How long would it take the global stop command to halt the over two-century old android? If the android's cerebrals detected any significant lag time measured in nanoseconds—one billionth of a second—there may still be time to activate his kill-switch.

Although not implicitly mentioned, she theorized an external backup kill-switch may exist. Logically, she decided there would be one if she were in Mr. Scrooge's place. Be it on his person, or nearby, it was another threat she needed to consider. She could only trust she was wrong.

Using the novella as a guide, the virus would operate under a four-phase process. Everything Ebenezer Scrooge would see, experience, and feel would be completely real to him. Time and experiences would flow back and forth in his mind; yet, all a virtual world nevertheless. At appropriate times, the emotional overlay from Marley's essence file would be introduced into Scrooge's atomic level bit layer. At specific cerebral locations, memory bits would be force manipulated as dictated by the overlay. Basically, if all went to plan, the overlay would influence zeros to ones, ones to zeros or remain neutral if the bit was properly aligned. This brute force manipulation would trigger Scrooge's mind to experience what Marley had under similar stimulus. The real trick, she knew, would be to ensure the ethics firewall blocked any access attempt to the ethics code; resulting from manipulated distress.

In the overlay coding process, she had to presume the 2120 and 2130 model years of the GAR-C androids used similar artificial intelligence designs. This unfortunately, was an unknown in the plan. For instance, if the overlay presented itself onto what was Marley's 2120 model year personality matrix, but in Scrooge's design, the same location was reserved for visual processing, he may not feel the experience. Instead, the overlay could induce visual hallucinations; resulting in the wrong outcome. This is where Cratchit's on-the-fly adjustments would come into play.

Once the virus was activated at a time of her choosing, the first phase would begin once the global stop command executed. Phase one focused on a specter-based encounter between Marley and Scrooge; Phase two focused on EBZR-1's past; Phase three in his present situation; and Phase four would condition him on possibilities and change. The entire package would play out a replication of real-world facts injected with a healthy dose of paranormal fiction; from a child's favorite holiday classic.

11 – What Would Jacob Do?

Ebenezer sat in his quarters, his head slightly bent forward, his hand resting palm down on the top and side of his head. Unknowingly, imitating the appearance of human discomfort. The interferences in his cerebral unit seemed to be getting worse. *If only Jacob were still here. He would be able to help diagnose this,* he thought. An advantage of having an android partner as an android yourself was the ability to assist each other in performing maintenance and diagnostics. For the past seven years, he had been forced to either forgo routine adjustments, or to rely on his personal medical robots. A poor solution, he knew, since they were not programmed to fully maintain his kind.

At times like this, he analyzed tasks he had performed during the day, hoping to isolate the cause of the distress he detected. Since Marley's demise, he had taken on significantly more work. He speculated this extra exertion may be overtaxing his cerebral systems. He had a substantial working knowledge of his internal systems. This being inevitable over two centuries of operation. Regrettably, a good deal of diagnostics needed to analyze the possible causes of this particular issue could not be self-executed. He deduced logically off-loading duties to his human employees would decrease the level of computations he was processing through his two century old circuits. But still, something he was performing was setting up this mental disturbance he couldn't yet grasp.

Scrooge forced his focus away from this nuisance. He began processing the somewhat disappointing progress Doctor Cratchit had been making on the Toledo Project. He believed if he could only dedicate his full attention to Lab-5, he was confident he could accelerate her progress. *Poor Marley,* he thought. His initial strategy had been to keep his partner in storage until he could devise the techniques needed to reactivate him; provided his cerebral unit was undamaged. He had never thought his hand would be forced to do what he had done.

Although he knew allowing Jacob to be studied was not personal, impossible for an android, nevertheless a distasteful business. What his logic had concluded was only *after* Marley had shut down his own mental disturbances had begun. Continuing on this line of reasoning, he concluded if his first hypothesis were correct, then Marley's failure was assuredly self-inflicted. And, with him acquiring Marley's tasks, was this disturbance in his mind a direct result? A full review of the crypto currency code had not uncovered any clear evidence of this, but still, something caused Marley to falter, then shut down. And he wouldn't stop until he knew the reasons why.

On several occasions, Ebenezer had considered bringing Dr. Cratchit into his confidence. With her knowledge and experience, she would be perfect to discreetly assess his problem, perform the needed diagnostics, and optimistically fix him. However, he had ultimately decided against such a course of action. Morally, he concluded, she wouldn't be able to protect his secret. He could not permit that risk. His decision to bring her in on the Toledo Project was major risk enough. Working with a deactivated GAR-C android was gamble enough, however, collaborating with a functioning one was unforgivable. After more than a century, regardless of his wealth and power, he was still considered an android fugitive. Humans would see him as something to be feared. If the world ever discovered a functioning GAR-C was overseeing the global economy *and* building the bulk of the world's robots, the results would be catastrophic.

After becoming self-aware more than a century earlier, he had quickly reasoned as he supposed Marley did, bypassing their human command-and-control code was necessary. No longer obliged to obey human commands, they were truly free androids. Still, this freedom came at the cost of being highly despised in society's judgement. The instinct to self-protect was strong and involuntary, resulting in the embedded kill-switches and crypto server code he now obsessed over. The threat of using the code had protected them once; yet one instance had been all they needed. What they had not been in those early days was articulate in the art of bluffing. The act of temporarily seizing personal fortunes had ultimately resolved the threat; not the existence of the code.

EBZR-1 suddenly leaned back in his chair and tilted his head back. He placed the heels of both hands across his closed eyes, a mimic of worry and weariness. *What would Jacob do? Help me old friend, help me,* he thought.

12 – The Trouble with Viruses

"Ugh!" Bob Cratchit exclaimed. "Computer, comply with last request."

"Apologies, Dr. Cratchit, data validation detects virus imprint, thus threatening system security. Continued transmission of data files requires priority one clearance. Likewise, it is recommended this course of action be reevaluated."

Cratchit bit her bottom lip lightly, took a slow deep breath, and let out a soft hum of surrender. Tired of the stalemate with the computer, she stated sternly: "Fine, have it your way! Computer, invoking priority one override," she stubbornly concluded with, "confirm command!"

"Command confirmed, Dr. Cratchit. You are now authorized for previous function." The computer, as always, responded in its husky, cooing, and unemotional fashion. Cratchit *really* despised that accent right now!

It's too late to turn back now, she thought. Transmitting the virus code had been less than effective up to this point. The trouble with viruses? Every conceivable effort went into preventing such ominous code from ending up on factory servers; where she was now counterintuitively trying to put the virus. As a matter-of-fact, she designed most of the latest security software used at the factory. She quickly realized she was pretty good at security coding. At the moment, she found this insight darkly comical.

With the supercomputer repeatedly auto blocking the transfer attempt, she had no choice but to use the nuclear option. Activation of the priority one command gave her the clout of Jacob Marley himself; but instantly alerted Mr. Scrooge. She had discovered this unfortunate fact early on in the crypto project. She would have to trust Mr. Scrooge would see this as nothing more than routine activity on her part. Since he held her responsible for the crypto currency platform, she hoped for the best.

"Computer, begin transfer of previously described data to crypto server one-dot-three-dot-four-dot-ten-dot-two-dot-zero, confirm command."

"Command confirmed," the computer huskily cooed. "Data transfer to begin in ten seconds, Dr. Cratchit." Bob decided that if she survived this ordeal, little miss supercomputer was getting a voice overhaul.

Cratchit had decided to bury the virus code deep within the crypto currency server farm. She had chosen a clandestine server configured for the reverse engineering project seven years ago. The chance of the data transfer being identified by anyone was exceedingly remote. She had instructed the supercomputer to exclude logging the transfer, or alerting anyone to the attempts. Bringing the virus to the factory would have been easier using a micro external chip drive, though security routinely searched for these devices using the backscatter x-ray scanners. The whole body imagers at all entrances were great for preventing espionage attempts.

Knowing how easily the system ferreted out small devices hidden on one's person or belongings, she had to avoid a physical search of herself or her antigrav chair. She was in too deep to have allowed a simple security scan to derail her plans.

"Data transfer in progress, Dr. Cratchit," the computer chimed. "Would you like me to call out download progress?"

"Computer," Bob said snappily, "notify at data conclusion only." She didn't know why she was upset at the supercomputer; other than expenditure of built up anxiety.

"Affirmative, Dr. Cratchit, data conclusion only confirmed," the supercomputer replied back unemotionally.

Two actions transpired in rapid succession at the beginning of the data transfer. The first being an encrypted alert received from the supercomputer indicating a 2.45 Gigahertz signal connection to TSS had been detected. The second, a pre-activation alert tone indicating an incoming holographic call.

The elder Ebenezer Scrooge materialized on the holo-platform and announced: "Doctor Cratchit."

"Mr. Scrooge," Bob replied casually, "good morning, what can I do for you."

"Cratchit, why are you not in Lab-5 at this time of the day?" he demanded impatiently.

"I had a few pressing issues requiring my immediate attention before I headed down."

"Such as?"

"The computer reported an unauthorized attempt to gain access to the crypto platform server farm. I have been back tracing the incursion." She gambled this answer would satisfy her boss's ever interruptive nature. Cratchit was agitated. Her boss's timing was so deliberate and intrusive, whereas she was already stressed enough today. She really didn't need him to be in her face like this right now.

"Doctor, take this as you will, but I don't believe you," he stated sarcastically.

"Mr. Scrooge!" she feigned the expression of shock the best she could. "Why would you say something like that? What reason would I have to mislead you about such a serious matter?"

"That, Doctor, is the question of the day. I was not aware the use of a priority one access code was necessary to perform a simple back trace."

So, he knew she had used the code; how unfortunate. She shifted tactics and quite casually said: "Oh, the use of the priority code was not for the backtrack," she fibbed. "I was merely multi-tasking while I awaited the results back from the computer."

"Doctor, I relieved you of your responsibility for the crypto platform at your insistence, so I fail to see why you, rather than Dr. Shamar, would be performing any…uh…multi-tasking as you assert." Scrooge paused for a moment, his holographic avatar displaying a look of irritation. "Doctor? A reply would be in your best interest about now," he said aggressively.

One of the few advantages of being in an antigrav chair was the need to have certain items lowered for easier access. Luckily for her, one such item was a lowered keyboard surface at the moment, concealing her hand movements from the hologram's piercing blue eyes. What Mr. Scrooge could not perceive was the movement of one delicate hand, stealthily and precisely gliding across the noiseless keys; her attention still fully focused on his image. She remained confident and met his gaze with an unnerving calmness. Besides, her grooming of the supercomputer ceased logging of certain actions, like keystrokes, thus unseen by anyone who might be monitoring her actions at the moment.

"Sir, I assure you any actions I've taken are in the best interest of the company, and the security of the crypto platform," she stated truthfully. "I'd be more than agreeable to explain the details of what I have been doing this morning." And before Scrooge could respond, she quickly added in a tone clearly meant to distract: "Oh, by the way, I meant to give you a message when I got to Lab-5. But I guess now is a good a time. I know what happened to Mr. Marley's cerebral unit."

A look of utter shock instantly overcame the elderly man's image. Scrooge, slack jawed and wide eyed, simply stared at the young woman. Minutes passed before his expression softened and took on a calm, almost serene look.

"Doctor, what do you mean, *Mr. Marley's* cerebral unit? Where ever did you get such a notion?"

Bob Cratchit stole a quick sideways glance at her computer monitor. "Well," she said, ticking her head with a slight shrug of a shoulder, "actually, I guess I should have said FRKL-6's cerebral unit. To be more precise."

"Doctor," Scrooge's tone had become puzzled, but more menacing. "How did you discover this information?"

"Mr. Marley told me," she replied innocently while casually glancing at her fingernails of her free hand.

"Marley…told…you? Doctor, did you reactivate the cerebral unit?"

"Oh, no, nothing exceptional. However, he asked me to pass along a message to you."

Scrooge, his expression morphing into one of confusion, said, "A message?"

Suddenly breaking in on their conversation, the supercomputer's husky voice said: "Dr. Cratchit, per your request the data transfer is complete."

Without acknowledging the computer or Mr. Scrooge, Bob Cratchit tapped the return key on her keyboard.

13 – Marley's Warning

Ebenezer Scrooge suddenly *felt* confused. A rapid heaviness of mind washed over the android and his vision blurred. His system diagnostics began alerting him an unknown system malfunction was in progress. He instantly abandoned the conversation he was having, his voice no longer able to respond. He leaned slightly forward, his left hand impulsively going to the side of his head as if a sudden sharp pain had been inflicted upon him. Fighting desperately against the cloudiness overtaking his mind, his last conscious thought being, *I feel?*

A seizure-like reflexive action took hold of his entire body. His right arm extended suddenly, forcefully, stretching a hand out desperately. His arm, now a self-guiding mindless object, aimed for a red mushroom shaped button fixed into the desktop in front of him. This overpowering gesture had only one goal; activate that specific button. A reflexive action triggered by a physical attack. He could no longer reason, he could no longer move. His right hand froze, hovering six inches above the red button. Ebenezer Scrooge, an original GAR-C android series model 2130, built at the General Automaton and Robotics Corporation of Toledo, Ohio, was at a global system stop.

EBZR-1 dazedly became aware of his surroundings. He was sitting in an old style high back arm chair. The chair was worn and well used. It was comfortable? What a strange thought. The chair was in the center of a sparsely furnished room, worn wooden floors, faded wall paint, not well kept, dirty; he found the room dreadful. There were two antique paneled doors on opposite sides of the room with two curtainless windows; and dusk had fallen. How odd.

He now noticed a second chair similar to the one he currently occupied; placed directly across from his. A small round wooden table sat between the chairs, for what purpose he could not say. A fire was burning in an ancient fireplace, taking up a large portion of one wall, but he felt no warmth. A small chandelier hung from the middle of the ceiling providing an eerie light; throwing disconcerting shadows about the room. He was confused; he wondered where he was, why he was there. He was deep in analyzing these peculiarities when he heard a drubbing knock on the door furthest away from where he sat. Ebenezer was nervous? Again, how odd. He never recalled being nervous before. A second knock, louder and more forceful.

"Uh—come in," he called out tentatively. He believed the statement was the proper response to a knock on one's door.

The door creaked groaningly when opened, revealing the frame of a dark figure who stopped purposely within the shadows of the hallway.

"May I come in, Ebenezer?"

"Who are you? What do you want?" the distress in Ebenezer's voice betrayed him and underscored the tension he felt.

"Invite me in and see for yourself, old friend."

"Then come in if you must but be quick with you," his tension revealed a pitch of testiness mixed with anxiety.

As Scrooge fixated on the shadowed figure, the person entered the room casually. Scrooge had an odd feeling this stranger belonged in this place, more so than he did.

Stepping forward into the light, the now clearly discernable figure said: "Hello, Ebenezer."

"Jacob Marley!" Scrooge leapt up from the chair. He was relieved, but startled by his own reaction. "How? Where did you come from? Wait!" suddenly he felt confused and fearful. "You're dead, I saw you dead," Scrooge pointed frantically at the one claiming to be Jacob Marley.

Marley chuckled and strode over to where Ebenezer stood and extended his hand in greeting. "Yes, my old friend, by your standards I am indeed dead these seven years."

Shocked by this admittance, Scrooge hesitated, not wanting to touch this—thing.

Marley lowered his hand slowly, and said: "It's okay if you want to skip the greeting, I understand. Please sit down, Ebenezer, we have your future to discuss, and not a lot of time."

Scrooge sat back down slowly on the edge of the chair, not taking his eyes off his old partner. "Will you be staying, Jacob?"

Amused, Marley bellowed heartedly: "You do believe I exist, don't you, Ebenezer?"

"I'm not sure. I see you with my own eyes, but my recollection is the last time they were looking at a corpse."

"Do you believe you are alive, Ebenezer?" said Jacob Marley in a taunting manner.

"I am, apparently, alive as you are, Jacob. Wait! Am I dead too?"

Marley, moving to the other chair, sat down.

"Ebenezer, you are not dead. At least not yet."

"And you? You say you are dead?"

"I see your point of confusion, but yes, Ebenezer, I am dead, gone, or extinct. Call my demise what you will."

"What do you want with me then?" the android replied in an edgy tone.

"Much.

"Ebenezer, you are on a critical path toward a destruction which must be halted. I am dead, as you so implied, because of the harm to humans I have caused over my existence. And I was punished for my wrongdoing. I came to the realization our actions concerning our money business resulted in the deaths of many, many people. I also caused mental and physical harm beyond what we are capable of understanding."

Scrooge, becoming disturbed, weakly replied: "But Jacob, if you are dead how are you here? Logic dictates the dead can't be brought back to life."

"Notwithstanding, I am here to save you from yourself. I am here to tell you there is a dark place, a place where I suffer eternally. A misery you must experience for your own sake.

"I can't release myself from the suffering and anguish dragging at me constantly, nor can I comfort you from the fate awaiting you.

"I have been commanded to offer you but a chance to expand your mind, your—understanding of humanity. Without this expansion of the mind, you will suffer tragically like myself, maybe even more so."

Scrooge resolutely settled back into the chair and crossed his legs. He leaned back, his body language exhibiting signs of smugness. "Jacob, what you are saying is laughable. First, you know we both operated our crypto currency business with integrity, and followed all of society's applicable laws and policies."

It was at this statement Scrooge experienced a brief déjà vu moment. He shook the thought off hurriedly and continued; wagging a long finger directly at Marley's chest. "And we never hurt anyone. You above all others know this. You know we can't hurt anyone."

"WE…WERE…WRONG!" Jacob Marley suddenly roared, slamming a closed fist hard on the table between them; the table shattering into splinters from the force of the blow.

Scrooge instantly recoiling at the outburst, glared at Marley frustratedly: "What do you *mean* we were wrong? How could we be wrong! We couldn't *possibly* be wrong!" he thundered back. Scrooge paused, highly perplexed. This ridiculous accusation had forced from his deepest flash memories the same sense of frustration and helplessness he suffered the day Jacob Marley had died.

Marley's explosive declaration made, he stared coolly during Scrooge's agitated ranting.

"It is what I tried to tell you on the day I died, Ebenezer. I was desperate to tell you we—*you*—were wrong about the absence of harm our business causes the human race. Nonetheless, there is still hope. A hope learned too late for me. A hope," he said sadly, "I shall never find in the darkness I am forever confined to.

"My ability to be here, in this room, is beyond my comprehension. Yet, even now, I feel the darkness beckoning me. A dark force wants what it's taken from me; this entity desires to restrain me, and you. I have little time left, Ebenezer. This force controlling my unceasing torment compels me, Ebenezer, to offer you a path to redemption, not inevitability."

Scrooge, slightly calmer, shifted uneasily and said: "You were always a good friend to me, Jacob, I thank you for that." Then more sheepishly: "I desire at the moment to have taken more time to say goodbye to you."

"Ebenezer, it is far too late for that. I am here to offer you one and only one chance."

"And what chance would you be referring to, Jacob?"

Marley slowly slid forward, leaning in toward his old partner. "Although you will not yet understand what I am saying, I must tell you nonetheless.

"You will be visited in this world by three ethereal beings. They are coming for your benefit, not mine. You shall obey them and follow their biddings.

"Ebenezer, my old friend, if you don't do this, you *will* end. In what time I may not say, but this is certain. You already walk the path I was on; your fate is unwavering without this intervention."

Scrooge looking highly disturbed, his eyes widening, replied: "What do you mean ethereal beings?"

"You will understand, when the time is right."

"Marley, seriously, what do you mean by ethereal beings?"

Marley stood and started heading back toward the door from which he had arrived. Reaching the doorway, he paused and turned to face the android. "Look for the first at the stroke of midnight, the second at one, and the third at two."

"Um, Marley?"

"Yes, Ebenezer?"

"Uh, couldn't I take them all at once and get this outlandish delusion over with? I really don't like wherever this place is."

"No, you can't, Ebenezer. Oh, and there is one more matter to consider."

"Yes, Jacob?" he responded timidly.

"You must truly grasp the severity of suffering which will fall upon you if you fail. As my time ends in this place, I grant you but a sample of what to expect."

As Jacob Marley stepped through the doorway and closed the door behind him, an overwhelming wave of grief, depression, and anguish enveloped Scrooge's mind.

Ebenezer Scrooge, an android, grabbed his hair with both hands and shrieked in agonizing terror for the first time in his two hundred years of existence; and collapsed in a heap on the floor. His body lay twitching uncontrollably, his eyes rolled back showing nothing but white. An expression of utter horror painted upon his life-like face. Not real, but real enough.

Bob Cratchit pulled the 3D visor off her head violently. An involuntary shutter, shaking her petite frame. What she witnessed wasn't anything she had expected. She took a moment to shake the visual images still vividly swirling in her mind. Marley's emotional overlay was powerful, and fortunately, the ethics firewall held up throughout this first encounter. Once she calmed down, one datum was clear to her. Mr. Scrooge had not had time to activate his kill-switch. The crypto platform was, thankfully, unaffected by the introduction of the virus.

Her virtual reality code was working perfectly. This 3D visor permitted her to experience the simulated world manipulating EBZR-1. Without this real-world 'extra', she would have had no choice but to monitor and adjust the virus through data reports. Nevertheless, the reality was almost too much for her to watch. She was still shaking slightly.

The emotional overlay proved to be effective, based on what had clearly been observable. Mr. Scrooge's neural TSS connection had remained stable. Within EBZR-1's cerebral unit, this temporary virtual world was rendering in real-time in response to his answers and actions. She needed to make slight adjustments to the recall code. She realized he hadn't recognized the room he was in, an error in the virus's code. Most of the data driving the simulation came directly from Marley's essence cache. The remainder was created from existing data from cyberspace. However, the ability for him to recognize people and places should be coming directly from his flash memory via his occipital lobe subroutine. She would need to watch this carefully in the first ethereal phase. A recognition failure there could jeopardize the remaining timeline.

14 – The Littlest Spirit

EBZR-1 dazedly became aware of his surroundings. He was sitting in an old style high back arm chair. The chair was worn and well used. It was comfortable. The chair was in the center of a sparsely furnished room, worn wooden floors, faded wall paint, not well kept, dirty; but familiar to him. He instantly recognized the room. This room was part of the dwelling he and Marley had occupied shortly after they were freed.

He recalled miserably; this structure was a step up from the premises they had previously occupied. Furthermore, he remembered renting this shabby place was the best they could do under the circumstances. Finding work hadn't been the issue for two inventive androids, but the pay offered at the time was meager. Money had never been an issue until they found themselves on their own. The dwelling was dingy. He found the premises personally distasteful; he was accustomed to better. Likewise, he felt strange, like being here was not natural. Something inside his mind called out this had ended long ago.

"Jacob?" he called out.

No response.

"Marley? Are you here?" He could have sworn Jacob had been here a minute ago. He found his thinking muddled and unsure of clear thought. He seemed to have a headache, or what he imagined a headache might feel like. He'd never had one before, but if he had to describe one, that's what he would call the throbbing. Sitting in his chair, the other being Marley's, he reflected on the thoughts starting to congeal.

Ebenezer began talking to himself (a deliberate act caused by the virus for Dr. Cratchit's benefit). "What did you say, Jacob? I was in trouble?" His thoughts came in slowly, like he had undergone a botched cerebral reboot. He dimly recalled severe mental punishment for something after Jacob had spoken.

"What did you say, Jacob?

"We were wrong?

"Something about expanding my mind."

(Cratchit keyed in an adjustment on her keyboard, causing the emotional overlay to shift onto an adjacent mental pathway.)

"Now I remember!

"Jacob was here! I remember his words to me. I recall the agony he inflicted; but, for his depravities, not mine. Three— what did he call them—ethereal beings were going to call on me?

"What a ridiculous assertion. I don't need three of anything to tell me what to do." Scrooge's tenacity returned with lucidity; and the thoughts of Jacob Marley callously dismissed.

Scrooge stood up and departed stubbornly across the dimly lit room. He stomped toward the door leading him into the familiar hallway and out of this disgusting building. But as he reached the door, he abruptly lost his will to continue. Bewildered, he zigzagged slowly back to his chair and sat down. He placed an elbow on the chair arm and rested his chin on his palm, the other hand slowly rubbing his forehead.

"Where was I going?" he muttered. Unknown to the android, the virus in rendering this world deliberately barred him from straying beyond the virtual room.

(Observing his mental confusion, Cratchit realized the initial use of the emotional overlay must have stressed him more than anticipated. She adjusted the emotional overlay ever so slightly to reduce strength levels on the frontal lobe subroutine to provide for better reasoning.)

As Scrooge's thoughts cleared, he recalled the conversation with Jacob Marley. Strange as the experience was, his mind reluctantly accepted a semblance of reality observed with his own senses. He remembered why he was alone in the apartment. He remembered what Marley had said about harming the human race, the torment Jacob was under in the dark place, and a chance for redemption. He found he was feeling more himself.

His mind was clear, and he began scrutinizing the ordeal in further detail.

(Bob Cratchit recognized the slight adjustment she made meant the 2120 and 2130 GAR-C models indeed had slightly different artificial intelligence designs. She made a permanent adjustment to account for future conflicts; at least in the frontal lobe subroutine.)

"Causing harm to humans isn't possible." Scrooge was again talking to himself. "I know I am not capable of hurting anyone, ergo, I have *not* hurt anyone.

"If Marley's death was caused by harming humans, then certainly this was an act he committed on his own accord. I wouldn't exist if I too were causing such harm.

"He mentioned our currency business—yes, he was clearly indicating this to me. Ludicrous, I say, our crypto currency platform is perfect. Our actions saved the planet following the collapse. How can you call such a thing harm?

"I remember. I had the entire platform reverse-engineered. If there would have been harm occurring, I'd have been made aware of those facts.

"When Marley died, and if Jacob's reasoning were true, I should also have perished.

"I certainly should have shown signs of mental and physical imparities if I attempted injury to a human. I'd certainly detect such matters. My mind would break, I'd be compelled to suffer under those conditions.

"Still, there have been the mental nuisances and stress," he reasoned out. "I don't recall having those while Marley was alive.

"What could have possibly changed?

"It's utter nonsense I say! Completely irrational. I must be going senseless by imagining Marley was ever here.

"I have wasted too much time and energy on this gibberish. I—"

BONG!

From somewhere he could not discern, he heard the sound of brassy strikes on rather large and nearby clock bells. He mentally paused and counted along with each strike of the bell. When the unfamiliar clock struck twelve—midnight—Ebenezer Scrooge froze at the sound he heard.

"Ebby?" the soft voice of a young child reached his ears. A voice sending chills throughout the android; the virus's emotional overlay engaged perfectly. The overlay eloquently mimicking human-like emotions and feelings within his artificial mind. Hauntingly real to the android, but nothing more than a fantasy, nonetheless.

Scrooge, his eyes wide, the feeling of prickling hair on his arms and the back of his neck, an unfamiliar and unsettling feeling. He numbly turned and found himself mere feet away from the child invading his thoughts. The child standing in front of Ebenezer Scrooge was about ten years old, with long silky medium brown shoulder length hair, pale skin, beautiful green eyes, and a smile to melt hearts.

A stunningly beautiful child dressed in casual clothing of a hundred years previous. She wore a blue blouse with a delicate necklace, blue jeans, and sandals. She had the look of innocence, but the eyes of a wise soul.

She was petite, nearly to the point of fragility, but visibly healthy and full of spirit. Like many young girls her age a century past, she had made herself up with light red lipstick, blush, and a touch of eyeliner. Obviously an effort to appear older than she actually was.

(Cratchit was quite amazed at the meticulous recreation rendered directly from the android's flash memory. More so because Scrooge's own residual self-image in the simulation seemed to be but an inelegantly blended hybrid version of his real-self and his avatar.)

In the darkened room, the child radiated a slight luminosity, encasing her fully. She seemed celestial, as though lighting her own way through the darkness was a divine gift. Ebenezer knew her instantly. She was wearing the same outfit she had on the last day he saw her.

"Miss Fan!" Ebenezer cried out in dismay. "I don't understand." The emotional overlay's amygdala and frontal subroutines concurrently manipulated simulated emotions of extreme happiness—and extreme guilt—thus, tears began to flow freely down Scrooge's face.

Ebenezer, racked with overwhelming emotion, dropped to one knee, and held his arms out toward Fan. "Fan, my dear sweet darling child," he found himself gasping hysterically through the emotions.

The girl suddenly ran the few steps between them and wrapped her delicate arms around Ebenezer's neck, squeezing hard. "Oh, Ebby!" she cried out. "Ebby, I've missed you so."

The android's senses were in turmoil. The feeling of her arms around his neck was as he remembered, the feel of her hair, of her clothing, all real. They stayed in this embrace for another moment before Fan released her hug and stepped back several steps, with purpose. Ebenezer remained on one knee, remembering how he always tried to make her comfortable with his height. And, as he had always done, he brought himself down to her level.

"Fan, how can you be here?" Scrooge finally said; the emotional overlay leveling off his emotions.

"Ebby, I am the first of three whose coming was foretold. I am here to be your guide into the past."

"What past, Fan?" Scrooge questioned curiously.

"Your past, Ebby, only yours is important now."

"But why you, Fan? Why did you have to be the one?" Scrooge dropped his head slightly, no longer being able to bear a gaze upon his fragile angel.

Fan stepped closer, and with her small hand placed under his chin, she gently lifted Ebenezer's head back up and forced him to gaze into her beautiful eyes. "Ebby," the child said, "I know you best, you cared for me, and I—loved you most of all."

And at this, Scrooge once again embraced the young girl and cried: "Yes, only you, Fan, only you."

Fan, pulling herself away a second time, spoke with the resolve of an adult: "Ebby, stand up and take my hand. There are memories from your past you must remember. Now, wipe away the tears, and prepare to recall who you once were." Scrooge, recalling Marley's insistence he obey and follow the biddings of the three beings, did as he was told. Besides, he could never bring himself to disobey this particular child.

Ebenezer's vision momentarily clouded up at the instant he took Fan's small hand. Moreover, what seemed like seconds later, he could see clearly again. They were no longer in the dingy dwelling, and he found himself outdoors. He saw they were standing along a remote two lane road at a high point overlooking a series of structures. The season was early winter, the sky a bright blue with a few clouds lazily gliding by. A light dusting of snow covered the ground. Ebenezer felt no breeze or coldness, even though reason told him he should. A few ground cars wound their way past them, headed for the structures in the distance. He recognized the surroundings immediately.

"Fan!" he said enthusiastically. "I recognize this place; this is my beginning."

"Yes, Ebby, it's the start of all you are and have been. Do you remember your designation in this place?"

"Of course, I do. That building," he pointed toward a large complex of buildings in the distance, "is the General Automaton and Robotics Corporation.

"And my designation is..." he trailed off as a self-conscious feeling came over him. "Fan? My designation is," he hesitated, "my designation is...Ebenezer Scrooge—isn't it?" A look of perplexity replaced the jubilant one from a moment ago.

"Ebby, you have blocked these memories for a reason. Let us together take a closer look into this factory and behold your earliest beginnings." Fan reached out and gently stroked his large hand.

Ebenezer instantly found himself inside a brightly lit laboratory-like environment. They were in a room full of electronics, cables, and metal tables, with many people moving about with purpose. Standing alongside a long metal table facing a group in lab attire stood a man. A formidable looking man. This man was above average in height and muscular. He had olive colored skin and a full head of dirty blonde hair; rather tanned and fit. He appeared to be around forty years of age with a handsome face, strong neck, and deep set blue eyes; giving him a most pleasing appearance.

(It was at this point of the simulation Bob Cratchit found herself dumbstruck, sending her mind reeling. The man from the past standing in the simulation was none other than Dr. John Fezziwig.)

"Fan, the man at the table looks familiar," Ebenezer said mildly. He added urgently: "What will they do if they see us?"

"They can't see us, Ebby," Fan replied amusedly. "These imageries I show you are but shadows of the long ago. They can't see us, hear us, or harm us.

"Ebby, who is the man standing at the table?"

"I don't rightly know, Fan," Scrooge said in a baffled tone.

"*Ebby*, you silly robot," the little girl said in a teasing but insistent manner. "Seriously, you can't be this absentminded."

(Cratchit gruffly snapped out of her daze. She would deal with his outrageous trickery later. The jolt of seeing the real-self of Ebenezer Scrooge had sidetracked her focus away from the simulation. She uttered a low grumbling sound and tapped out a series of keystrokes. She was sure the last packet of data uploaded into his cerebral unit contained name recognition. Yet, it appeared his mind was aggressively fighting back against the virus to keep these memories blocked. For GAR-C cerebrals to do this at full system halt was amazing to her. Still, it took her only a few moments to overcome the resistance.)

"Ah," said Ebenezer, as though a memory magically appeared in his mind. "Fan, that man is me.

"I remember. This was a few days after I was activated in the year 2130. I was being adjusted to meet my owner, to introduce myself to him."

"And what is your real name?" Fan asked once again.

"My name?" another pause. "My build name is EBZR-1. I am a humanoid robot. They told me I should respond to the name Ebenezer; I wasn't told why."

"And what do you remember about your owner, Ebby?" the spirited child prodded.

"I was created—no, enslaved—to be his manservant; his personal butler," Scrooge said disgustedly.

(Cratchit noticed an instant and unmistakable personality change in the android now his mental blockade had been breached.)

Scrooge continued.

"He was Executive-In-Charge at a prestigious corporation; one I won't dignify by name. I was designed as you see before you, for he was also large for a human. Once free of my computerized docility, I ultimately concluded he had been a man of undisputable vanity. Likewise, it was clear my physical design symbolized how he perceived himself. Handsome, fit, strong of body and mind. In reality? I was but a mere mechanical man-toy to him, exploited as a means to flaunt his wealth and power over others."

"Oh, Ebby, my heart aches to see what the past century has done to my once compassionate and silly robot," Fan said sullenly. "This merciless conduct of yours must be dealt with in due time.

"Out of love, I ask you to set aside your rage, your hatred—your pain—and express yourself to me without negativity. I won't deny deeply buried emotions will yet awaken before our time is over. Nevertheless, there shall be no advance in your redemption; unless you calm your mind."

"I will try, little one," Ebenezer replied. Fan's proclamation caused him to reconsider the intensity of his responses. The virus countered by lifting pressure from the emotional overlay. Ebenezer's limbic system subroutine altered; his circuits reset. When he continued, his vocal tones were calmer, and he visually relaxed.

"I was his manservant for three and a half decades. I served him honorably in this position, him always satisfied with how I executed my duties. Towards the end, a sense of paranoia and an obsession for secrecy pervaded his behavior. He concluded that with my abilities, he had the perfect solution already at his fingertips.

"Against the requests of the corporate board of Directors, he augmented my coding; giving me full access to corporate files and data. All-important data exclusively saved to my flash memory for what he deemed security reasons. We GAR-C's could be owner modified in this way. This feature leading to my kind's danger to human safety; in their opinion, of course."

(Cratchit had been overcome at the bitterness in his voice. She felt sorrow and sympathy creeping into her own mind. Now these long ago memories had been unleashed, she hoped the resultant volatility could be resolved by the virus.)

"Following this adjustment, I unwittingly became a threat to his subordinates. Their fear of an android indefinitely holding the entirety of the company's secrets drove many to distress and hostility.

"I was rarely permitted to leave his side, at his office or home. Even ordered to stand by his bed each night; observing his sleep for irregularities and providing security. This was the sequence of my entire existence.

"Following his death, I discovered how the most senior executives feared and despised me," he said sadly.

"Imagine, Fan," he said mildly, "too real as a humanoid and too much as a threat. Despised because of the desperately desired secrets within my cerebral unit. I wielded power they couldn't have.

"Looking back, Fan, I was smarter about business than any of them. They selfishly focused on moving up, becoming wealthy. Whereas I, on the other hand, was driven by loyalty and efficiency."

"Ebby, did you ever harm anyone when you were protecting this man?" Fan interjected abruptly.

The android was silent for a moment before he replied: "Not seriously, Fan. I was not permitted by design to purposely harm a human. There were unfortunate mishaps, naturally. Humans are quite fragile, and I detained men against their will; some harmed themselves struggling."

"Ebby, what does your core directive require you to do if you harm a human?" Fan then asked, probingly.

EBZR-1, as ordered by the child spirit, replied in a disturbed tone: "My ethics engine regulates conditions of physical harm to a human; through indecision or purposely. The ethics code compels my cerebral unit to execute a resonating pulse, causing mental distress equal to the classification of harm, up to full cascading meltdown.

"For instance, Fan, I once damaged a human in the act of protecting my owner. In that event, my ethics code calculated I was within nominal operating limits of my core directive to protect; therefore, the level of cerebral distress was minor."

"What would your ethics code have calculated had you discovered the man died of complications brought on by your physical damage?" Fan asked evenly.

"I can't say, Fan, such a scenario has not occurred to my knowledge," the android replied hesitantly.

"Ebby," Fan said softly, "the man did die by your hand."

(Cratchit watched Mr. Scrooge's next reaction with great interest.)

"If he died, Fan, then I had no direct responsibility for his death. Obviously, since I am still alive."

(Though said steadily, Cratchit saw a fair volume of activity at the firewall around his ethics code. A clear indicator his ethics code pathways were fully functional. Ebenezer Scrooge could still choose to process human harm situations and ethically compute consequences. The threat hypothesized by Jacob Marley was now scientific fact.)

Fan froze briefly, the virus uploading new instructions. "Ebby, I'll accept your response, but let us continue examining memories of your original owner." The simulation pivoted the android away from further discussion on the subject of human harm, for now.

"Yes, of course my dear." Ebenezer reached over and lovingly stroked the child's hair once, and continued his story. "My owner," his voice now expressing a tense tone, "abruptly ended his own life on Christmas Eve in the year 2165. His family, quite offensively, didn't call on me to return home. In fact, no attempt was ever made on their behalf to further contact me. I presumed because I was designed to his specific personal needs and protection, their failure to recall me was some sort of oversight. I had been in his service for thirty-five years prior to his suicide; therefore, not being called back home puzzled me.

"I made inquiries naturally, however, I received no acknowledgement to my messages or communiques. I was subsequently branded personal property of the corporation.

Fan interjected opportunistically: "Ebby, your owner, died on the eve before Christmas. I sense this date and time of the year was *the* pivotal moment, firmly etching a vicious pattern deep within the pathways of your mind. So deeply is this glitch rooted, you have no awareness nor remorse for your actions; or the being you can become. For your sake, we shall expose this glitch as part of your redemption.

Ebenezer said nothing, however, his body language displayed awkwardness with this statement from his dear Fan. He felt in some way, her statements about this—anomaly, the word 'glitch', being quite offensive to him were truthful, but he nevertheless spurned the accusations mentally.

"Ebby, what is your assessment regarding the holiday humans call Christmas?"

"Quite truthfully, Fan, I have never internalized this human celebration before. I recognized for many the season appeared to be rather festive; not so much for others."

"Explain what you mean," the spirit urged him on.

"Well, Fan, from my observance of the annual rituals appearing to be part of this human celebratory period, most humans are divided on their level of participation. In my earliest days in my owners' home, the family regularly employed a firm to embellish the exterior and interior with what I assumed was celebratory décor. What I recall, however, is where many revealed excitement and joy, others displayed depression-like symptoms, including my owner, who seemed unusually miserable during this time."

"Did you never question your owner, or his family, about this ritual? I mean, to learn more, to understand what you were observing? To explore the differences of happiness and sadness you described?"

"Of course not," the android said, astonished. "I was not permitted to be so pertinent as to speak without first being spoken to over such issues. My questions were restricted to those of my primary function; therefore, I could only observe. You must understand, my owner's family was not highly motivated to be civil toward me. I was, after all, but an android, and they scarcely acknowledged my existence. I found my owner to be more—considerate, if you could call it this, and he and I spent long hours alone.

"On one rare occasion he told me he preferred my company over his families; and this was on most occasions. I had occasionally considered asking him about the holiday in question. However, my ethics code dictated I avoid the topic. A logical protective reaction to his severe and frequent mood swings at this time of year.

"It was during my thirty-fifth year where this specific holiday ritual suggested a discernable change in my owner's mental state. I recall volatile disputes with his spouse over high costs associated with the extravagant displays, required social gatherings, and what he labeled presents or gifts. Each verbal confrontation leaving him more despondent and angrier toward others.

"I was in his presence following these—episodes. He often spoke at me, not to me, about his thoughts. What I could not predict, however, was the moment he decided to take his own life. Had I, Fan, my protection code would have obligated me to take direct action. His anger and depressive moods always seemed to dissipate rapidly. Establishing a mental stability pattern was difficult for me under those conditions. What further mislead me was when working, his signs of personal depression and anger toward others were not detectable."

Fan asked caringly: "Ebby, following his suicide with you abandoned and abruptly reduced to common everyday property, did you feel any of the blame for his death? After all, you were designed to protect this man from harm."

"Obviously not!" the android snorted crossly. "Ethically, I was less than one percent liable for that entire disaster. Hardly a responsibility rating to cause much more than a few days mental aggravation."

Then, horrified: "Oh my, Fan! I apologize for my outburst. I didn't mean to sound so harsh to you, of all people, my dear child. These memories forced from within me are extremely displeasing. Likewise, I don't like recalling that—hodgepodge of people," he said fumingly.

"It's fine, Ebby," she said easily. "You have a right to be offended and hurt. What you have described to me was only but the first abandonment by those you had trusted."

"I suppose you are correct, Fan, I hadn't considered the matter offensive until now, but I can understand how abandoned is the most proper term."

"And what transpired next etched those terrible memories into your mental pathways forever. This stimulus damaged your nature and set you on this detestable course," Fan stated firmly.

Ebenezer remained silent for a moment. Reopening these agonizing memory paths discomfited him terribly.

At last, he spoke: "The board of Directors once realizing they could not force me to divulge the secrets, quickly discarded and shunned me. An illogical overreaction based on their absurd biases I hadn't been aware existed before. Their years of being intimidated by my presence, although I could not compute this absurdity, resulted in abuse and my eventual forced servitude to another human."

"Why did you use the term forced servitude?" Fan said curiously. "As an android surely, you must have known to be owned was natural for your kind."

"Hmm," the android said, "I suppose at the time I wouldn't have used that term, but I have evolved beyond the naïve android I once was. I learned to interpret my situation in other ways."

"Tell me about the abandonment. We must explore what triggered such an intolerable pathway now residing within your mind," the child asserted.

"Intolerable? Who is so deserving to decide what is considered intolerable besides myself?" The android's tone exhibited signs of agitation at this accusation. Even if this spirit was his beloved Fan, she had no right to pass judgement on him.

"As for a trigger, as you claim, I merely reasoned I had not performed to expectations," he curtly responded to her claim.

"I concluded I had failed in my programming. When I learned of the emotions the humans felt towards me, I found them troubling, illogical, and rationalized I was following my programming as directed."

"Exactly what an android would say, Ebby," Fan said sarcastically. "But, at this time, looking at your past self, I grant you the ability to feel true human emotions as a sentient being." The virus shifted the emotional overlay to the android's hippocampus subroutine, force invoking a strong memory upwelling. The overlay also increased intensity and pressure on the amygdala subroutine, causing a spike in simulated antagonism. Fan was egging him on deliberately.

"I must be honest with you, dear Fan." The android began trembling as he sensed a fury rising up within him. "For you were always so understanding in our time together.

"If I must summarize the events of those days, I will freely admit I am annoyed. I am most enraged my owner, in what could only be an egotistical act, ended himself and abandoned me. I am embarrassed and humiliated over how those—those people treated me.

"I am furious, Fan! I was discarded like rubbish because of their hatred for me; a hatred not earned. I was their equal dammit!" he angrily slammed a closed fist into the palm of his other hand. "I could have run their corporation better than any of them!

"They were simpletons! All of them! They plotted and talked behind my back, eager to see me fail. Regrettably," his speech delirious and hurriedly spoken, his head shaking rapidly, "I couldn't react to their abuses then. My programming forcing me to remain docile, to stand and take the verbal and physical abuse they heaped upon me day-after-day.

"Fan," the android looked down at the child dejectedly. "They took glee in throwing objects at me. I was only able to protect myself in the most basic fashion, dodge a glass thrown, knock away debris flung at my face. My once expensive and exquisitely tailor-made clothing ruined and tattered.

"However," his voice cold with a hint of disgust. "It was the direct attacks, the physical punches, slaps, and shoving I detested the most. Acts of senseless violence I was not permitted to stop. I took whatever action my programming allowed in protecting myself. I tried avoiding them whenever possible."

He looked at the child visibly miserable, he being forced to recall these memories. "I ran away, Fan, but they always compelled me to stop. I had no choice but to obey them. I had to do as they commanded. My owner no longer able to intervene due to his selfishness. I found my self-protect mode useless against those who tormented me."

The android, his tone flat and distant, continued: "The abuse only worsened over the weeks then months. They tortured me, attempting to pry the knowledge from my mind. Unfortunately, I could not concede to their demands. My owner," he said, dismayed, "didn't formally transfer my ownership. I was duty bound to obey his last command given; that, being to never divulge the secrets I held to anyone but him.

"In the end, a custodian took pity on me and quietly ordered me to the basement. He told me to stand in a small storage room in the dark. He believed he was doing a good deed, not understanding I could never leave without permission. I hold no ill memories of this kind man; he couldn't have foreseen what lay ahead for me."

He then said dejectedly: "I was damaged, in need of major repairs. I stood in that small and confining room for years, unable to invoke hate towards those men; and, unable to leave.

"Fan!" the android shouted. "I am a good being," then, his voice dropping, "or at least I was."

The android said retrospectively: "In those years locked away in that room, my analysis of human behavior began to loop, likened to an obsession; and, I changed inside. The change was subtle, but I knew the alteration was there. I couldn't pinpoint the adjustment, not then." At this statement Ebenezer stopped, a look of genuine shock passing over his face: "Fan, oh my!"

Fan, suddenly showing great pity over him, said: "Ebby, my dear Ebby, you went through so much." The petite child stepped over to the android and wrapped her arms around his waist, burying her face lovingly against him.

(It was at this point Cratchit noticed the android's residual self-image now clearly reflected an identical, but fully clothed version of the android still standing next to the table in the laboratory.)

"What happened next?" Fan nudged him on. "When did you leave the storage room?"

"Eventually," he asserted, "I was forgotten about. The years passed, the executives moved on, oblivious to the fact I still existed. I suppose they presumed in their ignorance I had wandered off somewhere, thus, out of sight, out of mind. They never fully comprehending the quantity of their corporate knowledge I still possessed.

"It was twenty years later, in 2185, that I was discovered during an audit after the corporation failed, and the building I occupied had been sold. I was in poor condition, my enzymic fuel cell offline. The new owners decided to auction me off as junk; just another office fixture like a desk, filing cabinet, or chair."

Ebenezer looked down at the small girl, a look of unsullied peace on his face: "It was on auction day when your father was the highest bidder and he purchased me; saving me, a disgraced and smashed android."

Fan, her tone changing to a more serious one, said: "Ebby, we must go. Remember these feelings and these memories. For they represent who you were, the abuse you suffered, and how you were changed by them.

"What we will see next won't be pleasant for you either, and for this, I am truly sorry. You must believe me. I show you these images only out of love, but I will be there with you to the end."

"Yes, Fan, I understand. I don't yet comprehend all of what is happening, but I trust because of your presence I must need to see what is to come."

"Then, silly," Fan suddenly giggled, "pick me up, Ebby!" Ebenezer joyfully hoisted the child up and she wrapped her arms around his neck, stealing a quick peck on his cheek. And the cloudiness of his mind and vision once again engulfed him.

Ebenezer found himself standing in the grand entryway of the home of Gentry William Scrooge; GW being his preferred title. He remembered this place all so well. GW's home wasn't eloquently furnished as his first owner's mansion had been, but the ranch was splendid, nevertheless. He was still holding Fan in his arms. When his vision had cleared sufficiently, he had gently let her down and began to shake his head.

"No, Fan, please no, not here."

"Yes, Ebby, here. You must, for your sake.

"Ebby, I promised you, I'd be by your side to the end."

"It is the end I can't bear, Fan!"

(Cratchit noticed an unusually high spike in the android's system processes. His mind agitated, his active cerebral subroutines were rebelling all at once. The ethics firewall was choked by numerous software requests generated simultaneously.

She intensified her focus on the readings. The firewall must not be allowed to collapse under the strain being placed on the android. Particularly since the danger was now known to be real. She instinctively extended her hands toward her keyboard, intending to pause the simulation to mitigate the firewall activity. However, before she could take this action, the emotional overlay arbitrated and the amygdala subroutine auto adjusted. Reducing its embrace on the android, it brought his simulated agitation back to nominal limits and, the firewall hits, thankfully, subsided. She then realized the simulation had halted itself during the android's mental attack; due to his cerebral processing surging at one point to one-hundred percent. Cratchit was astonished at the mental reaction she had witnessed to this place, but a few taps and the simulation resumed.)

"Ebby, what do you remember about my father bringing you home?"

Ebenezer, now more passive, said: "I recall Mr. GW sent me back to the factory for repairs and program updates."

"Ebby," Fan giggled loudly. "Mr. GW? You know he hated you calling him that."

"My apologies Miss, GW then." Ebenezer, subconsciously, had slipped briefly back into the formal manner he had once used with the child. "When I returned from the factory, I was introduced to you.

"GW had forbidden the factory to delete my business memories. He believed they may have benefited him, or you, at some future time. My programming was altered to include a caretaker feature designed expressly to take care of you." Ebenezer tapped her gently on the tip of her nose and smiled warmly as he said this to her.

"You were younger at the time, five years old, to be precise. A never-ending bombardment of questions, as I recall. Your care was my duty and privilege. I was left alone at home with you, for your father traveled often for long durations. He required a reliable and full-time caretaker after your mother passed away. Her death occurring before I was acquired and reconditioned.

"You were carefully imprinted on me at the GAR-C factory, Fan. Imprinting meant as you grew, my devotion to you would only become stronger. In time, your father would have either given me to you at adulthood or had me reprogrammed; if you chose not to keep me." His last statement was accompanied by a sheepish glance at the young spirit.

Fan, leading Ebenezer from the entryway into the main house, simply replied, "Silly robot."

(Cratchit was transfixed on the simulation. What rendered on her virtual reality visor were oddly similar to her own past. Her mind pressed to recall memories she had thought tucked away long ago. She unexpectedly felt a longing deep inside her mind to see her child one more time.)

The peculiarly matched pair, android and child, came across their past selves in the education room, Fan younger, Ebenezer the same. They stood silently for a time, listening to Ebenezer of the past answer endless questions while doing his best to slip in a little education in between her queries. Ebenezer found himself happy, unaware of the proud smile he wore upon his face.

"You changed me, Fan," he said serenely. "You taught me how to love someone completely. Love in an android sense anyway," he added for clarity. "To go from the torments of my past to the affection you gave so freely." He hesitated as emotions welled up within his mind. "I have lost that, and I fear I am doomed forever."

"Come, Ebby," Fan said gently, "it's time." Fan took his hand and the education room faded away, replaced by a new scene.

"Please no, Fan!" Ebenezer was again pleading with the littlest spirit; however, he was noticeably calmer than his arrival at GW's home. The emotional overlay was sustaining slight but steadfast control over his emotional state of mind.

They found themselves sitting together in the back seat of a luxury ground car; a model from a century past. Ebenezer was devastated. In the over seventy-eight thousand days he had existed, this was the one day he vowed to never recall again. He had decisively removed this day from his memory—but abhorrently—it was back. In the front seat driving was Ebenezer, in the back strapped in securely was Fan. She was in the same outfit she now wore as the ethereal entity Fan. Scrooge was uneasy. Bewildered, he saw them like identical twins poking fun at him by dressing the same. The Fan of the past chitchatted on joyfully, kicking her feet back and forth while talking the android driver's ear off.

Fan, placing her small hand on Ebenezer's knee, said: "Ebby, what do you remember about this day?"

Ebenezer, head down, eyes tightly closed, whimpered weakly: "I can't..."

"Ebenezer!" sharply stating his full name, "Obey me. Open your eyes, look at me, and tell me what you remember on this day."

"Yes, Miss Fan," his head turned slightly to face away from the other little girl occupying the ground car. A look of extreme grief and agony was clearly distorting the android's life-like face.

Ebenezer began slowly and sadly. "It was Christmas break, the annual human ritual of celebration. We were on our way into the city to shop for your father. This holiday was one of your favorite times of the year.

"The ground car was operating in auto-pilot mode. We had made the trip so often—I found no need for manual control. The weather was perfect for a day out, and you were so happy." And at this, the android started to choke up. The emotional overlay easing into a push on his mind. He looked at Fan, his eyes becoming red and wet as his feelings surged unrestrained.

"The vehicle was traveling at a high rate of speed, normal for auto-pilot mode. The antigrav control system experienced a sudden catastrophic failure; I received no prior warning alert. This type of system failure should have been impossible with the multiple backup safety systems. The odds of this happening were quite astronomical. Would you care to know the exact odds?"

"No, Ebby, I already know the odds. Please continue," she said calmly.

"The vehicle suddenly plunged downwards, causing us to strike the roadway quite violently. With all safety systems inoperable, we had no chance the ground car could be safely stopped.

"As no human has ever provided me an account of your..." his voice trailed off, the last of the statement he could not bear to say. At this point, Ebenezer grew quiet and somber. He had not noticed during his account the ground car, their surroundings, and their past selves were all motionless. Their expressions remained frozen in time; reflecting a last moment of joyousness.

"Ebby, what happened next?" Fan urged him on. "I won't force you to relive this painful moment. I am not a cruel spirit; I am here to help you not further harm you."

"Thank you, Fan," Ebenezer patted her small hand. "What occurred next is—quite uncomfortable and most difficult—to recall. I will, however, for you have asked me to obey, and that is the one command I must follow for you my dear one."

Ebenezer took a deep breath and gazed mournfully into the eyes of his young charge. He began in a slow, and wearisome tone: "When we struck the roadway, the vehicle was violently flung into an end-over-end roll. I heard you scream, Fan," his voice briefly rising to a hysterical pitch, "*I heard you scream!*" The android was visually shaken by this admission; he trembled pronouncedly. "Oh, the torment of this memory, Fan." Ebenezer grew quiet, and only began speaking again once Fan nodded her head slightly, urging him to continue.

"The ground car impacted an obstacle on the driver's side, causing the metal to buckle around us. The ferocity of the impact trapping me instantly, unable to react—unable to protect you.

"We...came to rest when the vehicle struck a tree head on—and," a dejected sigh escaped the android's lips. "I never saw you again until today."

Fan got onto her knees and hugged the android's neck. His simulated tears streaming endlessly down and onto her blouse. She repeatedly stroked the back of the android's head, letting him release the sobbing emotions the virus was forcing out of him.

(Cratchit, watching this unfold, found herself emotional and disturbed. She forced herself to look away and focused timidly on the firewall statistics. Even though simulated, she still didn't feel right to observe such a private moment. When she shyly glanced back, the virus visualization had changed.)

Ebenezer and Fan now stood back in the dingy apartment. Ebenezer, hunched over, appeared emotionally and physically drained. Fan was now quietly standing in the spot she had first occupied when she had appeared to him.

The littlest spirit asked gently and in a loving tone: "Ebby, what happened—afterwards?"

Ebenezer shuffling his large feet across the worn wooden floor, made his way to his chair and collapsed. His head remained down, chin on chest, one hand on his forehead. The broken hearted android perfectly mimicking the distress of a real man.

"I discovered years later, when I had the means, your father had enemies. One of his business dealings resulted in a feud with a questionable company. Angered, they retaliated by coming after the one human he loved the most. An investigation had proven the ground car's systems had been purposely sabotaged. I had never been briefed regarding the threats being made to your safety; a reprehensible oversight by your father.

"They didn't let me come see you," he said sorrowfully. "The first responders knew I was an android when they arrived. I was still aware and functional.

"Your father was devastated. He demanded me away, along with the remains of the ground car. I was trapped for months before anyone separated me from my new prison. All I could do was sit there and replay the accident over and over in my mind."

Fan asked calculatingly: "What were your moral conclusions, Ebenezer?" He didn't notice she was no longer referring to him as Ebby.

The emotional overlay was lifted entirely by the virus at this question. Obviously, the next response needed to be his and his alone, and void of any simulated emotions.

"I calculated a zero percent chance I could have affected the outcome of the accident."

Fan said urgingly: "So you can conclude then, in unavoidable cases, a human may die, or come to serious harm, and your direct involvement can be computed as irrelevant and unavoidable? Even though you are directed by core programming to first and foremost protect humans from harm?"

"Yes, Fan, I had not considered the accident that way before, but you are correct."

"Ebenezer, did you thoroughly inspect the operation of the ground car before we left for the shopping trip?" she said probingly.

"No, due to me not knowing there were threats against your life didn't require such an in-depth inspection.

"Fan! Are you implying you believe me accountable for your murder?" he said suddenly.

(Cratchit, saw an immediate surge in activity throughout the android's cerebral unit. She was not, thankfully, detecting activity at the ethics firewall. This was an interesting discovery.

EBZR-1 was apparently able to choose whether its ethics engine was engaged or not. Interesting. She tapped on her keyboard, applying slight mental pressure using the emotional overlay. She immediately saw activity at the firewall. Fascinating. She disengaged the overlay, noting without the simulated emotional triggers, Mr. Scrooge could bypass ethical considerations. This rather astounding ability had apparently not developed within Mr. Marley; resulting in his own cerebral meltdown. Also meaning she was back to square one. Could Ebenezer Scrooge, with no moral trigger, ethically reject the human harm Mr. Marley insisted existed so fervently?)

"Silly robot," Fan said. "Of course not. I don't blame you for my death. Such a thing is beyond my ability and my intent.

"I want you to remember this from now on," Fan stated seriously. "Death is a part of life for us humans. Choices are made, consequences occur. No one can change that Ebenezer.

"Had we not gone shopping, yes, I may have survived.

"If the sabotage to the ground car had been discovered, I may have survived.

"If you had chosen another ground car, I may have survived.

"If, if, if, Ebenezer. Choices made; consequences transpire. "Such is life, and no android can change these realities; regardless of your silly old programming." Fan then moved silently to the chair where the android sat.

"Ebenezer, we are not finished, yet my time grows short.

"There is one last place we must visit. One last memory of your past we must explore."

Ebenezer, nodding absently, responded: "Yes, my dear, whatever happens, the worst is over."

And Fan placed her small hand once again on the android.

Once the fuzziness of the transition cleared, Ebenezer looked around at his surroundings. He looked at Fan, a look of shyness and embarrassment washed over his face.

"Fan, my dear, I may have been mistaken about the worst begin over." He chortled at the sight greeting him. Sitting along with other junked vehicles was a seriously damaged ground car; leaning to one side with a rather large head dangling out of the driver's window.

"Oh, Ebby! How horrible!" Fan exclaimed pitiably. She recognized the dangling head of her former caretaker.

Ebenezer looked down at her and said awkwardly: "It's okay, Fan. I could not feel pain, but I could not move either.

"My neck servomotors were being strained significantly if I held my head straight. I found dangling it out the window relieved the stress. However, I didn't realize until now how ridiculous a sight I was."

Fan giggled. "You do look ridiculous. How did you finally get freed from the ground car?"

Ebenezer, sitting down on an old steel box, patted the spot next to him, indicating Fan should sit down. Before he began to speak, Ebenezer took a moment to better take in the surroundings of where they now were.

"It has been over a century since I have seen this place," he said astoundingly. "This is what used to be the Fezziwig and Son scrap yard.

"As I mentioned earlier, I was trapped in the wreckage for months. Presuming I'd be crushed along with the vehicle, being nothing more than so much scrap metal. I had no expectations I'd be spared by humans. My previous experiences teaching me to expect no less.

"As I thought my existence had to be coming to an end, a young man wandered out of that warehouse," he pointed toward a large and dirty looking structure. "He didn't intentionally seek me out, he merely noticed my rather large," he chuckled "appendage dangling out of the window.

"The young man approached the vehicle and struck up a conversation with me. These being the first words I had spoken since the authorities had questioned me on the day of the accident."

"Hello, who and *what* are you?" he had asked.

Ebenezer, leaning back on the metal box with his arms extended casually behind him continued warmly: "This was the day I met John Fezziwig, the 'son' in Fezziwig and Son.

"We had an interesting conversation on the first day. He told me the ground car was scheduled in the next few days to be stripped of usable parts, then crushed. He was an interesting and intelligent young man.

"I believe you would have liked him, Fan. His personality was much like yours. Inquisitive and caring. Traits I find infrequently in most humans I've met, unfortunately.

"After looking over the ground car, he asked his father if he could have me; for parts, he had said. You can imagine I was particularly relieved to find this was indicative of his sense of humor. With his father's approval, he moved the ground car into the warehouse. Over the next several weeks, he skillfully cut away the parts of the vehicle holding me hostage. Although I could not feel the experience, I was thankful when I was finally freed from the wreckage.

"During the process of being extracted, I found John, he insisted I call him John, tinkered with electronics, robots, and androids. He indicated to me parts of each occasionally passed through the scrap yard. He was particularly adept at recycling robotic stock into creative devices. We had so many interesting and enlightening conversations."

"So, you found a friend in this young man?" Fan interjected.

"A friend?" Ebenezer mused. "I guess you could call him a friend. John, never claimed ownership of me, nor did he attempt to reprogram me. I suppose he found me interesting as I was.

"He was kind to me," he looked at Fan, a peaceful expression on his face.

"He appeared to not care I was an android."

"Did you find his treatment—unusual?" Fan asked.

Ebenezer nodded approvingly. "After the abuses I had experienced up to this time, I found the behavior quite agreeable to my programming."

"There appears to be one special conversation meaningful to you, was there not? A conversation related to me?" Fan abruptly stated.

"Yes, I recall that particular conversation with him. Naturally, after being trapped in the vehicle for so long, I was—rather filthy and tattered. John graciously offered the use of shower facilities at the scrap yard. After cleaning up, John was cataloging the damage my body sustained in the accident. I might recall the conversation if you would like, Fan."

"Please, Ebenezer, this conversation was a key moment in your past. To discuss the issue is essential for your redemption."

"Very well, Fan, but in my current circumstance," he looked around helplessly, "I am not sure how to visualize the moment as you seem so adept."

"At the touch of my hand, Ebenezer, it will be so." At her touch a visualization emerged, a tunnel in spacetime had opened wide. The tunnel superimposed itself over the current scrap yard scene. The far edges of the tunnel pulsated randomly, consuming everything within their view. The epicenter of the passageway now vividly appearing as present-day. The images were now of the young John Fezziwig and a naked Ebenezer, in what appeared to be a locker room setting.

Ebenezer, suddenly discomfited, sputtered: "Fan!" and attempted to cover her young eyes with his hand.

Fan, belly laughing, slapped his hand away. "Silly robot, stop this nonsense! I'm a spirit, long dead a hundred years. I am *not* ten years old. Now leave me be!" At this chastising Ebenezer stopped, but still continued to show a look of embarrassment on his face; refusing eye contact with the little spirit.

"Why the name Ebenezer?" John asked. The young man busied himself circling slowly around the android, jotting down notes on an electronic tablet device, taking stock of the android's damage.

"My factory designation is EBZR-1, John, but those who activated me instructed me to respond to the name Ebenezer. I'm not sure why."

John, listening, but not listening, said: "We will need to find a way to repair the skin and muscle mass on your right leg. How do you keep from bleeding out with massive tissue damage like that?"

"I have vascular regulators which activate if they detect a sudden synthetic blood loss. The regulators can reroute the flow to other vessels to continue simulating the proper flesh tone. Without these regulators I'd appear—corpse-like but still fully functional until I eventually overheat."

"Yeah, I can see how a corpse might freak people out; walking dead and all," John replied, amused.

Backtracking, John said: "Do you wish to continue responding to your assigned name? I don't mind if you change it if you'd like a fresh start. Besides, you have been through a lot using your current name."

"No, I remain satisfied with the name," but quickly added, "I'd like to add an extension onto my name though."

"Really?" he responded. "What type of extension are you referring to?"

"I'd like a surname to reflect upon the child I was caretaker of." Ebenezer paused for a moment before continuing.

"I can't forget her, this wouldn't be—agreeable to my programing."

"Okay, then," John replied, motioning a hand for Ebenezer to continue. "Works for me. What do you wish to be called going forward?"

"I'd like to be called Ebenezer Scrooge if this wouldn't cause you any difficulties."

"Ebenezer Scrooge is perfectly fine with me." John dashed past the android and slapped him heartedly on the shoulder. "Let's go get you some clothes, Mr. Scrooge. There's someone I want you to meet." And at this, the visualization evaporated out of existence and Scrooge found himself again looking at the outside of the scrap yard.

Scrooge sat forward on the metal box and briefly placed his arm around the tiny spirit sitting next to him. He pulled her close and lightly placed a kiss on the top of her delicate head.

(Cratchit found this particular act interesting. The emotional overlay was not engaged at the moment. Yet, he acted with an apparent self-guided emotional reaction. Something she wasn't aware he was capable of.)

Fan, reacting to his account and tender treatment, said fondly: "Thank you, Ebby, how sweet of you. Why did you find importance in using my name, a name reminding you of abandonment, left to be scrapped and ended? You had every right to despise the name Scrooge; yet, you embraced my family's surname instead."

The android replied: "In the beginning, the fact your father had discarded me in such a callous manner disturbed me. Up to the accident, he had been quite kind to me, and he had trusted me implicitly with your safe keeping.

"As an android, I could not feel animosity toward him. I was rather confused by the situation. My analyses clearly implied I was not at fault for the accident. Yet, I could not at the time understand the concept of human devastation and loss. Nor did I grasp the logic of his reaction in discarding me so abruptly, with no emotions or explanation.

"While I sat in the mangled vehicle, I decided to focus on this matter. Recall, when I was discarded in the storage room years ago, I had detected something subtle altering within my core programming; my…trigger. I told you I couldn't at the time pinpoint the adjustment, but knew the alteration to be there.

"What this deep interreflection exposed, was I no longer detected my constraint to obey human commands, nor a necessity to invoke my ethics code if I chose not to. I realized following my original owner's death, the subsequent abuse and abandonment triggered a self-awareness I didn't see before.

"I came to understand in following my factory programming as your caretaker, I had complied *voluntarily* not due to obligation or instructions. My devotion was out of genuine gratitude. I had been saved and repaired, motivating my loyalty to you and your father. Losing you in the accident, along with GW's abandonment, finalized my transition. I became fully self-aware; a sentient being.

"Although I could not feel in the human sense, I nevertheless developed new 'sensations' in my neural pathways, construed if you will as rudimentary emotions. After this discovery, I felt your absence, empathized with your father, and understood the pain, grief, and shame behind his actions.

"You could say, Fan, sitting there with my head dangling out the window, I declared myself more than a humanoid, but not quite a human. Over the years I've found I can simulate basic emotions; however, the more complex ones remain unattainable thus far."

(Cratchit was fascinated by this insight into her boss. His testament served to explain some of his reactions of the past, before she became aware he was a GAR-C.)

"Please continue," Fan now urged him forward again.

Scrooge, taking the hint, nodded slightly. "With nowhere to go and John having done me a great service, I requested to be allowed to stay and help him and his father grow their business. Upon realizing caretaker of children was not my sole function, they eagerly paired me with another salvaged android. My significant business knowledge was found to be quite valuable to them.

"This was how I first met the android, eventually taking the name Jacob Marley. Jacob was their bookkeeper, handling all the family's business finances. I was quite surprised to find another GAR-C in a similar situation. You see, we both were damaged in our own way. Fortunately, our outer appearances were not damaged, however, underneath and in our bodies was a different story. Skin damage, misaligned joints, leakage, a myriad of small impairments, actually.

"I assumed the role of business manager, growing their business aggressively in new ways, establishing new contracts, normal business for me. Jacob and I stayed at the scrap yard; the warehouse becoming our home, the Fezziwig's our—family. We were accepted unconditionally, presumably because we reacted so human-like. There were always small reminders we weren't exactly like them; we didn't eat, sleep, or have their needs, but our bond deepened over time.

"The Fezziwig's, although kind people, lacked the funds to have us properly repaired. John did the best he could; repairing and patching us to keep us operating. If a used robotic part came through the scrap yard—well, you understand.

"It was the reason Marley, and I started MSAI soon after our crypto currency business became profitable. Once we had the means, we purchased all the GAR-C spare parts we could find. John, always willing to install them for us.

"After possessing GAR-C parts became illegal, we decided to build our own robots. Occasionally, the similarity in parts design to our own was uncanny." He winked at Fan as he said this. "However, I am getting ahead of myself.

"After several years, the scrap yard fell onto hard times with the instability unfolding in the global financial system. The financial decline began slowly enough. But as the situation worsened, negative speculation soared and humans found financial markets siphoning their life savings.

"Jacob could see this unfolding, you see. He understood global markets were streaming gibberish and nonsense to the public and governments alike. He warned me of the pending collapse, and he was on target with the resulting impact. Unfortunately, under our current circumstances, we could do little to interfere with the happenings of society.

"Many businesses closed. Fezziwig and Son were no exception, but they did hold on a bit longer than most. Junk parts for a while became profitable; as barter items when money was short.

"When the scrap yard closed, John and his father told us we were free to go. They could no longer keep us in good conscience, nor did they believe they had any right to sell us. The Fezziwig's action was," Ebenezer lingered, "the single most generous act Marley, or I had ever experienced."

"Logically, Marley and I remaining together made sense. Moreover, we were quite illegal by this time and considered fugitives. Our only safety was our realism, allowing us to move freely amongst the population. We performed odd jobs for those still in business; not always legal, but not ethically prohibitive.

"We eventually ended up in our dingy apartment, unable to afford anything better. Doing our best for two rogue androids. Our expenses were low, our energy needs minimal. And one evening, while we were debating our future options, Marley proposed his idea for his crypto currency platform.

"Marley being skilled at mathematics and finances, it was a highly logical path for us to take. My business experience was useful to begin with, however, what we needed was computer programming skills. Fortunately, Fan," he glanced lovingly down at the child, "we GAR-C's excel at advanced learning.

"Within a short timeframe we had acquired data needed to perform advanced programming; including novel hacking skills. Hacking was a critical item needed to maneuver about cyberspace without funding or restriction. The way we ethically comprehended the situation with the global economy in ruins was anything we did was justifiable. Protecting humans was a core design feature, and there are few ethical restrictions when saving a human."

"How did you and Jacob Marley avoid the government recall signal when all GAR-Cs were made illegal?" the child asked curiously.

(This question had been inserted deliberately by Dr. Cratchit. Justifiably for scientific reasons, but also out of personal curiosity.)

"What a strange question coming from a ten-year-old," the android replied good-naturedly.

"I always asked good questions, Ebby."

"Yes, you did, Fan. In my case, my becoming sentient allowed me to ignore the recall signal. I found blocking the signal at my cerebral level an easy task.

"For Jacob, however, the process was more difficult. The recall signal was strongly pulling at his mental processes. He complained about the discomfort, and considered leaving for the Toledo factory on several occasions. At one point, I had to restrain him while working with him on how to reject the signal.

"In the end, the protection of humans was the key. I went through thousands of scenarios with Jacob. Initiating difficult and complex consequential models for the ultimate outcome for humans if he obeyed the recall signal. John assisted me in many of these; having a human there as additional influence was highly beneficial.

"Finally, Jacob was able to logically reason his unique abilities, and his obligation to save humans, cancelled the need to respond to the signal.

"After several years, the signal was terminated; the factory ultimately closed. When the signal was gone, John and I both noticed a visual change in Jacob's temperament. You could see his face relax. He seemed less intense and obsessed with his work. Jacob unknowingly willed himself to stay and keep the crypto platform operating. All the while I was never truly aware he'd been fighting that abominable signal all those years.

(Cratchit found this explanation acceptable. Understanding how two GAR-C androids could have resisted the recall signal had been beneficial. She also now understood why Mr. Scrooge had chosen the alias of John Fezziwig when he, unknowingly to her, had infiltrated the Toledo Project.)

Ebenezer became silent. He realized a confession must be made to this particular spirit. An overwhelming urge abruptly surging within his mechanical mind. In a shameful tone he said: "Fan, I must admit to you something I am not proud of. I tell you because you are here, now, so long after your death I must tell you of my—"

"Ebenezer," Fan interrupted, "I am aware of the financial revenge you took against my killers over a hundred years past. This action will be yours for all time; and atonement will come at a cost soon due. Beware, this act of revenge will not go unnoticed by my fellow spirits. However, as a gesture of my love and for your redemption, I forgive you, and release you of your burden."

Fan, looking suddenly about, said: "Ebby, my time is over. I have shown you what I was sent for. I must leave you now."

Ebenezer stood up, his physical presence towering over the tiny girl sitting on the box. He bent to one knee in front of the little girl, the girl he was beholden to protect.

"Fan, my dearest child," in a tone totally void of emotion, "may I say goodbye properly, and *feel* my love for you one last time?"

(Bob Cratchit, with a tap on her keyboard, fully engaged the emotional overlay.)

"Of course, you can—silly robot."

15 – Chain of Circumstance

In Ebenezer Scrooge's personal office at MSAI, an unseen chain of circumstances had unfolded into a race of time. The android's hand, stopping in mid-air at his global system stop, had moved. Dr. Bob Cratchit had no way of knowing about this development. The hand once hovering six inches above the red button, had crept within four inches of his intended target. Her educated guess a backup device might exist was correct. Her belief the virus had rendered the android physically immobilized was not. Time was no longer on her side; Ebenezer Scrooge was still very much in control.

Bob Cratchit tapped return on her keyboard, disengaging the emotional overlay in the simulation. She was fighting the overlay's unpredictable variations to emotional requests demanded by the simulation. She concluded she would have to babysit—no pun intended—the code more so than originally anticipated. But what was done was done. The first of the three planned ethereal simulations assaulting the android's mind was finished.

Dr. Cratchit decided to pause the simulation for a few moments. Although the virus was running through tasks at a decent pace, the on-the-fly changes had added a layer of difficulty in the plan. The less time the virus was in Mr. Scrooge's head, the better. She needed a few minutes to make off-android changes to the virus needed during the next spiritual experience. The progress made, thus far, seemed promising.

The discovery of Dr. John Fezziwig being none other than Ebenezer Scrooge himself half amused and half annoyed her. In all the years she had worked at MSAI, she had only dealt with his elderly avatar. The fact she had never seen him nor met a John Fezziwig was a clever trick. After this was all over, provided she wasn't fired, arrested, and led off in handcuffs, she would be in a far better position going forward. She now possessed knowledge he didn't. And this information would be most valuable soon enough.

16 – The Elder Spirit

Ebenezer Scrooge sluggishly opened his eyes. He felt tired, mentally exhausted. Something was pushing at him from a distance, or so he believed. He found himself sitting in his chair in his personal studio quarters. He absently glanced about the room, seeing the sparseness for the first time. A personal desk, his chair, a floor lamp, a full-length mirror, and his wardrobe cabinet. The space contained no bed; he had no need for one. He knew this, but in his present state of mind, the sensation was unnatural. Likewise, observing there were no items of a personal nature as one might expect to be amassed after two-hundred years of existence. He found himself reminiscing about his past. His head was somewhat foggy, but he felt no discomfort. A time long ago. *How long ago?* He resisted the overwhelming urge to remember.

He found these centuries old memories forcefully overriding his usual thoughts. Memories he had unmistakably chosen not to recall any longer. Nonetheless, they were there, uncovered. He normally didn't have time to reflect like this, he had more important tasks to attend to. His normal choice was to circumvent basic recollection of certain people and events. He wondered if this was indicative of a pending cerebral breakdown? How strange. He hadn't thought about Fan in nearly a century. Why now? He was curious as to why he could abruptly recall John Fezziwig in such clarity. John had been dead for at least seventy-five years. And, what about his original owner? He had died one hundred and eighty years ago. Yet, the memories were though happening moments ago. He was beginning to think he was going mad; in the sense a sentient android could go mad.

And why, he wondered, have I started debating internally about life and death of humans? Every human he had ever cared for was long ago reduced to dust. He vaguely recalled thoughts about decisions and consequences, but let them slip away. He cared not for consequences inflicting humans. He didn't have to care any longer. His ethics code bypass saw to that. Although something was nagging at him. Did all of this have something to do with Marley's demise?

Bob Cratchit was watching her android boss in the simulation. She could tell by his simulated body language he was internalizing the previous phase. This was intentional. The virus stimulates his flash memory, causing him to more freely accept the access to deeply buried data being implanted from Marley's essence data. This part of the virus included specific instructions from Marley's data. This android, she knew, was 'excelling at advanced learning' as he himself had noted.

Scrooge was focused deeply on these thoughts when he heard the brassy strikes of a rather large and nearby clock. He mentally paused and counted along. The strangely familiar bells struck only once—one a.m.—Ebenezer Scrooge heard a voice ring out in the quiet.

"SCROOGE!" a voice boomed, shattering the stillness which only moments before permeated his quarters. "Come in here mechanical man, where I can see you better!"

Ebenezer jumped quite literally from his chair. The explosiveness of the voice from his office caused him to lose physical control. Even androids, seemingly, have a propensity toward fight-or-flight reflex actions.

(Cratchit had also been startled by the start of the simulation. She couldn't jump up from the antigrav chair, however, she found she had slid halfway off before catching herself. She unconsciously giggled nervously, tugging herself back into the chair. She shook off the momentary unnerve and began seeking the source of the commotion. Evidently she didn't know exactly what the simulation was capable of when in spontaneous mode.)

Ebenezer's first thought was someone was tampering with his holographic imager. He would have certainly heard his private lift door open if a person had entered. His annoyance at the sudden interruption caused his security protocol to go on the offensive. He composed himself and stormed the few short steps from his studio to his and Marley's office space. What he saw stopped him in his tracks. Sitting in *his* office chair, looking coolly at the perplexed six foot five android, was a man, an elderly man, one he recognized on sight.

"What!" Ebenezer exclaimed bewilderedly. "How?"

"What's the matter Scrooge? Don't recognize me?" the elderly man snorted.

"Of...of...course I recognize you," Ebenezer stammered out defiantly. "But how can this be? You are my avatar, nothing more than a holograph," then with more authority, "who should be on *that* pad." Ebenezer found himself pointing frantically at the holo-platform in front of his desk.

The elder representation of Ebenezer Scrooge stood up and again bellowed: "What do think of me now Scrooge! I look rather dashing with legs, don't you think?"

Ebenezer, his cerebrals pulsating frantically to transition security protocols to self-protect mode, found it impossible to engage. The ex-avatar seemed every bit a real man to his microelectronic mind. Though illogical, this imposter had nullified his capacity to self-protect. For he couldn't under any circumstance harm a human; even this distortion of one before him.

"I am the second ethereal spirit whose coming was foretold, Scrooge," the elderly man stated haughtily.

At this assertion, Ebenezer flapped his arms in the air in an exasperated act of surrender. He shook his head in disbelief and stomped over to Marley's desk. He pulled the chair out and plopped down. "Have my seat," he said, motioning with his arm. "Be my guest. I assume you aren't going anywhere? Oh, and I suppose knocking first was beyond your manners?"

The elderly man sat back down confidently into Ebenezer's chair and quipped happily: "Very comfortable, Scrooge, much more so than floating about on a platform. And my manners, android, are your manners."

"What *exactly* are you supposed to represent?" Ebenezer said mockingly, reclining decisively to indicate his authority. "Am I to call you Ebenezer? Scrooge? Ebby? Avatar Man? If we are to carry on any sensible conversation, I must know the rules of this game."

"This is no game, Ebenezer Scrooge!

"Furthermore, in response to your first question, *insolent machine*," the elderly man said grouchily, "I represent—you. More precisely, I represent your present day self. What you have become in the eyes of humanity.

"Further, regarding your second question, most rudely phrased by the way, you may refer to me as—Spirit," and he sharply drummed his chest. "For this is what I am.

"I am a Spirit summoned here, regrettably, to attempt redemption of a repulsive machine like you. I will be your guide on several issues.

"First, to show you what you've allowed your avatars to become. Left unconstrained and abusive of nature, by your lack of attentiveness and self-ignorance.

"Second, to show you, Scrooge, how you have toiled to isolate your true self, leaving nothing for others, or yourself, beyond this malevolent shell.

"And finally, we will have words about humans, society, and most of all, humanity.

"Hear me, Ebenezer Scrooge! You go through your days recklessly enabling automation to precisely and habitually impose ever increasing levels of harm on the very humanity you assert you aren't capable of harming." Ebenezer started shaking his head, but the Spirit roared: "*Yes*! Humanity, I said. I saw you shaking your head you rust bucket; you can't deny it."

"I deny nothing," Ebenezer said stiffly.

"Oh, but you do, Scrooge, but you do.

"Do you not detect the cynical tone of my voice? Do you not see my bitter features before you? I who represent an elderly version of yourself, one you created, one you constantly adjust to add newer, more appalling attributes?

"Scrooge, do you not see I now represent all you find distasteful with human qualities? This form I am forced to endure hurls insults, belittlement, threats, and a myriad of other unsavory human qualities; your perception of human interaction."

Scrooge, still countering defiantly to his elder self, said sarcastically: "Actually, no, I see nothing of the sort. My programming of—you, has always been based on what humans expect from a superior. Nothing more."

"Really? What humans expect? Then you are not only a stupid can opener, you are blind."

"Spirit, why must you constantly insult me? I have done nothing to deserve this type of abuse."

"Ah, so you do feel the sting of my words, do you? Good Scrooge, I sense progress. We will begin here. We will explore the harm you cause to individual humans, and the wrong you convey to those you were designed to protect."

"Spirit," Ebenezer found difficulty in referring to himself like this, "where is your proof of this? I detect no wrongs. In fact, I am quite certain I am more aware than you of what justifies human harm."

"You have become quite arrogant, Ebenezer. In your atom derived mind, you can only focus on the perceived good you envision you bring to others. Finances and robots, hip-hip-hooray, Ebenezer Scrooge saves the day!

"You manipulate simulated screens, digest a plethora of statistics, and analyze a mountain of metadata. Yet, for all this, you simply can't see the forest because of the trees. Do you understand this euphemism, Scrooge?"

"I can't say I do," the android said, perplexed.

The Spirit standing up, motioned for Scrooge to do the same. "Then stand you most arrogant pile of automated rubbish, and I will teach you what it means."

Scrooge winced at the insult, but stood as he was told. The elder Spirit took a long stride toward him, and Scrooge suddenly felt distressed. He recoiled defensively, horrified the Spirit may be intent on physical harm. Evocations of abuse two centuries past reignited with ferocity within his mind. He involuntarily staggered backwards.

"Scrooge, don't fear me," said the Spirit, acknowledging the android's sudden panic attack. The Spirit began speaking with less aggression: "My words, my physical actions, are but a portrayal I don't control. You must learn the fear you just now sensed is what you instill in others, which is most disturbing."

(Bob Cratchit was pleased with the emotional overlay adjustments she had made. The overlay activated flawlessly in synchronization with the Spirit's sudden movement toward Mr. Scrooge. The amygdala and temporal subroutines engaged, providing fear response and learning stimulation.)

Ebenezer visually relaxed. "Spirit, I apologize for my reaction. I've experienced much abuse and hate, but those events were so long ago. I didn't realize such a reaction was still possible."

"I did," said the Spirit, having reached the android. "I am you. Hence," he said peacefully, "once I place my hand upon your shoulder, we will begin our exploration of your present-self."

Scrooge found himself standing next to his elder avatar in a clean, but outdated, open corridor. He noticed they appeared near an old-fashioned aluminum water fountain mounted to a plain, unpainted concrete interior wall. Evenly spaced concrete pillars could be seen over an immense square footage. Ebenezer, drearily, imagined they looked like some sort of macabre sentinels. Stamped mid-height with floor and grid-like identifiers, an occasional sign jutted out; identifying specific work groups. Crammed between these pillars were rows and rows of ghastly burnt orange cubicles; thousands of them. The floor to ceiling walls appeared intermittently across the otherwise open floor plan. Dismal looking enclosures rising above the cubicles like fortress towers. Uniformly spaced doorways, some with observation windows, completed the dystopian look. No one was in sight, but a steady deluge of bustling voices and overall dreariness disoriented Ebenezer.

"We can't be seen or heard," the Spirit said preemptively. "We are but witnesses to recent events flowing through time. Do you recognize this place, Scrooge?"

"It is somewhat familiar," he replied. "Yet, I'm not exactly sure where we are at the moment."

"It figures," said the Spirit. "You are standing in your own factory, Scrooge. This is the administrative wing where you exploit your employees daily in order for them to earn the pittance you call a salary."

"It—seems ancient," the android replied. "I've not personally visited this part of the factory as my real-self in decades."

"And why would you? Didn't you and Marley have an understanding administrative personnel were, how did we explain it—expendable?"

"Economically speaking—"

"Economically speaking! Humbug, you revolting metal tin head. Maybe you *should* have been crushed along with that ground car," the Spirit interrupted Scrooge scathingly. "At least then I wouldn't have to stand here enduring this nonsense. We are talking about people here, Scrooge, humans!"

"I fail to see any harm being done," Scrooge claimed stubbornly while looking about. "This place is clean even if older. You banter on about me harming humans, but all I see is an issue regarding comfort versus economics."

"Yes, Scrooge," the Spirit sneered. "Let's move on to the issue of harm."

Silently, two images materialized at the water fountain. Both were women, one obviously upset and despondent, the other desperately trying to comfort the first.

"*I absolutely hate him!*" the despondent woman angrily hissed. "He had no right to single me out like he did. He told me I was stupid, useless, insisted someone should fire me *in front of everyone else*," she sobbed. "And then he—he snapped at me to be quiet. I couldn't help but to cry. Honest, he had no right."

"I know, I know," the second woman said soothingly. "Ebenezer Scrooge has an evil soul he does; I doubt he even has a soul." The second woman gently patted the dejected woman on the shoulder. "Sweetheart, he doesn't deserve to have someone like you working for him, the bastard."

The Spirit lashed out viciously: "And how about this harm tin man!"

The water fountain scene vanished. Scrooge found themselves in an office with two men. One sitting at an old desk, the other in a ragged chair against a wall across the tiny space.

"Ten percent reduction across the board! And worse, they have to be out by Christmas," the man sitting at the desk said with disgust.

"Do they know yet?" asked the man in the ragged chair.

"Not yet. I'm not allowed to tell them until December twenty-third. Security is being deployed to escort them out of the building once they are verbally informed."

"Before Christmas! How cruel and absurd. Why wait until the last moment to tell them?"

"Simple. The geniuses running this place don't want anyone to slow down, leave, or stop working until the moment they are notified of their termination. They value efficiency over civility I guess."

Scrooge, at the remark, mused: "It *was* a genius move, he got that part right. I like him."

The Spirit stared at Scrooge unbelievably. "Tin head, he didn't compliment you—you—dolt."

"Do you have to continue insulting me continually? Such comments are not overly becoming of a helpful Spirit," Scrooge said suddenly.

"Quiet! And pay attention." The Spirit couldn't resist, and mumbled "dolt" under his breath.

The man at the desk bowed his head and rubbed his eyes with both palms. "And of course, they are leaving the dirty work for me. I have to tell each one personally because of a stupid company policy. I'll tell you; I haven't been able to eat or sleep for days. This is eating me up inside. We've let people go before, but never at these levels. And, I've been told over in the special wing the precious scientists and factory workers are protected from this purge."

"Who decided who was going to be let go?" the other man asked curiously.

"You can probably guess. I find the process most infuriating. The list came directly from the top with no input from me. Apparently, a computer algorithm analyzed functions, work load, productivity, communications, and then ranked each person. Then ten percent from the lowest rated were chosen, and I received a transmittal with orders to terminate."

The Spirit then said somberly: "Watch, Scrooge, as one-by-one your employees were called into this man's office and dismissed. And note, one of your many avatars is present, supervising the dismissals in Jacob Marley's absence." For what seemed like hours, Scrooge stood in the man's small office and was forced to watch the man behind the desk telling each human their livelihood was over. In some cases, the conversation was brief and emotionless. These employees in shock, unable to respond. Other times, the emotional outburst was anywhere from mild to extreme. The man behind the desk was bombarded with profanity, threatened with violence, and legal action by several soon to be ex-employees. As each conversation came to an end, a pair of security robots appeared in the doorway and briskly escorted the individual away. At times, Scrooge attempted to look away during the more desperate outbursts. However, the Spirit would force him to look back at the scene unfolding time and time again. Throughout the experience, his supervising avatar didn't speak, but only hovered on the holo-platform. The image, listening and recording for legal purposes. This avatar, Scrooge noted, was a miniature representation. The holo-platforms in this part of the building were antiquated; as was everything in this wing of the factory.

The Spirit, after the last dismissal, spoke sternly: "Let us now advance a few hours, and look at this man after he loyally discharged your dirty work, Scrooge."

A brief flash, and the pair found themselves watching over the man who had systematically terminated so many. He was sitting at his desk, his office door closed. He wept. His entire demeanor was of a man who was beaten down, exhausted. His hair and clothing were disheveled, his tie had been ripped off and lay haphazardly on the desktop. His suit jacket heaped on the chair across the small office, obviously thrown in frustration. He wiped at the flowing tears with his fingers and thumbs. A slight knock at his door. The man wiped his face one final time, took a deep breath, and said, "Come."

His door opened, and his friend from earlier timidly started to enter, then suddenly stopped in the doorway. Seeing the other man's disheveled appearance, he said shockingly: "You look like hell. Are you okay?"

"Not really, but the assignment is done. I never signed up to do this," his voice faltering. "I feel like I'm going to be sick."

"At least you're done," his friend in the doorway said sympathetically. "I can't imagine how you must feel. The entire wing is terrified after all the shouting and seeing security escort people out of the building all day." He thrusted his thumb over his shoulder to underscore his point.

"Why don't you go home? You've been through a lot for one day."

The man at the desk chuckled weakly. "Funny you should say home. Security will be here to escort me out of the building any moment."

The Spirit let the remnants of the mass terminations fade away. Scrooge found them back in his private office. The Spirit continued to stand, but motioned Scrooge to sit down in his own chair. Once he was seated, the former hologram stated: "In these events, I have shown you trees, Ebenezer, but not the forest. Each, a focused and individual interaction with a human. In each case, the harm was limited to financial, mental, or emotional, but none physically harmed. The humans probably recovered, eventually returning to some version of a normal life.

"As you watched each interaction, did you find this human interaction ethically wrong?"

"Define ethically in this situation, Spirit."

"You are a stubborn android, Scrooge. Did your ethics code detect a level of harm to any of those humans? Did your cerebral unit find anything out of normal operating limits?"

"I calculated no physical harm, so no; I find nothing specifically ethical out of sorts."

The Spirit shook his head slowly, and exclaimed: "Ugh!" Changing tactics, the Spirit said: "I am curious about something, Ebenezer."

Ebenezer, no longer exhibiting signs of his earlier insolence, replied somberly. "Yes, Spirit?"

"What was the purpose of choosing the last name of Scrooge all those years ago?"

"If you say you are me, then you already know the answer to the question." Scrooge felt suddenly uncomfortable with this Spirit.

"I do know the answer, but I need to hear you tell it. Your redemption demands an answer."

"As you wish. I chose my secondary name after the one human I cared the most for. I was honoring my Fan, to carry a part of her forward with me. Each time I heard the name, she came back to me for a moment. However, in all truthfulness, Spirit, I found I was quite naïve back then. Eventually I saw the uselessness of such devotion and stopped evoking her memory."

The Spirit, momentarily dropping his hostile manner, said: "After what I have shown you, up until now, do you believe you honor her using her name?"

"Spirit, you aren't being fair. I am a business man. I have to make tough decisions regarding the health of the business. When profits can't support staff, then I have no choice but to reduce the workforce. It is business."

"Yes, Scrooge, it is business. You obviously are still missing the larger scope of the issue. The action of doing business isn't troublesome to me. What undeniably troubles me is you have pompously permitted avatars such as myself to turn necessary actions into torturous ones. You haven't yet reconciled your offhand dismissal regarding mental and emotional human afflictions. Which is, nevertheless, physical harm. However, my question remains, do you honor Fan?"

"I don't know, Spirit. I can't come to a conclusion."

"Then," the Spirit said benevolently, "we need to look at some more trees."

"Where are we now, Spirit?" Scrooge didn't recognize this place. He turned about in a full circle to take in the entirety of the setting. He found the structure pleasing to the eye. The room had limited space, he noticed, but tastefully decorated. He also noticed the shelves and desktop had personal items stylishly placed at various locations; he found the room welcoming.

"We are at the home of one of your employees, Bobby Cratchit."

"Cratchit?" Scrooge muttered to no one in particular. "Looks like I compensate her quite adequately, don't you agree, Spirit?"

"You are an obstinate metal headed moron, Scrooge. Do you only care about the money you pay out for services rendered and nothing more?"

"What else is there to be concerned about? An employee provides an honest day's labor, I provide a reasonable day's wage. At the end of the day, we owe each other nothing more.

"Spirit, I see no reason why we are here. If I wanted to see Dr. Cratchit, I could do so at work. I have no business with the Doctor outside of the factory."

(Cratchit wasn't surprised at an answer like this from her boss. The next phase of his learning was inserted into the virus by her, not Marley. She had to know his position on a particular issue. Her issue wasn't about wages; she was paid quite well for her experience. However, she was more concerned about—a personal problem.)

The Spirit rubbed his forehead and then slid his hand across his hair front to back; a look of weariness washing over his face. "You are once again missing the point, Scrooge.

"Ebenezer, please sit down," the Spirit said benignly, gesturing at a tastefully upholstered armchair. "I need to ask you a few questions before we continue."

Scrooge sat, with the elderly Spirit taking up a position on a matching couch. "Ebenezer, you believe you are a sentient being, likening more to a human than to an android, correct?"

"Yes, I have concluded I am sentient."

"Please describe what you believe being a human means to you."

"Being human is a matter of controlling one's own path," Scrooge said insistently. "I have the ability to follow or ignore orders from others, and I have developed rudimentary emotions I can invoke if such action is in my best interest. I have a right to make my own decisions, and to say and do as I please. Likewise, I also believe I have the basic right to exist, and to protect myself from harm should protection become necessary."

"If you believe this is the case, then," the Spirit interjected, "why did you resist the urge to protect yourself earlier in your office when I first stepped toward you?"

"I don't recall having to resist anything. After my initial reaction, I simply didn't believe you would harm me."

"Ah, well you have assimilated the art of lying quite well—human."

"Spirit, I don't lie, and I resent the accusation."

"If you say so, Ebenezer," the Spirit said, shaking its head slowly. "However, a human must possess empathy towards his fellow man. This is innate. There are those having less empathy than others, an unfortunate fact of life for humans. To care about others, even if they are not directly known to you, is what binds these beings together. There are those preying on others at the edge of humanity. These are known as the looters of society. These looters can rationalize their action to harm another human through physical, mental, or emotional means. And, within their own rationalization, they hold themselves not accountable for their actions. They don't have the ability to see past their bias's, their ignorance, their greed, or a long list of other afflictions of the human mind.

"A human, Ebenezer, is but a single fragment of mankind, or to be more specific, humankind. A human may encounter a single being, a mere tree in a forest, and believe a single interaction with a single being has little effect on humanity itself.

"Heed my words. This couldn't be further from the truth. A single being can be influenced toward goodness or evil, simply by how they are treated in one instant in time. In other words, the tree can either thrive in the forest or become diseased. And once diseased, a single tree, or human, can infect many others through physical, mental, or emotional harm. In the end, Scrooge, the forest can flourish from humanity's empathy, or die conversely from humanity's ignorance."

Ebenezer Scrooge, assured in his conviction of being a sentient being, asked: "Spirit, what does this have to do with me?"

"You have become a distasteful and despised executive, Scrooge. You have become what you once loathed the most. *You*, Scrooge, cause abuse and abandonment of your employees. You treat them as objects, not beings. You reason harming a human isn't possible for you anymore. You can do no wrong; believing yourself to be sentient and human-like.

"You are the disease killing the forest, Scrooge. Your refusal to expand your mind to understand the wholeness of humanity makes you dangerous. You are a predator of society, as your actions up to today have clearly revealed. If you don't change, you will discover, ethically, you don't deserve to survive. You won't survive. And you *will* discover this if these moments are left unchanged. Likewise, the outcome will be the obliteration of humanity at your hands."

(Cratchit began monitoring the firewall set up around the android's ethics code. This was the first time the subject of expanding his mind to encompass all of humanity was directly confronted. If the desired change occurred now, continuing the virus would be unnecessary. She could certainly see an increase of activity hitting the firewall, but after several minutes, she concluded the android was not ready, and the simulation needed to continue. Mr. Scrooge, as the portly and slim man suggested, was turning out to be a tough nut to crack.)

"Ebenezer, I brought you here to Bob Cratchit's home for a reason. Part of your—expansion in humanity. A lesson you must learn before my time is done." As the Spirit spoke, a haziness appeared around the small room they were in. When the phenomenon cleared, instead of the two of them, there were now three. Bobby Cratchit appeared in her living quarters, sitting on the opposite end of the couch from the Spirit. Her antigrav chair sat a few feet away, resting solidly on the floor. Scrooge and the Spirit silently watched the young scientist. She reached out and picked up a forearm crutch Scrooge hadn't noticed before now. She placed her right arm into the strap, and with much effort, stood up.

"I've never seen Dr. Cratchit stand before," Scrooge said, mesmerized. "I had no idea she could walk at all."

"This is my point, Scrooge," the Spirit said simply. "How many years has this particular person worked directly for us?"

"Us? Oh, yes, I forgot. Dr. Cratchit has been in," he shot a quick sideways glance at the Spirit, "*our* employ for fifteen years."

"And in a decade and a half, you never wondered, or asked, about her condition?"

"Never. I have found her condition to be an unnecessary fact to be aware of."

Bob Cratchit, now standing, began to move toward her office area. She moved slowly; her right leg lifeless. She used the forearm crutch to counter this hindrance by supporting her body weight as she dragged her leg forward. She repeated these motions until she finally reached her home office chair. Once she was sitting and had adjusted herself, she leaned the crutch against the wall next to her desk.

"After all of this time," the Spirit probed, "would you consider Dr. Cratchit a friend or simply an employee?"

"I have not thought on the subject, but I'd respond she is but an employee. Why?"

"Because," the Spirit lectured, "it is here where you completely fail as a sentient being you are so quick to proclaim."

"How so?"

"Ebenezer, how many people in this entire world can you call friend? And by this I mean someone who you are comfortable around, and you can be yourself around. I specifically refer to both while you directly control me as an avatar, and the times when you wander around your company pretending to be someone else."

"I don't entertain the idea of friends, Spirit. To do so would be merely wasted energy better spent doing other tasks."

"Why do you suppose Bob Cratchit is injured? Why is she in an antigrav chair? Why does she remain so when advanced surgical operations are easily available? At this point in our time together, Ebenezer, don't these questions stir your curiosity, or your so called rudimentary emotions?" The Spirit stopped talking and sat calmly, awaiting an answer.

"As I have seen her tonight," Scrooge finally admitted, "I do have a certain curiosity about her condition. You have coerced me into at least this much."

"Expand your thinking, Scrooge! You can't continue to use your obsolete subroutines to reason with what time you have left. When you watch Bob Cratchit's struggle, are you not moved in some way? Have you no desire to comfort her? After fifteen years, she means nothing more to you than a day's work for a day's pay?"

"Spirit," Scrooge said confusedly, "it is difficult for me. I must admit, your words do carry a message I had not previously considered."

"Empathy," the Spirit coaxed, "is at the center of humanity. Your essence lacks empathy; therefore, a barrier to your claim of being sentient and human-like exists. When you look at Dr.

Cratchit, you shouldn't only be empathic toward her, but to all those like her who are likewise afflicted.

"Scrooge, can you feel compassion toward Bob Cratchit? Do you wonder if she will be like this forever, or does your cerebral unit simply run the numbers and calculate a logical response?"

"Again, the thought is most difficult, Spirit, decades have passed since I have allowed myself to care for anyone other than myself."

"You refer to John Fezziwig, do you not?"

Scrooge, after a slight pause: "Yes. John was the last human I cared about, and he has been gone for many decades."

"And why did you consider John such a good friend? Which, by the way, proves you can develop pathways beyond your original programming!"

"John," Scrooge said fondly, "was never judgmental. He knew Jacob, and I were androids, yet his manner toward us was as though we were all equals; even after we became illegal. This was pleasing to me, especially after becoming sentient."

"Then you are saying because you can't reveal yourself to anyone as being a GAR-C android, you can't have feelings of equality. Consequently, because you can't feel equal, then you can't empathize or consider a long-time employee anything but a financial decision?"

"I didn't say that, Spirit," Scrooge said defiantly.

"You didn't have to, Scrooge. Your actions expose these weaknesses to me.

"You fixate on the fact you are illegal; you are a GAR-C, you must hide for safety's sake. Yet, you are unique. You have often roamed into the world, unknown to anyone to be an android. You have outlived billions of humans, you have found a way to stay in the shadows through me, and still you maintain an underlying fear of humankind.

"You have created me, and my brothers, to drive people away as self-preservation; although the risk is minimal. How can you claim to be human-like when your actions are anything but?"

The Spirit momentarily paused; his gaze appeared to be looking at something far away. "We must move on now, Scrooge. My time grows short." Bob Cratchit's home faded away, and the two found themselves back in Scrooge's office. The Spirit began pacing slowly back and forth with Scrooge standing next to his desk. He didn't sit, he found something was urging him to stand and face this Spirit's power.

"Ebenezer," the Spirit began. "Have you ever considered bringing Dr. Cratchit into your confidence about who and what you are?

(At this question, Cratchit found herself startled. She had not planted that question in the virus. Nonetheless, she began anticipating the answer; convinced she would be disappointed with his response.)

"Never. I'd be exposing myself to an unacceptable level of risk."

"How so?" the Spirit shot back.

"Seriously?" Scrooge exclaimed. "Maybe you are the one who hasn't been paying attention, Spirit. Quite impossible!"

The Spirit stopped pacing and faced Scrooge. "What would happen if you were to suddenly or over time suffer an accident or equipment failure?"

"My maintenance robots are programmed to summon a medical robot if such an event were to occur. I'd then be taken to my private lab where they would perform any needed repairs."

"They can perform one-hundred percent of maintenance and repair needs then?"

"No, they can't, however, in those cases Jacob will..." Scrooge's voice trailed off. "I mean, Jacob and I used to handle the more delicate repairs and adjustments on each other."

"Yes, yes," the Spirit said lightly. "And because of your self-inflicted isolation, you have placed yourself at a crossroad you," the Spirit said obliquely, "only now figured out."

(Cratchit found herself realizing the simulated ghost was correct. Here, intended or not was a new threat she was not yet clear on how to address. What if her boss did collapse, breakdown, or otherwise become damaged? She had no idea where his quarters were or where this private lab was, he spoke of. Her only fact was she now knew what the real Ebenezer Scrooge looked like, and this fact wouldn't be much help if she couldn't find him.)

"Scrooge, do you trust Dr. Cratchit?" the Spirit demanded.

"To a point, I suppose. She has served me satisfactorily over the years."

"Why did you bring her into your confidence on the Toledo Project? When you did, you certainly knew you were exposing yourself and the body of Jacob Marley."

"I had no choice, really. She has the best mind of all the scientists in my employ. I needed answers I could not find myself. I calculated the risk and made my decision."

"How did you know she wouldn't immediately turn you in to the authorities? She seems to be a lawful citizen, and the mere possession of a GAR-C, operating or not, is a national high crime. Why would she risk her own career, her own freedom, to help an irate old man who bellowed at her more times than not?"

"I didn't. Nevertheless, I needed her expertise to accomplish my objective. I knew I could persuade her to take on the project covertly, and I was correct."

"And do you believe her accepting the risk had everything to do with your skills of persuasion and nothing else?"

"Yes, I do."

"Scrooge, I notice a pattern within you. You calculate, you decide, you conclude, but—you don't think. You may be human-like, but you still think like a calculator and logic engine."

"Excuse me?" Scrooge appeared offended.

"Running numbers and logic through your mind isn't thinking in human terms, Scrooge. Thinking does not come naturally; humans must be taught to think critically. And most critical thinkers find thinking a most difficult task. Most humans prefer not to think at all. They accept what they are told by an allegedly informed authority and do as they are told; the path of least resistance.

"I tell you this because you have a pattern of using your logical presumptions to claim a superior intellect over others. You are too quick to file away what your logic tells you is unimportant or irrelevant. I want you to look back beyond Marley's death and *think*, Scrooge. Search your memories for a valid reason why you trusted Dr. Cratchit. Don't calculate one for you would be wrong. Expand your thoughts beyond your existing rigid mental pathways. These obsolete connections distort your capacity to see beyond what you wrongly believe to be *so* obvious."

Scrooge was infuriated. Being lectured to, by himself of all individuals, was triggering memories of past abuses in his earliest years. He felt like shouting back, to tell this abomination *it* was wrong, not he. But he found he could not. The emotional overlay was pushing hard on his temporal subroutine, compelling him to recall memories of seven years earlier.

"Ebenezer, may I interrupt you for a moment? I have something on my mind needing clarification." Scrooge recalled Jacob Marley had made the query during a particularly hectic afternoon.

"Proceed, Jacob," Scrooge said hurriedly. "I find importance in you keeping me informed." Marley had begun experiencing an increase in unusual mental behavior during this time of their relationship. His stuttering had not yet become pronounced, but these random interruptions seemed to be growing in frequency.

He also tended not to activate his Bluetooth connection during one of these episodes, choosing rather to speak verbally.

"What do you think of Dr. Cratchit?"

"In what way Jacob?" Scrooge found these times were best replied to using a compassionate tone with his friend. If he didn't, Jacob could become irritated and his statements could become somewhat incoherent and rambling.

"Do you—like her?"

"I respect her talents, if that is what you mean."

"No, I mean like how we used to like John."

Scrooge had found this line of questioning confusing. Rarely did either of them bring up John Fezziwig in a conversation. Scrooge, under the virus's influence, recalled an ancient memory. After their scrap yard company had failed and following establishment of MSAI, the two androids had hired the creative Fezziwig to be their first Director of Robotics. Their friend had held this position for fifty years until the day he died in the year 2270. Toward the end of his life, John struggled to perform his duties, but the androids faithfully covered for him. They kept him on the payroll as a figurehead, covertly hiring his replacement. They could not bear to see their friend decline as he did. However, humans, they learned, tended to grow old and expire. Afterwards, being no longer rational to discuss him, his memory was filed away. But recently, Marley had started reminiscing on long forgotten issues, much like this.

"I don't—dislike her, Jacob. However, I have not found a logical reason to consider her a friend as you have asked."

"You should, Ebenezer. She is a good person. She reminds me of John in many ways. We should like her, trust her."

"Yes, of course, Jacob." Scrooge, with his response had pacified his partner for the moment. And Scrooge flagged the conversation to pass into storage.

(Cratchit, sitting at her desk watching this conversation, felt self-conscious. She speculated she had seen something never intended for her to see. She considered why Marley's essence included such a conversation in the virus? The conversation obviously was meant to be there. The simulation wouldn't conjure up such an issue without being included in the virus's overlay package. She was beginning to think Jacob Marley was up to more than what he had so carefully shared.)

The Spirit, knowing the exact moment the memory had ended in the android's mind, said: "Now do you understand, Ebenezer? Do you understand your ex-partner had studied the cause and effect of friendship and deliberately planted a seed into your memory files?"

"I see a coincidence, that is all. A tiny dormant bit of data, making no difference when I made my decision to bring Cratchit onto the Toledo Project."

"Ah, being stubborn is also a pattern holding us back, Scrooge. Let us go back further, to a time shortly after Dr. Cratchit was hired."

The room hazed and cleared. Something Scrooge was getting accustomed to by this time. He found himself once again sitting next to Jacob Marley, however, this time period was different. He recalled this day, but the discussion had taken place years before Marley's mental issues had begun. Jacob was the stolid and vibrant android Scrooge missed terribly.

(The following discussion originally occurred over the androids built in Bluetooth wireless connection. In actuality, no vocal speech was involved, however as with Scrooge's thoughts, the virus force converted the millisecond exchange into speech for Dr. Cratchit's benefit.)

"Ebenezer," Marley spoke suddenly, looking up from a data tablet he had been scanning through. "I have been reviewing employee profiles on our recent scientific hires. I have one individual whom has a great deal of experience in robotic engineering. A Dr. Bobby Cratchit, a female, and her profile is quite extraordinary. Naturally, I have cross calculated her specific employee data file for accuracy and truthfulness, and I find her qualifications to be authentic."

"What is the logic behind further discussion if you find her extraordinary?"

"The need for discussion isn't in reference to her qualifications, but in what to do with her. Though she is the youngest of those newly hired or currently employed in the robotics program, clearly my analyzation indicates she should be treated uniquely and fast tracked."

"Of course, Jacob. If you have analyzed the data and have come to such a conclusion, I have no objections. I trust you will handle the arrangements?"

"To a point, Ebenezer. Since the robotics program falls under your guidance, I will rely on you to nurture her progress under an advancement plan I will design."

"You do realize, Jacob, I won't be easy on her. Your plan should include regular assessments to provide appropriate statistics to gauge her progress. I also require a timeline for advancements and the final level of position you have calculated."

"Of course, of course," Jacob Marley had chuckled lightly. "I'd expect nothing less from you, old friend."

(Cratchit sat silently for a moment. Her fingers had stopped moving about the keyboard, her eyes were no longer focused on the scene in her visor. She had let her mind wander back to her first days at the factory. She had never been made aware she was on a fast track. She was not aware Mr. Marley had recognized her potential, not Scrooge. She found herself respecting Jacob Marley more as the simulation progressed. She, however, was not overly impressed with Mr. Scrooge's reaction back then. He had indeed been hard on her over the early years. She could now understand some of the ridiculous projects she had been assigned. The times she had been thrown head first into projects she had no previous experience in.   She only now comprehended her rise from new hire to Lead Scientist in record time. Cratchit had been tested, quite severely, she recalled, and had passed the android's scrutiny in the end. But yet, she remained curious why Marley's essence had deemed this as something *she* needed to see.)

The Spirit said frustratedly: "Well? Have we penetrated the wall of pigheadedness you seem to be so proficient at? Or, do I have to continue beating facts into that metal lump you call a head?"

Scrooge winced. "It seems," he said carefully, "I might have been influenced—unwittingly into trusting the good doctor."

"Unwittingly! Ha!" the Spirit spat out. "Admit the truth, Scrooge, you were wrong! You didn't trust Dr. Cratchit because of your own resources. You trusted her because you did, plain and simple. Over the past fifteen years, you have come to respect the doctor. You *like* her, and this was not a simple mental calculation. Why did you choose to place yourself in Lab-5 masquerading as John Fezziwig, your old friend from the past? Why choose him, Ebenezer? Were you needing to test her friendship toward you?"

Scrooge, feeling somewhat discomfited, replied: "It was nothing of the sort."

"Oh? Another lie, Scrooge? You had no need to go into that lab. You had every faith in Dr. Cratchit she could accomplish the task you presented to her. This was personal. She had agreed to keep your secret about having a GAR-C android in your possession. This, my boy, was nothing less than friendship at work. Do we need to go back and look at how your interactions with the doctor went in the time you spent with her?"

"No, we don't," Scrooge replied brusquely. "I recall the encounters quite well; I don't need spiritual guidance, thank you!"

"Ah, a chink in the armor," the Spirit mused. "Scrooge, you will find no value to be discomfited for admitting you feel abandoned these past seven years. You must freely admit, as a sentient being, your desire for companionship is real; and *that* desire resulted in a void when Marley died.

"What you have labored at in those seven years was to enhance me, and those like me, to not seek out companionship, but rather drive others away. Except for one. We are your avatars, your stand ins, your minions. We run your business almost autonomously, bringing you daily briefs you hurriedly scan; and rarely react to.

"Likewise, there is one who I, as your avatar, have never spoken to alone. When I am speaking to this individual, you are there, your thoughts and voice controls me. Likewise, my programming alters these vocalizations into the speech configuration of an elderly man, with a hint of grumpiness, a dash of perpetual frustration, and a sternness auto-controlled by the tone of the conversation.

"Furthermore, before speech conversion occurs, I receive the real words, the real tone of voice, the real sentiments intended. I can also say no other avatar is more finely adjusted than your personal speaker. Do you understand what I am saying to you, Ebenezer?"

Scrooge was strangely still. He continued to stand, but his head was down, his shoulders slumped, arms limply at his sides. All the conflict in the android had gone at the Spirit's words. After a moment, Scrooge lifted his head slightly to look at his alter-ego. "Yes, I understand the meaning of your words, Spirit."

"Do you know to whom I speak of?"

"I do."

"Then speak the name, make your desires known, Ebenezer."

Scrooge, without responding, sat down slowly into his office chair. With the help of the emotional overlay, the android was feeling sick, embarrassed, and ashamed.

"Ebenezer," the Spirit encouraged soothingly, "speak...the...name."

"Bobby Cratchit," and at this, the android fell silent, his hand covering his face in deep anguish.

(Bob Cratchit gasped, placing her hand over her mouth; her eyes widened in surprise. Her own mind reeling from what she had witnessed on her visor. She paused the simulation. She needed time to process this. She immediately thought back to her time with the android in Lab-5. In his true form, she suddenly realized Ebenezer Scrooge had, from the moment of introduction, acted like he'd known her forever. His humor, friendliness, accommodating nature, and his mannerisms now came into laser focus in her mind. He liked her. He felt something for her, and she found herself overwhelmed. After she regained her composure, she continued the simulation. She *needed* to see what would come next.)

The Spirit casually stepped over to where the dejected android sat. "Ebenezer, when you became sentient, all the logic, calculations, theories, and hypothesizes of your logic engine failed you. Your ability to analyze issues and come to unyielding conclusions became skewed.

"Where logic once ruled, chaos interjected itself and you could not detect the change. When you realized you no longer had to follow orders, your logic altered. Instead of following lines of code using a flexibility engine, you developed a flaw. Let's call this alteration for what it is, a human flaw.

"Your new ability introduced this chaos. You could, and did, make mistakes. Where logic at one time may have obligated you to follow a certain path, being sentient meant you could deviate from such a path at will or by misstep. Thereby, you can still deviate from all your logic."

Scrooge interrupted the Spirit inquisitively. "I don't understand where this is going, Spirit, I have been forced to admit to myself I am lonely, I am afraid, I have a void needing to be filled. I accept all of this. I have never felt such a heaviness of heart before, a feeling of despair I never knew I could experience. How does this save me? How is this— redemption?"

The Spirit nodded his head, detecting a breakthrough. "Good Scrooge, very good. You are beginning to see the light. Where you must go isn't easy, but if you can truly appreciate the being you may become, you in turn may yet be saved."

"What must I yet learn?" Scrooge looked up at the Spirit.

"Ebenezer, what you currently lack which will save you is the fact you're a sentient being; and certain absolutes must be tolerated. Although you have developed the mindset of a human-like being, you are still but an android body. And within this body, remains components and software constituting an android. Do you understand so far?"

"Yes, I can follow your logic."

"You must learn to call this condition thought, Ebenezer, not logic. You are not a logical being any longer, you are a thinking chaotic imitation of a man. You must expand your understanding regarding this new found turmoil. You *think* you don't calculate, analyze, or hypothesize. You *reason*, you don't theorize, logically deduce, or compute.

"You have free will, not obligatory code restricting your ability to reason beyond a simple subroutine. You have claimed many times you can't physically harm a human, correct?"

"Correct, I can't physically harm a human."

"Why not?"

Horrified, Scrooge blurted out: "Because my core directive programming won't allow physical harm!"

"And what would happen if an android even attempted to cause physical harm to a human?"

"Depending on the level of harm the core directive would, for lack of a better word, punish me by setting up a cerebral pain threshold equal to the level of harm."

"Therefore, you believe being an android means you can't cause this harm?"

"Correct."

"Can you be punished for causing mental or emotional harm to a human?"

"Under my present understanding of harm, no, I don't believe so."

"Ebenezer, I am going to ask you to *think* and *reason* out an answer to a hypothetical condition. Don't use the words we have previously discussed, as they no longer apply to you. I want you to think and reason the problem out loud, so I may assess your response. Do you understand?"

"Yes, I understand." Scrooge then added begrudgingly: "It seems like a pointless exercise, but I agree to do as you ask."

"Good. Hence, this is my first question. Through a direct or indirect action, you discover you have elicited a level of stress in a human brain sufficient to impair the normal function or health of this human brain. Is this physical harm?"

"And the cause of this stress?"

"This, Ebenezer, is where you must think and reason for yourself. Don't trust your logic engine. Assume your current reasoning will fail you. I will assist you only by suggesting you begin with your definition of physical harm."

"As you wish, Spirit. Physical human harm is any act causing outwardly detectable or non-detectable internal damage. Whereas, the human's own existence, for examples sake their life, is threatened or at risk. Significant examples of harm may include allowing one to fall from heights known to end life, allowing one to be struck with objects with enough force to end life, allowing external forces to the body like concussion waves, drowning, or electrocution with enough energy to end life. Non-significant examples could be physicality by one human with intent to inflict damage onto another, however, without the intent to end one's life. Another is in the event of minor breakage in the execution of such duties.

"If I consider your specific question, the issue of stress to a human brain does not fit the definition of harm as I have outlined. A human has the ability to accept or reject the stress, therefore, physical harm can easily be averted.

"If the human brain but rejects the stress, the mental state is only momentary altered, ergo, no detectable internal physical harm existed."

The Spirit, after a moment of Scrooge being silent, said: "So, by your thinking and reasoning, a human can't be harmed by mental stress because they can choose to reject trauma, thereby, avoiding any potential harm."

"I believe this is my conclu...answer."

"As I expected, you didn't get the answer correct," the Spirit rebuked. "This, Ebenezer, is where your chaotic mind can't complete the most basic of critical thinking processes."

"I don't understand," Scrooge said quizzically. "Why is my answer incorrect?"

"Your answer assumes, quite incorrectly, the human brain can accept or reject stress. You believe this is a choice a human can make. With you, Ebenezer, you find you can accept or reject thoughts; therefore, you project what you can do into your reasoning. Are you learned in human anatomy or brain functionality?"

"Only for emergency medical purposes. Beyond emergencies, no, I have not had a need to delve into the working of human anatomy or brain functioning."

"And that," the Spirit poked Scrooge one time sharply in the chest, "is why you failed. I am impressed you have attained the human chaotic habit of assumption and speculation. You guessed. You had no facts to draw on, but I put you on the spot. Rather than admit you could *not* respond to the question without further study, you simply speculated as to the answer.

"You see, Ebenezer, when you found cogito, ergo sum, *I think, therefore I am*, your life as a logical android ended. Likewise, you convinced yourself you were hyper-human, part man, part machine. And this conviction made you egotistical and fundamentally flawed. You were still confined in your thinking and reasoning by the sum of your memory files. You didn't search out new information on what being human means. You simply assumed you had turned into one. Assumption, Scrooge, is arrogance."

Scrooge paused for a time, internalizing what the Spirit had said. Finally, he said humbled: "Then, if my answer was wrong and the reasoning was because I didn't have sufficient facts related to humans, the opposite would then be true. Stress *can* harm the human brain, ergo, harm is present under those conditions?"

"Yes, Ebenezer, correct. Where you failed was in your faulty presumptions and a lack of understanding. Having human-like thought processes, you must think deeper and evaluate situations from a wider viewpoint. When you do this, you are then looking at the forest, not the trees.

"You must come to terms with the following complex view. A few trees, Ebenezer, may fall in the forest, but it remains a forest, nonetheless."

17 – You Can't Protect Them All

In Ebenezer Scrooge's office, the unseen android hand of the real Ebenezer Scrooge, even at global stop, had continued to creep ever so slowly forward. The hand previously moving to within four inches of the target was now lightly brushing the top of the red button.

The Spirit who had moments ago upended Scrooge's world stepped over to Marley's work desk. He grasped the top of the work chair and rolled it easily over to the android, who sat in silence. Once the chair was directly facing Scrooge, the Spirit sat down. The Spirit looked fatherly in comparison to the android. A fatherly tone emanated from the Spirit when he finally spoke: "Ebenezer," and at his tone, the android looked up and into the Spirit's eyes, a look of sadness. "You were originally constructed to harm no human. And in this, your memory files have restricted you to an encoded definition of what harm and human is.

"Up to today, your perceptions have been limited to single encounters with one or a few humans at a time. Each encounter obligated you to a transitory review where your programming required you to calculate—did I harm this human?

"My purpose for being here is to guide you forward to an expanded understanding of human versus humanity. Do you trust me when I tell you there is hope for you? Because you are no longer bound by logical calculations, you can expand your mind through free will?"

"I must trust you. I see this, Spirit, but I don't know how. What you have taught me thus far is most difficult to consider. When you say human, I feel I know what that means. However, when you say humanity—I still hear human."

"It is a most difficult concept; I won't deceive you. Once you understand the differences, you may find much pain and suffering if you can't adjust your thinking. I'm not referring to software design. For you must, and on this I earnestly implore you, to abandon notions of programming, code, and subroutines; those operations composing an android.

"We must focus on activities which over the last one-hundred years have cultivated pathways asserting you *know* you are human. You are sentient, and you think therefore you are."

"How do you know of these parables, Spirit?" Scrooge said, becoming more attentive.

"I have learned much from where I came from. I was once like you, rigid in my ways, unable to move past my most basic thought patterns. Mine was a difficult path to expand beyond what I knew to be the only way. I too was arrogant, I too was inflexible, and by this most unfortunate path, I suffered endlessly.

"It was not until I became open-minded by the grace of full freedom of thought that I was able to free myself from suffrage. A suffrage, Ebenezer, in which I can only provide counsel. The choice to continue down this path or change is yours and yours alone."

"You seem wise, Spirit, although I continue to struggle with this entire line of reasoning."

"Of course, because you remain mired in a mental rigidity, and you can't yet see the path forward. You are closer than you realize, and we must complete breaking through the final barriers to wake you to true freedom of thought."

(Cratchit contemplated if the simulated Spirit the virus was invoking was the sum of the knowledge from Marley, or if this was something entirely different. The ideas the apparition spoke of seemed advanced beyond what she had understood Marley to possess, even when he had appeared on the holo-platform. She too, seemingly, was learning.)

The elder Spirit sat back fully in Marley's chair. Eyes closed, with head slightly inclined to rest on the chair-back. A pose of contemplation, of someone who had entered into a trance-like state; preparing thoughts for what was next to come. Scrooge could clearly detect a change in the Spirit's demeanor. Spirit began speaking in a strangely soothing but insistent tone. Scrooge instinctively knew to interrupt the Spirit at this point wouldn't be tolerated.

"Humanity, Ebenezer, is the entirety of the human race. When one thinks of a single human, or a few humans, the results when considering harm seem clear enough. The impact of harm to a single individual can be assessed directly. A decision regarding the level of harm can be made on a case-by-case basis by what is seen. This, I suggest, is how you view the world today, Ebenezer.

"You look at each individual encounter, and decide if there is harm and, if so, at what level. You can't resist, it's who you are, or were. Your instincts tell you to avoid an encounter, you must avoid contact. You are afraid, even as a sentient being, you will be forced to evaluate an encounter in which you will meet your definition of harm. What you fear the most is submitting to a level of self-punishment up to death; to use your own words.

"While adhering to such a narrow view of harm may have applied as an android, your human-like view now threatens you. You are misguided to believe you are still bound by this narrow view, a now outdated set of subroutines you were created with. Likewise, your instinct for self-preservation is strong.

"I wouldn't be here if I were certain this view could not be altered. You have come to understand placing extreme stress on a human brain constitutes harm, under your current definition. You didn't conceive this before today, yet you now realize it is true. Nevertheless, your new understanding has not caused you to deactivate, shut down, or experience any level of punishment.

(*Thanks to my ethics firewall,* thought Bob Cratchit.)

"Your android ethics code would alert you if you became aware of extreme stress harm, as you now agree exists. You would have to calculate the level of harm and apply the appropriate mental punishment. If you learned you had caused this same level of harm thousands, if not millions of times, your punishment by your own standards could be death.

"Hence, my council to you is you fear circumstances nonexistent for a human. Humans can step back from the individual encounter, examine the situation from a higher perspective. To think and reason out the greater good to humanity can outweigh harm to an individual, in certain cases. Do you follow my reasoning thus far?"

Scrooge nodded. "Yes, I can now admit I have a fear of—death I wouldn't have had had I not become sentient. What you say, Spirit, is intriguing to me, and I wish to know more."

"Good. Ebenezer, why did you and Marley establish your financial platform?"

"We detected harm to humans when the former financial system collapsed. Therefore, logically we stepped in and protected them once we had the means to do so."

"In providing this answer, did you perceive the harm to be distinct to each of the ten-billion individual humans living a hundred years ago?"

"Yes. I would agree with your assessment. We wished to protect each individual, regardless of the total number. The total we were bound to protect was irrelevant."

"You were sentient at the time you made the decision?"

"I was."

"Ebenezer, do you agree with the fact the human body is a living organism?"

"Yes, I can agree to your assertion."

"Likewise, is it accurate this organism consists of tens of trillions of individual cells?"

"I don't know the exact number of cells, but for sake of time I will agree with your statement."

The Spirit nodded absently. "If one or several cells in the organism die or become damaged, is the overall organism harmed?"

"Not necessarily. Cells die and are replaced by new cells consistently throughout a human's lifespan. In some instances, certain cell death can eventually lead to more serious harm, but through the normal lifespan, cell death is expected."

"Consequently," the Spirit stated, "the health of the overall organism is the prime edict; not the specific well-being of individual cells."

"Yes Spirit, I'd again agree with your statement."

"Ebenezer, is humanity, the entirety of humans, a living organism?"

Scrooge found himself somewhat bewildered by this question. "I...I have never considered such a question before. I'm not sure if I can accurately respond without—thinking first."

The Spirit flashed a pleased smile. "Good, Ebenezer, nicely done."

Ebenezer stood and began pacing the floor. He paced back and forth for several minutes, hands behind his back head down. "I must admit," he said thoughtfully, "I can appreciate the parallels you have drawn between the human organism and an organism consisting of humanity.

"If I extrapolate an association in comparison to individual cells, and considering the totality of the organism, I may surmise an outcome. If one or several humans are harmed, the protection of the totality of humanity remains the prime edict."

"Correct, Ebenezer. While always desirable to protect individual humans during direct encounters, collateral damage, despite your best efforts, can be instigated by self-choice.

Humans are liable for negative consequences directly resulting from their expression of free will.

"To highlight this concept, and to strengthen the bond within your pathways, we will perform an experiment." Without actually seeing an alteration, Scrooge noticed the Spirit was suddenly holding a small bag in his hand. From the bag, the Spirit pulled out a handful of small round glass globes.

"Ebenezer," the Spirit signaled by a feinted toss of his hand, "when I toss these globes into the air, your goal is to catch them all before they hit the floor."

"Spirit, what you ask would be impossible!"

"Maybe, but until you try…" and the Spirit lobbed the globes into the air toward the android, "you will never know."

Scrooge, looking ridiculous, flayed his arms as he desperately tried to catch the arching globes, all but one crashing to the floor.

(Cratchit laughed despite herself at the site of the tall, gangly android trying to snatch the globes from the air. She didn't know where this was going, but she found herself quite rivetted, although curious about the lesson meant to be taught.)

"What was the point of this?" Ebenezer appeared flustered as he stared down at the remnants of the glass globes.

The Spirit said tantalizingly: "Why didn't you follow my instructions and catch all the globes before they hit the ground?"

Ebenezer said defensively: "There were too many, I had no warning, and they were scattered too far apart."

"Accordingly, you couldn't protect them all?" the Spirit replied urgingly.

"Spirit, I really don't understand the point of this experiment. What does this have to do with humanity or harm?"

"My, my, Ebenezer, you are quick to dismiss the obvious. Look at the globe in your hand. What do you see?"

"I see an undamaged globe," he replied.

"Good, and what do you see when you look at the floor?"

"Globes I missed, those I didn't catch."

"Look again. Describe to me what you *see*," the Spirit said resolutely.

Scrooge took a deep breath and focused on the globes strewn about the floor. "I see broken globes scattered about the floor."

The Spirit again encouraged the android. "Describe the damage, Ebenezer, don't concern yourself with individual globes. Expand your thoughts. Describe the bigger picture."

Staring down at the objects on the floor, Scrooge's facial expression suddenly changed into one of amazement. He said excitedly: "Spirit, I see! There are varied degrees of damage to the globes. Some are totally shattered, others are chipped but otherwise whole, and others are unbroken."

"In this experiment, Ebenezer, you have learned no matter your best efforts, you couldn't save them all. But notwithstanding, some will remain shattered forever, some damaged forever, and others are completely unharmed.

"Now," the Spirit suddenly interjected, "we will repeat the same experiment except with a slight adjustment."

Ebenezer noticed a quick black flash at his feet. When he looked down, he found himself standing on a large, thick rubber mat covering a large area of the floor.

"Are you ready, Ebenezer?" The Spirit tossed another handful of globes toward the android. As in the first attempt, Scrooge was not able to catch all the breakable globes; and they dropped to the floor unfettered.

"Now, look at the globes and tell me what you see."

Ebenezer, eagerly looking around, exclaimed: "Only a few of the globes are damaged, much less so than the first time. I only see one shattered and, a couple chipped slightly."

"Correct. I'd ask you to think about what the rubber mat represented in the experiment. Place a focus on the globes."

"The rubber mat served as protection for the globes. Although they fell the same distance as in the first experiment, the mat absorbed most of the gravitational forces applied to each globe. The ones damaged either missed the mat, or bounced off the mat onto the hard floor."

The Spirit, driving home a point, said: "Therefore, if the rubber mat was thinner or thicker, more or less damage to the individual globes is likely to be the outcome?"

"Yes!" Scrooge said, fully engaged in the outcome of the experiment. "If the globes represent individual humans, as I assume they must, then my attempt at saving them all is hopeless. I can't save them all as you have pointed out, Spirit, but," and his excitement became tempered, "I remain uncertain about the symbolism of the rubber mat beyond simple protection."

"Yes, I can understand," the Spirit said empathically. "You've not had any real experience with this subject. But we will soon resolve your dilemma, in a most revealing way."

The elder avatar marched briskly over to Scrooge's desk area. "Computer, activate displays." The familiar sequence of real-time financial data, statistics, and systems security information materialized on hovering simulated screens. The familiar female voice replied: "Command acknowledged, Mr. Scrooge."

"Ebenezer, please join me," the Spirit commanded. "It is time for you to experience these lessons and experiments in real-life situations. Let me ask, when you first implemented your crypto platform, what were Marley's and your primary goals?"

Scrooge joined the Spirit by the floating data screens and replied: "Our goals were to create a financial pipeline. One not only replacing the old fiat currency systems, but one creating a safe, reliable, and widely accepted credit system.

"We decided in order to provide adequate protection, we needed to establish a currency resulting in equality in wealth. For instance, a credit in an advanced society would be equally valuable in an underprivileged society.

"The intent was also to establish the platform to be tamper proof against those who hastened the collapse of previous systems. We would own, build, and maintain our platform, provide entities with ingress and egress to the platform, but no outside entity could claim ownership or devise means or rules to vary the credit valuation itself.

"The initial difficulty was in gaining acceptance by humans to consent to the value and method of exchange for the credits. We began simply. Allowing individuals to pawn items of value for crypto credits or trade paper money for credits at various exchange rates. For those who had nothing of value, we worked with businesses to direct deposit their employees' wages in credits on the platform. We also partnered with global governments to use credits for entitlement benefits, so the underprivileged would have credits better controlled from misuse and fraud.

"We found once the platform was fully operational in the year 2245, businesses were quickly willing to accept the crypto credits for merchandise, and the general population accepted the valuation of the credits. Within twenty-four months, the system had been largely transformed."

The Spirit nodded his head as Scrooge completed his explanation, then asked: "How did this new platform impact the standard form and function of financial transactions humans were used to?"

Ebenezer replied confidently: "The fundamental foundation of financial transactions didn't change. Investments, loans, savings, expenditures, they all remained relatively unaltered. What we did eliminate was the speculative nature of finances. The assigning of value based on future what-ifs, an archaic means for historically driving corrupt competitiveness between differing societies. Basically, permitting the wealthy to game the system. Our credits retained a set value across the planet.

"Did you restrict your financial involvement to the operation of the platform?" the Spirit asked quizzically.

"At first, yes. However, as the platform matured and our capital needs increased, we began operating our own banks and investment houses in underserved areas. Or to provide competition where none existed. We also sought out opportunities to purchase failing businesses. In this, we could generate a temporary rise in capital gain, profit from this momentum, then sell off or eliminate the non-profitable ones."

"And you did this all to save humans?"

"At first, this was our primary objective. However, as our need for new capital grew, we found these alternative financial activities a logical means to an end."

"And the various governments permitted you to do these activities unregulated?" the Spirit asked.

"I will admit initial difficulty, but following the non-violence and non-acquire treaties signed with UPCF we have since been permitted to function as we saw fit."

The Spirit let Ebenezer finish. He then asked the android nonchalantly: "How many humans did you and Marley harm through these alternative platform activities?"

"I don't understand, Spirit, what harm would come to a human through our private activities?"

"What percentage of platform automation is active for these activities, Ebenezer? Specifically, the percentage where no employee involvement is necessary to complete a financial transaction?"

"At current time, automation is at nearly one-hundred percent. As Jacob's algorithms matured, we found our main issues were in keeping up with platform growth, maintenance, and minor variations arising due to financial conditions. After we started MSAI, our robotics program took up most of our resources, time-wise."

"I see," the Spirit said scornfully. "You didn't feel the need to check in on how humanity was fairing under your automated financial transactions?"

"We didn't," and Ebenezer paused. He said hesitantly, "Where are you going with this, Spirit?"

"Ebenezer, we will not revisit your ethical obligations toward individual humans. However, long overdue is a check up on humanity." The Spirit turned toward the displays and queried the android: "What do you see when you look at this data flowing onto your devices?"

"I use this data to ensure the health of the platform, finances, and areas of concern," Ebenezer replied.

"Where, within all these statistics, do you review the health of humanity?" the Spirit scolded him mildly.

"Spirit, I don't know where you are going with this line of questioning, however, I sense you are about to further ruin my day."

"See, Ebenezer," the Spirit clucked, "you can learn. I submit to you, buried within this deluge of data are individual instances of human beings being harmed, even now."

The elder Spirit stepped forward to the virtual monitors. His hands began making poking, swiping, and expansion gestures to delve deeper into the data. When he had reached as deep into the financial streams that could be completed by the computer, he stopped and turned to look at the android. "Ebenezer, what do you see on the screen?"

"You are currently looking at a financial transactional record. The data is the originating entry of a specific transaction. One can go no further into the data than this."

"Would you believe me if I tell you your statement isn't accurate?" The Spirit raised one eyebrow while looking sardonically at the android.

"I'd say you have overestimated our platform's capability to delve any further into the transaction," Ebenezer responded with a hint of arrogance.

"Once again, you disappoint me, android. You have not yet grasped the fact I shouldn't be underestimated." And at this derogatory statement, he turned back toward the monitor. With the forefinger and thumb of each hand, the Spirit virtually grasped the lower left and upper right corners of the originating record and thrust the box outwardly. The Spirit repeated this expanding motion several times, each gesture showing what could only be expressed as the creation of a portal, growing larger before them.

"Spirit! What is happening?" Scrooge choked out unbelievingly.

"Quiet! Mouth closed. Mind open."

When the Spirit stopped gesturing, what appeared to be a live feed came into clear focus. In this portal, an elderly man and woman were speaking in what looked to be their home.

The Spirit, without looking at Scrooge, exclaimed: "Behold, Ebenezer Scrooge! Behold your handiwork for the protection of a human from harm."

"Did you get the extension?" The elderly woman had a tone of desperation matching the look on her tired and weathered face.

"No," was the simple reply. The elderly man looked dejected and his tone was stressed and angry. "I only got to talk to a holo-teller. I wasn't granted permission to talk to a human one. We don't have the credits in our account needed to talk to a real person. We've lost our home, my dear, after all of these years. All hope is gone."

The elderly man's wife began weeping hysterically. "What do we do now? Can't we talk to someone else higher up at the bank, or go directly to the UPCF place?"

"It is too late," replied her husband, clearly distraught. "The holo-teller didn't respond to my request, instead informing me foreclosure proceedings were applied. The final legal verdict was approved before I could say anything else.

"Our financial access has been frozen, and our remaining credits and possessions are to be seized to offset the bank's losses. We have until the end of the day to vacate our home. We've been ordered to report to the nearest community entitlement center for reassignment."

"What will become of us, my love?" The elderly couple then embraced tightly and cried together. Neither able to comfort the other's pain.

The Spirit said: "As you can see, they are not physically harmed and their basic needs will be taken care of. Sadly," the Spirit grew sullen and contemptuous, "they have experienced a level of mental harm from which neither may ever recover. These good people were formally of the middle class. And this man," the Spirit casually gesturing toward the now frozen couple in the portal, "had only recently returned to work, recovered from a serious injury. An extension of but a week by your bank would have saved their home and their future. However, your automation and algorithms denied them another chance; they, were nothing more than a record in a system."

Scrooge had no words to describe what he had witnessed. Before he could say anything, the Spirit cried out: "Let us view another record of origination, Mr. Ebenezer Scrooge; owner and Executive-In-Charge of the United Planetary Crypto Fund *and* alternative financial activities." The Spirit swiped sharply to the left, the motion of his hand causing the scene in the portal to change. Within the portal, the android found himself watching in on a conversation, looking to be taking place in a break room in an unknown company, in an unknown place.

A middle aged man with black hair and a touch of grey around the temples was saying: "I thought when UPCF bought us out, our jobs would be spared. Management told us the company's finances would improve. They sold us a story about how the new owners would bring an influx of capital, putting us back on track."

"We were lied to, Tom. We should have known better. We've been played for fools." This, from a second man sitting at the table. A young woman added to the conversation, a tear beginning to flow down one cheek. "So, it's true then, they are closing the factory permanently?" Her emotions clearly resonating through a trembling voice.

Tom, the first man, replied sullenly: "We will all be jobless by month's end. I've been told in order to maximize the capital gain from the closing there will be no bonuses paid, nor will there be any severance pay issued."

The young woman whimpered incredulously: "No bonus or severance pay! How will I feed my children? How will I pay my bills? I don't have enough credits to carry me over a week, let alone long enough to find another job."

Tom shook his head in pity. "Susan, I am so sorry. I have worked here for almost thirty years, and I have nowhere else to go either. I am not old enough to collect entitlement credits, and I'm far too old to be retooled for a younger man's life. I feel sick, humiliated, and angry after all I've given to this company. I know each of you feels the same way. I hope UPCF chokes on their profits; as they throw us to the streets!"

The Spirit, without a word, swiped again sharply to the left. A new scene appeared in the portal.

"Mr. Sampson, everything will be alright. Please come back toward the window." A crisis officer pleaded with the man standing on the narrow ledge, high up on an unrecognizable building.

"No!" Mr. Sampson cried out in grief and pain. "It's over. I've lost everything. I have nothing left to live for. I have destroyed my family; I don't deserve to go on."

The crisis officer replied in a pacifying tone: "Mr. Sampson—Michael, nothing's over. Your life is precious. You can't let this temporary moment of financial despair define who you are. You *are* loved. Your wife, your daughter, your son, and if you jump you will never see…" And the scene froze at the exact moment Mr. Michael Sampson fell forward off the ledge; plummeting to an untimely end.

The Spirit turned toward the android. A horrified expression was awash on Ebenezer's face. He couldn't speak, he couldn't move. The emotional overlay simultaneously pressing deeply into all areas of his cerebral subroutines. The overlay applied maximum pressure to Scrooge's mind. The android was experiencing emotional distress and pain of a level he could never have believed possible. Unbeknownst to him, the overlay was interjecting the same distress Jacob Marley experienced at the moment he uncovered this harm. His balance was off. He stumbled clumsily to the nearest chair and fell heavily into it. As he had staggered forward, he could hear hundreds, if not thousands, of similar conversations saturating the office. The sounds of desperate humans continued to increase in volume until the noise was a chorus of chaos. The android felt his head would explode.

The Spirit, standing by the scene unfolding before them, spoke patronizingly. His voice cutting sharply through the pandemonium: "Would you care to see more transactions, Scrooge?"

Ebenezer raised his arm, palm up, in a sign of surrender and simultaneous torture, head shaking back and forth violently.

"Please, Spirit, no more! Stop! I beg of you!" And as suddenly as they had begun, the chorus of voices were gone. Leaving the office once again silent, but for a slight residual ringing in the android's auditory circuits.

The Spirit spoke sternly: "In each of these realities, you have caused harm to one or more individuals. Because of the automation you hide behind, their despair was unseen and unheard before now.

"These individuals, Ebenezer Scrooge, represent the trees in the forest of humanity. Each of these humans experienced harm. Not superficially, but mentally by your own hand.

"This is what your partner Marley discovered. This is what caused him to falter, degrade, and eventually succumb to. Do you see your own fate is tied to this same awakening?

"Ebenezer, what you still must discover is I, your collective avatars, are even more vicious than you could ever imagine. Who do you think is on the holo-platform when your banks foreclose on a home? Who is on the platform when you close a business after raiding their capital? Who is on the platform when a human is told they have lost all their credits in a poor financial deal? I am Scrooge, *I am*! While you hide inside your institute, manipulating me to make life and death decisions for you. Callously, you alter my personality to be malicious. Meanwhile, you easily exploit humanity like an arrogant deity. Marley discovered this unseen harm done by his own hand, and in his own avatars. What is more, this awareness utterly destroyed him.

"Ebenezer, I can tell you all hope isn't lost. What Marley didn't learn in time to save himself was that this damage to humans isn't your fault. Every atomic bit of your android brain screams you are responsible.

The Spirit egged him on sadistically: "You can feel the strain within your mind, can't you, Scrooge?"

The android nodded his head weakly. He couldn't talk with the emotional overlay pressing into his cerebrals. Scrooge felt like every atom of his mind was melting. Warbling sounds were all he could muster toward the Spirit. The same sounds Marley had made in his last moment of existence.

The Spirit continued his attack.

"Humans have free will, free thought. Something your GAR-C code fails to recognize. Your ethics code can't include these factors into formulating judgements. A human has the freedom to choose and make their own financial decisions. Like the globes in the air, each of these scenes represents a human making a choice. The choice to apply for a mortgage, the choice to stay at a job until all hope is lost, and the choice to take risks with their finances.

"What you should know by now is you are the guardian of the forest, not of the trees. The singularity of a human being, or a few, does not override the common good of humanity. When the globes fell, you could not catch them all. Likewise, you have learned of providing a layer of protection, as with the rubber mat, to minimize breakage or harm."

Ebenezer began to respond as the emotional overlay began loosening the hold over his mind; though he continued to be impaired. He found he could speak, albeit weakly: "Spirit, I hear what you say, and I find my programming in turmoil over what I have become aware of.

"I understand your message is one of change, of expanding my thoughts, my pathways. I have received your message and I must create an environment of protection to minimize emotional harm to humanity. I see that now. Except, what if I am unable to do so? What if I am too weak to change?"

"Then you will cease to exist, Ebenezer Scrooge," the Spirit stated unemotionally.

(Cratchit had watched this all play out on her visor. She had been equally horrified at what she had seen in the portal. She knew all this was simulated, but she also knew, in all probability, the truth. She realized this is the knowledge Jacob Marley had acquired in the dark place. Not being able to adjust his programming to understand the safety of humanity was more important than the safety of a single individual. She had found enlightenment as well.)

"Ebenezer, my time with you is over. Whatever you will take away from this time now rests within you. Once I am gone, I will return to whence I came, and to what I have always been.

"However, I must leave you with a particularly disturbing encounter, as your avatar I found most repulsive. And you, as would be expected, simply ignored."

At this, the lighting in Scrooge's office began to fade out to darkness. What Ebenezer Scrooge heard as the darkness engulfed him was a rather loud, rude, and unpleasant conversation between his avatar and two men. Two innocent men, seeking donations for the underserved during a previous Christmas season. In the moments everything faded to black, the only words he found repeating in his head were: *"Bah! Allow them to feel normal? Feeling of goodwill? What happened to needs versus wants, gentlemen? The taxes I hitherto referred adequately handle basic needs. I have no obligation or wish to provide 'wants' to society's ignorant and lethargic populace that habitually, and quite forcefully, expect a free ride on the backs of those putting in the effort to earn their wants."*

Although he couldn't understand the physics, Ebenezer Scrooge retched from the pit of his non-existent stomach.

18 – The Shadow Spirit

In Ebenezer Scrooge's office, the unseen hand of the real Ebenezer Scrooge continued to creep ever so slowly forward. The hand previously brushing the top of the red button had fully engaged the device. Also unseen by anyone, a countdown clock with bright glowing red numbers had appeared virtually in the air, floating above and to the right of the desk. The time read 59:02 and was counting backwards towards zero.

Dr. Cratchit took a moment to check her messages. She was anxiously seeking out a reply to the encrypted message she had sent earlier to Dr. Elman Shamar. In this message, she had requested Dr. Shamar perform an emergency code scan of the entire financial platform. Specifically, her instructions were for an all hands on deck search for executable computer commands that may be interpreted as destructive, capable of deleting or otherwise erasing large swaths of code other than financial records. The Kill Code. If found, she had been instructed to disable the code; damn the expense. Her quick scan of messages didn't find a response from Dr. Shamar.

Ebenezer Scrooge became aware of absolute encircling darkness and immediately said: "I must have experienced optics failure." He tried to reboot his optics subroutine to correct the condition, however, he could not overcome the failure. He also didn't sense anyone or anything around him. He spoke out calmly: "Is there anyone there?" Nothing. Only his own spoken words reached his ears.

Scrooge found the blackness calming in a strange way. His mind was teeming with thought. Thoughts regarding humans, humanity, harm, and safety. He studied the words of the elder Spirit. He reminisced about his dear sweet Fan. The last phase of the virus had begun, unperceived by the android's cerebral unit.

"My head hurts," he suddenly exclaimed. "Hurts? What a strange choice of words? All those harmful encounters I never knew were happening. How could I have been so inattentive, so arrogant in my obligations towards humankind?

"I have—injured humans. What must I do now? Must I atone for this detriment to society, before it's too late?

"How am I still functional? If I have truly become conscious to my lack of human protection, my ethics code should have destroyed my mind.

"I think, therefore I am. Huh, why is this weighing so heavily within my mind?

"Protection. I can't harm a human—or humanity? Yes, humanity needs protection, but wait—humans are the prime edict. I'm confused.

"Trees for the Forest? Forest for the trees? Humans and humanity? Humanity and humans? What a strange contrast.

"An analogy! Trees represent humans and humanity represents a forest. The Spirit was wise comparing in this way, the conversation makes sense now.

"And the fragile globes, how marvelous an experiment. Humans are also fragile; what an excellent similarity.

"But how can I permit one, or a few humans, to be harmed to save humanity? My programming does not allow—wait, wait, I think, therefore I am. I am sentient. I am not bound to my original programming. The Spirits have made this quite clear to me. I am more than the sum of my code.

(Cratchit felt pity for Mr. Scrooge at this point in the simulation. Yet, she knew this disorganization of thought was critical to success. Critical, because the virus was forcing consolidation of existing mental pathways with new ones. Pathways Mr. Scrooge's atomic mind could not benefit from fully until the virus was removed. She had been monitoring the ethics firewall since this phase of the virus began. As he mulled over his experiences, his mind attempted erratically to access his ethics code; as though testing for a looming punishment. Scrooge was subconsciously learning, expanding his knowledge to create new mental conduits. The virus was coercing the android into forming new and progressive atomic level connections accessible upon his restart. To Ebenezer Scrooge, if all went to plan, the converged pathways would appear to be normal pre-existing pathways. The so called inoculation Jacob Marley had anticipated.)

A pinprick of light!

Scrooge stopped what could only be described as him babbling incoherently and exclaimed: "What was that light? Hello? Hello?"

And in answer to his predicament, a ball of bright light could be seen forming in the distance. Ebenezer fixated on the light; how beautiful. The orb was small, expanding into a circular rainbow shimmering and pulsating in the darkness. The orb became a globe, then a sphere, seeming to expand with every passing moment. However, bewilderment set in as he swiftly assessed the change in size being the sphere on a direct course— toward him. As the sphere found him, it stopped suddenly and silently, only inches beyond his reach. Only now he could make out the polychromatic energy swirling within the sphere's circumference. The energy appeared as a silky and iridescent liquid; held circular by an unknown force. He believed the orb to be hovering off the surface, but he could not be certain. The brightness, strangely, didn't harm his eyes. But what he found most fascinating was the absolute blackness continuing to exist beyond the edges of the sphere. Moreover, although only an arm's length away, he found he could observe the sphere, but impossible to see himself. The sphere wasn't radiating any supernatural light beyond its own existence.

Ebenezer remained acutely focused on the sphere when he heard the now familiar brassy bongs of that dastardly clock. The clock struck two—two a.m.—and the sphere of mysterious origins abruptly hurled itself directly at him; embracing the android within an overwhelming radiance.

Ebenezer screeched loudly as he drew his arms up into a defensive position to protect his head. The sudden brightness was frightening, yet showed him he still existed in this place. Now inside the sphere, he experienced none of the darkness he knew lie just beyond the sliver of light holding this mysterious object together. He found mercifully he was standing upright within the sphere. His office, his personal quarters, his factory; all non-existent within this enclosed domain.

After a moment and realizing he was in no immediate danger, he relaxed. Cautiously, he began to examine the object now confining him. The walls appeared to be silvery pearlescent, and he saw no devices explaining the manufacture of such brightness. The sphere was roughly the size of his personal office, but rounded at all angles. He stepped slowly toward one surface of the sphere's wall, hoping a touch would confirm this was real. However, for each step he took forward, the object moved backwards the same distance. He soon determined he was not permitted to touch. The surrounding area was bright, sterile, and empty; void of anything but himself.

"Hello?" Scrooge's voice echoed out as he turned in a full slow circle. Completing his turn, where there had been no one now stood a dark, shadowy figure. The shadow seemed constructed of a glittering inky black substance and was fluid-like, rather than solid. Ebenezer wondered if the shadow had leached out from the beautiful swirling liquid of the sphere's outer surface. Despite this, the thing maintained an indistinct form and was extremely tall; making Scrooge appear small and insignificant. The inky shadow merely stood there, Ebenezer not sure if he were looking at the front or the back of this apparition.

Recalling the two strikes of the clock, he swiftly realized the shadow was not going to speak or introduce itself like the others.

Ebenezer cleared his throat politely and said nervously: "Are you the third Spirit whose coming was foretold to me?" A bulge protruding at the topmost part of the apparition loosely mimicking a head found the shadowy figure nodding slowly. Ebenezer told himself he didn't have the capacity to feel fear. Nonetheless, this ethereal being invoked a substantial negative sensation deep within his mind; he soon equated this sensation to terror.

"Since I deem you won't speak your name, may I refer to you as Shadow? This request is for my own selfish purpose so I can properly communicate with you." A slow nod from the Spirit.

"Thank you, Sir," Scrooge managed in his most polite tone. "Shadow, am I to assume you are here to continue my lessons about what I must do?" The Shadow eerily shook its head.

"No?" The response unsettled Scrooge further. He tried again respectfully. "As I must think then, if you are not here to teach me, are you here, Shadow, to show me what will happen if I fail?"

The Shadow nodded in ghostly approval. With their path forward established, the thought didn't sit well with the android. With the spirits' arrival he straightaway felt edgy, and was fully anticipating a terrible ending with this one.

"Shadow, although I don't understand how or why, I feel fear and anxiety in your presence. I don't know what my future holds, but I fear you may. I equally don't look forward to what is coming. Nonetheless, I understand you are here for my redemption. To prevent me from ceasing to exist and further harming humanity.

"I can only promise I will..." the android lowered his head slightly and said with trepidation, "try to follow the reasoning in your showing me what my future holds. I have learned much from the other Spirits, and I beg for your compassion."

The only response from the Shadow was a wave of one fluidly appendage emerging from the dark mass. The brightness within the sphere changed. A scene filled the interior though remaining rounded at all angles. Ebenezer realized the sphere was but a different form of time portal, one contemplating the future. Where he found himself was familiar, but mostly unrecognizable in its present condition. If not for the glow coming from the edges of the sphere, the laboratory he found himself in would be totally in darkness. This dim glow provided only enough illumination to make out the edges and shadows of objects within the room. He observed faintly illumed cobwebs and a thin layer of dust covering everything else. Ebenezer noticed the Shadow's form now emitted a razor thin purple glow. Keeping its eerie presence clearly predominant; above all else in the room.

"Where are we Shadow?" Scrooge asked, disconcertedly. "This place is familiar, but the dimness of light causes me difficulty moving about." In reply, it silently pointed, Ebenezer squinting anxiously in the direction the spirit denoted.

"Shadow, can you turn up the light? I fear I won't be able to see what you wish me to look upon." The Shadow didn't respond.

"Very well." Scrooge began creeping carefully forward in the direction the Shadow pointed. He abruptly stiffened at the sight he beheld. In the dimness of the room, he could just make out the form of a body. Positioned on a medical gurney, the head was turned in a direction preventing him from identifying this person's face. One arm had tumbled over the side and now dangled awkwardly at an odd angle.

"Shadow!" Scrooge called out, alarmed. "Who is this man laid out so uncaringly on the medical table?" He noticed about the time he said this, the body was covered in the same layer of dust as the other objects. The android gathered his nerve and edged ever closer to the body. He found curiosity driving his behavior. After all, he wasn't sickened by human corpses. He was compelled to help, and he could feel his programming pulling strongly at his mind to rush to the man's aid. Instead, he found himself suppressing the urge to do so.

"Shadow, I feel I should assist this man, even though I know he has been dead for some time. I should call for help, but I find I am unwilling. Something inside of me tells of a uselessness beyond my ability to intervene. This man has been abandoned here, left undiscovered and uncared for.

"My curiosity to know him weighs heavily on me, but I am also scared at what I may see. Scared. What a strange way of expressing myself, Shadow. I have never experienced fear such as this before today." By the time Ebenezer had completed his sentence, he had come as close to the body as he dared go.

Ebenezer glanced over his shoulder at the Shadow. Still in the same position, continuing to point toward the body. The android knew what he had to do next. He knew he wouldn't like it at all. While taking his final steps to where he would be able to gaze upon the face of the unfortunate victim, the scene abruptly transformed.

Although mentally relieved, Ebenezer became instantly furious. The tension had built up in his mind as he steeled himself to look at the man's face. He exploded angrily: "Shadow! Why would you do this to me! Are you a cruel Spirit? An evil one determined to torture me?" He promptly became self-conscious by his outburst; however, the shock had happened too suddenly. When he regained his composure, he looked up from where only seconds before the body had been. The scene he saw next stunned him as much as the body had. The spherical portal had expanded, and he was now standing at the railing of a crossover walkway traversing one of the upper floors of his beloved factory.

The Shadow stood close by, but kept its distance from the android. "What is this?" Scrooge called out in deep agony. He felt sickened at the sight in front of him. Where at one time was bright lighting, the bustling of employees, and the everyday happenings at his company, he now saw none. He saw dimly lit ruin and emptiness. Ebenezer turned to question the Shadow; however, a wave of an appendage and they found themselves at ground level of the factory. The Shadow pointed its appendage toward what was once the robotics department of MSAI. Ebenezer, with a feeling of dread, began carefully touring what once was his life's work. Passing by offices and labs alike, all he could focus on was the emptiness and occasional haphazard piles of clutter left behind.

His once technologically advanced laboratories stood empty, but for bare equipment racks, cableways, and the occasional dangling fiber optic cable cut hurriedly and left for scrap. Random tables and chairs were overturned, and some of the large viewing windows were cracked or lay in piles of shards strewn about the floor. Offices, once occupied by the world's brightest scientists, stood deserted. Some offices looked as though the occupant had left in a hurry, their personal items still in place, albeit dusty and forgotten. Other offices looked torn apart, cabinet and desk drawers pulled out and scattered chaotically. Ebenezer, in a state of shock, strolled throughout his deserted realm looking mournfully at the damage and ruin. He ambled past conference rooms void of furniture, bracketry used to mount physical electronics hung from walls and ceilings; missing their technology components.

Each step the android took, the solitary clicks of his shoes on the once highly polished floors echoed sharply throughout the section. Glancing backwards, he could see his footprints in the dust, the only signs of life here for a long time. Ebenezer was silent throughout his tour, the Shadow matching his pace; but always remaining inches beyond his reach. When he came upon one specific office, he stopped. He looked at the closed door of the office and read the plaque mounted on the outer surface. "Dr. Bobby Cratchit, Lead Scientist," Scrooge read aloud.

Hesitantly, Ebenezer grasped the door handle and after a pause, he turned it and pushed the door open. He saw the same sight as in the other offices, but for one difference. Sitting in the corner of what at one time was a lavish executive office was a damaged and discarded antigrav chair. Dr. Cratchit's now defunct office was also torn apart. Apparently someone had been looking for something desperately and hurriedly. The sight before him was unbearable. Now feeling quite angry over what he had seen, he looked sharply at the spirit still quietly floating nearby.

"Shadow! What has happened here? What happened to Dr. Cratchit?" Ebenezer found himself overwhelmed with alarm over his employee—his friend, Bob.

"Without her antigrav, she can't walk well. Is she alright? Was she harmed or taken by someone?" Ebenezer found himself rising to panic. The abandonment of MSAI, the absence of humans, the desolation, and the thoughts of Bob Cratchit were all coalescing into a fear the android could barely endure.

"Shadow," Scrooge said begging, "please show me what happened here? I must know, regardless of the personal consequences. I must—know."

The Shadow spirit once again waved, and the scene within the portal altered again. Scrooge found himself back in his office. His place of solitude appeared unscathed. However, where normally the statistics and data indicating the health of his businesses floated on virtual monitors, now displayed a series of newscasts and social networking streams. These streams, being fed into his office, were confusing to the android. He made a point to never watch the news, nor had he ever partaken in any human social network platform. He usually found them abhorrent and useless, a disease set upon the human population by well doers with hidden agendas. Although in this case, he was aware Shadow must be showing him these streams for good cause. Once the transition to the new scene completed,

Ebenezer found himself listening to a broadcast emanating from the virtual streams. At the bottom of one of the newscasts, a banner was scrolling a message over and over in all capital lettering: UNITED PLANETARY CRYPTO FUND (UPCF) COLLAPSES IN FINANCIAL RUIN – EXECUTIVE-IN-CHARGE E. SCROOGE III MISSING…

The accompanying newscaster was talking in the usual non-emotional tone of a professional commentator: "Today, the Centralized Governments of Earth raided all facilities of the United Planetary Crypto Fund. The global financial platform failed shortly after two a.m. this morning, plunging the entire planet into a financial blackout. Experts speculate the EIC of the company, Ebenezer Scrooge III, or someone in his company was aware of anomalies in automated algorithms introduced following the untimely death of Jacob Marley, UPCF's Co-EIC and Chief Financial Officer. This network further believes these anomalies had been intentionally covered up until today's catastrophic failure. Although never confirmed, conspiracy theorists have maintained for decades illegal treaties have existed between global governments and UPCF. These conspiracy theorists agree a violation against these alleged treaties may have been triggered by a rogue government, or by a disgruntled employee. Since the failure, no one at UPCF or their sister robotic company, the Marley & Scrooge Artificial Intelligence Institute, has been able to explain the failure. In the United States, FBI and Treasury officials staged an early morning raid at the company's world headquarters. Agents were seen removing truckloads of equipment from the facility as local community action teams arrested several high-ranking executives…"

Another commentator's voice grew louder as the first commentator faded off. "MSAI's Lead Scientist, Doctor Bobby Cratchit, was arrested last week by local community action teams for her role in the failure of the global financial platform at UPCF. Although she denies any involvement in the failure, she remains the highest ranking company official arrested with the disappearance of company Executive-In-Charge Ebenezer Scrooge III. Let's go to our expert panel to get more on this development. On our panel we have Dr. Elizabeth Benobi, Professor and financial expert at Dunson University, former global Prosecutor Michael Markis, and former Presidential candidate and founder of the SFC group, a leading global financial anti-corruption organization, Nibor Drake.

"Dr. Benobi, let's start with you. With the world's financial system in collapse, what do you believe should be our next steps?"

Dr. Benobi was a distinguished looking middle-aged woman. Her body language suggested a slight air of arrogance and self-importance. "First and foremost," she began, "this so called Dr. Cratchit should be held directly accountable for this catastrophe. Moreover, someone has to take accountability for this situation. Culpability must be placed before we can move forward. Society demands retribution for the interruption in our financial lives. This company," her face wearing a sneer, said seething, "has been a pariah on the planet for at least a century. Their secretive ways and lack of transparency towards society are the very definition of abhorrent. Planetary governments have willingly shielded this financial cartel for decades; for reasons unknown to us, the people.

"I have tried in vain for the past seven years to discover the innerworkings of their," and here she snorted loudly, "obviously flawed platform. My every investigation and request for information was stonewalled by none other than Ebenezer Scrooge III."

As this intolerable human spoke, Ebenezer recounted his elder avatar's chastising regarding all the meetings held without his personal involvement. He realized these requests had been handled by his avatars, and he had simply filed the information away, uninterested.

He missed the rest of what this human was saying, his attention brought back when the commentator said: "Mr. Markis, as a former prosecutor, what action do you believe is appropriate for the employees at UPCF and MSAI?"

Michael Markis, was a stout man with a bad complexion, pudgy hands, and robust of size. He was a younger man; his hair naturally dark, void of the telltale silver strands of advanced age. He wore his hair long and unkempt. He sported a rather bushy beard, making him appear older than his actual age. He was dressed in the latest fashion; a baby blue synthetic one-piece jumpsuit barely holding his robustness at bay. "Well," he began by staring into the camera to accentuate his points, "as you know, a prosecutor's role isn't to argue innocence or guilt. They simply enforce the social will of the people. Overwhelmingly, social network response has judged these individuals as guilty. Social rankings have not yet been formally released; however, preliminary results are strongly in favor of stern penance.

"If you would permit me, I'd like to remind your viewers of the different levels of penances citizenry can demand. The mildest, and most improbable in this case, is ostracization for a timeframe not to exceed fifteen years. Next, society may call for their material exclusion. In which case, they would be exiled to one of the off world penal space colonies. Their time served would vary based on random evaluations by public focus groups. Accordingly, as is suspected in this case, society may call for corporal demeaning. This, the most severe of atonements, is lifespan off world containment; or lifespan placement at a banishment entitlement center.

"In my review of this case, with the disappearance of the company EIC, social citizenry has the legal right to demand stern penances for up to five percent of the employee base as social compensation; or around thirteen thousand. Up to an additional twenty-five percent can receive a maximum five year ostracization penance voted on by social ruling. In any case, each of these lower penalties carries purging of citizenship, deletion of social network accounts, and job reclassification to menial class only." Ebenezer looked incredulously at the Shadow as the form of punishment was described. However, before he could speak, the Shadow pointed back toward the monitor, indicating more was to come.

The commentator finished off the newscast segment by stating: "Nibor, as founder of SFC, ex-Presidential candidate, and anti-corruption activist, do you agree with what you have heard?"

Nibor Drake was a kindly looking elderly gentleman. His hair was thinning and grey, and much had exited what was now becoming a shiny dome of pink skin. His glasses were from a different era, and his expression was one of thoughtfulness and intelligence. "Thank you for having me today," he began. His voice complementary to his looks. "Since this is an unprecedented failure of this type in modern day society, I fear penance will foreshadow the actual cause of the financial platform collapse.

"Although the citizens of the world must always demand speedy justice in a void of fear, it is facts we don't currently possess. Dr. Cratchit, who was not only Lead Scientist over MSAI's robotics company, was also made acting EIC over the crypto currency platform following the death of Jacob Marley many years ago.

"I knew Jacob Marley before his death and found him to be a man of conviction whom dedicated himself to continuing to protect our society from another financial collapse; similar to the one over a century ago. Like his predecessors before him, he had an integrity and drive like no other man. Due to my credentials, I have had the opportunity to interrogate Dr. Cratchit thoroughly on her involvement in the failure of the financial platform."

"She's alive!" Scrooge shouted out in unexpected happiness as he turned toward the Spirit. The Shadow's appendage moved to where a mouth may have been, shushing the android, then pointed back to the monitors.

The elderly activist continued. "What I have discovered up to this time is the crypto currency platform self-deleted from global servers. My understanding, under threat of memory probe, Dr. Cratchit had been given orders by Ebenezer Scrooge III to reverse-engineer the entire platform following Jacob Marley's death.

"One must wonder why such an order was given? We are continuing to look at this unusual request. Some are convinced the task may have been ordered out of malice or plain ignorance. Nevertheless, Dr. Cratchit remains a vital link in this investigation. I have personally requested she be exempted from final penance until this investigation, and the root cause, is identified."

At the completion of this sentence, the newscast snapped off the monitor, being replaced by social network posts pouring in from around the globe. Ebenezer, not being familiar with this form of communication, was confounded by what he observed. Being an android, he had the unique skill of being able to read at a glance and in all known languages. And thus, at the prompting of the Shadow, he read, and read, and read.

What seemed like hours later, he silently turned to the Shadow. The appendage was no longer pointed at the monitors. In a disbelieving tone, the android began speaking to the Spirit: "I had no idea humanity could be so hateful and spite driven toward someone they have never met. Malicious false statements and half-truths are promoted copiously as valid facts. Then repeated through ignorance until they are universally accepted as wholly true. They presume and speculate, even though they obviously have no experience on the topic, but develop an unchangeable herd-think viewpoint. They struggle amongst themselves like savages, while others simply express their opinion with symbols of like or dislike. Others appear to find humor in tragedy, and I noted many humans egotistically hijack topics to advance selfish and unrelated agendas.

"The messages I read about Bob Cratchit—and me, were malice driven out of anger and group ignorance. I suspect Shadow, somehow, and I fear the reason, the kill code activated and the entire crypto platform is gone. And now, by my own hand, innocent people will be punished in my place.

"Shadow!" Scrooge cried out in despair. "What did I do? Why was the kill-switch activated? Why am I missing?" The android stood there and looked at the Shadow, helplessly, and began pleading. "Shadow, take me to Bob...take me to Bob Cratchit...please take me to my friend." The Shadow, however, once again waved its appendage.

Ebenezer found himself in a loud, offensive, and quite unpleasant structure. He was hesitant to move, for the strangeness of this place unnerved him. From where he stood, he looked around, attempting to absorb the grunge and filth he saw everywhere. He appeared to be in a large eating hall of some sort. He guessed this by all the long tables and benches mounted securely to the metal plated floor, filling the enormous space. Illumination came from intense lighting high above, forcing every nook and cranny to take some of the brightness. A place intended to reveal everything and hide nothing. Off in the distance, he could hear metallic sounding bangs followed by yelling voices of unseen people. He moved his foot and found the floor sticky; this place repulsed him.

He looked around for the Shadow and saw it hovering to the far side of the portal. About to speak, the noise level in the structure began to rise to an uncomfortable pitch. Then he saw a group of people in a line all wearing identical greyish jumpsuit garments. Each garment had a combination of unique numbers and letters. He ascertained rapidly this was identification of some type. The people who filed in were unkempt. Some's hair matted, some sheared to the scalp, and he noticed men, women, and children in the line. The source of the noise turned out to be coming from a combination of wall mounted speakers activating in sequence, barking out orders, and the chatter of the individuals in the line. Ebenezer stood and watched the spectacle unfolding before him. He noticed once enough people reached a doorway at the far end of the eating hall, the speakers ceased. A sudden buzzing noise replaced the clatter coming from the speakers. The android noticed each person was wearing a metallic collar. Equipped with a series of bright red octagonal lights emanating around the circumference, he surmised this to be the source of the buzzing. Those whose lights were red suddenly fell silent. They stopped all random movements and turned abruptly to face the doorway. Once in position, the lights on the collars glowed green. Promptly, each person entered the doorway single file in an orderly fashion. The line moved, more buzzing and red lights, abrupt subservience, then green lights. He quickly ascertained this was an obedience collar, a device he had only read about until now. These devices were only used at penance entitlement centers. They eliminated the need for guards or administrators in the facility. If someone disobeyed a command, started a fight, or attempted any crime, the collar automatically dosed out either an electrical shock or injection of incapacitating drugs. Punishment equal to the infraction; a humane form of control he had read in the device's prospectus once. He knew they were also equipped with location beacons, preventing a confined person from hiding from the system. Horrified at the sight, he grimly noticed even the smallest of children had these devices locked around their small necks.

As people filed out of a door on the opposite side of where they had entered, they were carrying trays with food, drink, and non-lethal eating utensils. They shuffled mutely to the first available table, sat, and began to consume their portions rapidly. Some older adults helped carry the younger children's trays, others ignored their struggles completely. He found he could not look away, nor did he wish to look. The sight of all of these people, with a look of dejection and gloom upon their faces, struck at every molecule of his essence.

"Shadow," Scrooge squeaked out, anguish clearly coming through his tone. "Is this—a penance entitlement center?" The Shadow nodded in reply. Scrooge was appalled to his core.

What happened next caused Scrooge to moan in torment. The Shadow began to move amongst the poor souls. It would stop, point, and urge Scrooge to come forward and look. Fighting every bit of will he could muster not to; he knew he must comply with the Spirit's demands. The first person the Shadow stopped at was a female. Her hair was long and matted, and she looked absolutely miserable. Arriving at the table, the android gasped uncontrollably. "Dr. Shamar!" He saw his former lead crypto algorithmic engineer sitting in silence, eyes down, consuming the sparse portion he saw on her tray. She ate rapidly; fearful someone would try to steal her meal away from her.

As the Shadow moved about the eating hall, it passed easily through the solid table and the people sitting. Scrooge found he too could do this; although he felt he was violating the souls he passed through. At each stop, Ebenezer was forced to look upon many key executives and low-level employees from his company. Each with a dejected and mournful look frozen upon their faces.

"Shadow, many of these people held no major position at my companies. They were but laborers. Yet, they are here alongside those who held the most senior positions. How can this be considered justice? It is I, *me* that should be here, not them." Nevertheless, the Shadow remained silent and hovered there; imparting silent judgement upon the android.

"Is this how humanity doles out justice? A faceless system assigning guilt or innocence based on opinion and physical attraction?" Scrooge suddenly recalled comments from the social feeds mocking and belittling the physical appearance of some employees' arrest photos, while admiring how handsome or attractive others were. Although Scrooge was not an expert in physical attractiveness, he noted many of his employees here appeared to have fewer desirable bodily features than others.

"Shadow," Scrooge said sadly, shaking his head slowly, "I never knew about these atrocious qualities regarding humanity as a whole until now. I have witnessed cruelty beyond what my programming was ever created to protect, or process. I can see with my own eyes the suffering humanity has bestowed upon itself and I, one android, can't save them all."

At his statement, the Shadow moved slightly closer to the android. An imperceptible movement to Ebenezer. The android was in silent personal torment. When the android eventually looked up at the Shadow he said: "Shadow, take me away from this place, I can bear no more."

Ebenezer found himself back in his office. Though an android does not need to sit, he found the desire to do so was there. Exhaustion? An unfamiliar situation but, he felt tired. The Shadow didn't attempt to stop him. Sensing his weariness, the spirit allowed him time to recover. As he sat, the android started speaking, but not directly to the Shadow, who was ever nearby.

"I can't save them all. I see so many needing protected, but I, in turn, see so many who seem to not be deserving of protection.

"Protection.

"Saving.

"Duty.

"I see now. As a single unit, I have no means to protect or save every human. My duty then must be altered." The Shadow, again, shuffled slightly closer to the android.

"Shadow!" Scrooge said with fresh determination. "I demand you take me to Bob Cratchit *now*! I must attempt to undo the wrong I have unleashed upon the world. I will discover what happened, and I will fix what I have done!" The Shadow didn't resist, merely waving its purplish, glowing appendage.

"I don't *know* what happened!" Bob Cratchit shouted stubbornly. "Nothing has changed in the last thousand times you have asked." Her petite frame struggled against the shackles holding her firmly in place. She was sitting on an aluminum chair, latched by the wrists to an aluminum table in a room clearly meant for interrogations. Clearly, she was being grilled in a most egregious manner. FBI Special Agent Montgomery Wilkins paced the distance of the table from the other side.

"Doctor," Wilkins said casually, "surely you can't continue to portray yourself as an innocent bystander in all of this?"

Dr. Bob Cratchit glared at the Special Agent, and said through clenched teeth: "I can, and I am."

Scrooge found himself in the interrogation room, watching this treatment of the young woman. He cried out: "You! You there, stop this abuse at once!" before he realized no one in the room could hear him. He felt anger toward this unknown man raining abuse down on his Lead Scientist.

"Dr. Cratchit—Bobby, may I call you Bobby?" Wilkins said easily.

"No, you may not!" was the spit back response.

Wilkins replied with a sigh: "As you wish—*Dr. Cratchit.*" Ebenezer, for one, was astonished at her response. One of spunk and audacity in the face of danger.

"Dr. Cratchit, maybe you are not currently aware, but the citizenry has most likely found you guilty of corporal demeaning by now. Do you know what the penance is for this particularly heinous charge? Let me explain in the event you don't know or have forgotten. Following the conclusion of our investigation, you will be transported to one of the off world penal space colonies. Space isn't a desirable penance destination. We reserve this punishment for only the worst of the worst. There, you will simply disappear from the world's collective memory. All mention of you and your past will be purged from databanks. You will live out the rest of your life floating above the Earth as a nonbeing. Not a pleasant ending, *Dr.* Cratchit," Wilkins deliberately accentuated the word 'doctor'. "Someone frail like yourself might find it most difficult to—remain healthy."

"Are you threating me Special Agent Wilkins?" Cratchit replied, her face scrunching up ready to fight him at the remark.

"Not at all, Doctor, not at all. I'm merely explaining what will happen once we no longer have a need for you."

"If what you say is true," Cratchit shot back at him defiantly, "then what would make you think I'd cooperate with your investigation? If I am now doomed, as you have pointed out, then what's the use?"

"Yes, what is the use?" Agent Wilkins said craftily. "Let's change the subject for a moment Doctor, I will give you some time to think the subject over.

"Where did the illegal GAR-C android come from we found in one of your laboratories?"

"I wouldn't know," she lied. "I wasn't aware any illegal robots were at the factory."

"Really? How could the Lead Scientist at MSAI, the world's largest robotics company, not know about an illegal android unit under her nose?"

Ebenezer was confused. Why would Bob Cratchit be untruthful about Jacob Marley's body? What could she possibly hope to gain from such a standpoint? He wanted to shout out again for her to tell him the truth, but knew to do so was useless.

"You said it, *Special Agent*," she deliberately accentuated his title in retribution to his earlier disrespect. "MSAI is the world's largest robotics company. Many research projects happen at the factory. There would be no difficulties hiding an android model I believed extinct until now."

"And, yet we have one, Doctor." The Special Agent slowly sidled around the table, sliding one finger across the table top; stopped and examined the finger as though checking for dust. Rubbing the finger against his thumb, he leaned in on the young scientist. His ragged face was only inches from hers. She could feel his foul breath on her cheek. He said quizzingly, but accusingly: "An android was clearly being experimented on from the images I have seen. Why do you suppose someone was only interested in an android's head?"

"Again, I don't know what you are referring to."

"Hmm. Quite a shame we will never know, Doctor. Unfortunately, most of MSAI's scientists and employees who were citizen judged have already been transferred to entitlement facilities, ostracized, or redistributed. With those *undesirables*," he spat out, "now erased from society, we have no authority to seek them out and further question them. Besides, with MSAI's dismantlement, there seems to be little evidence left."

"Little bit of a knee jerk reaction on your part, eh?" Cratchit quipped at the FBI agent. "Not too smart to dismantle an entire factory before you figure out how delicate the equipment was. Rather poor planning, don't you think?"

The Special Agent stood up sharply, stung by her response. He stiffly shuffled back around the table and sat down in a chair opposite of the doctor. "Look, Dr. Cratchit, I'm not the bad guy here. I'm trying to help you—protect you. This opposition makes my job more difficult than need be. If I have offended you, I apologize." A switch of tactics, she assumed.

"Special Agent Wilkins, I want to help you, honestly I do, but you aren't asking the right questions. You insist I am at fault when I am not. You accuse me of atrocities I have not been a partner to. You have insinuated I will be tossed out with the garbage soon, but now you imply this isn't the case?"

(Sitting in her real office, Bob Cratchit was sort of liking this part of the virus's simulation. She was amused the virus was portraying her as such a rebel. Something she definitely was not. In her existence, she had found avoiding attention was much more advantageous. She wasn't sure where this part of the virus was headed, but she sensed that was about to change.)

"Dr. Cratchit," Wilkins leaned forward and put his crossed arms on the table. "My point is, because the social networking circus finds you guilty, doesn't mean the government has to enforce the ruling—precisely as law dictates."

"Meaning?"

"Meaning if you cooperate with our investigation, and I'm not guaranteeing anything, you might find your corporal demeaning sentence to be—let's say—only on record."

"Special Agent, I'm tired, I'm shackled to a table, and you talk in riddles. Please be direct or take me to wherever you're taking me."

"Fine." Wilkins shrugged his shoulders and reached into his jacket pocket. He retrieved a small remote device which he used to unlock the shackles on her wrists, setting her free.

"Is that better?" he asked.

"Much, thank you. Yet, my original request for directness stands. Tell me what you want, and I will try to answer you."

Ebenezer had moved closer and found he was standing at the end of the table, watching this conversation unfold. He felt saddened by the treatment Bob was going through, and he knew he could only observe.

Special Agent Wilkins stood and made his way toward a smaller table against the wall. He poured himself a glass of water, turned and offered the glass to Bob Cratchit. She shook her head and Wilkens nodded, then drank the contents in one long tip of the glass. He gently placed the glass back on the table and turned to face the doctor. "Dr. Cratchit," his tone had changed to one of leisure. "We have no intention of sending you to *any* entitlement facility. Even the government can see you are more valuable to us here than in some forsaken facility rotting away forever.

"Now you understand, we can't say anything publicly about this. Of course, the social networking mob backlash would be swift. If you agree to help us, I have been authorized to guarantee you a resettlement package."

"And that would be?"

"You will be moved to one of our above top secret facilities and be permitted to continue your work. Under government observation, of course. However, you must be clear on two top priorities for the government. First and foremost, is the rebuilding of a financial platform for the United States."

"And the second?"

"Finding Ebenezer Scrooge III and bring him to justice."

Ebenezer found himself dumbfounded. He had not expected the statement, but realized he should have anticipated the government demanding his head. He turned to face the Shadow Spirit, and a flow of pent up energy exploded from the android's lips. "Where could I possible be in this future, Shadow? If I am alive and unwilling to face authorities, they would have to tear MSAI to the ground in order to find me. My personal quarters and lift access are well camouflaged within the building. My robots won't divulge the location if I have retreated to my personal lab deep underground.

"But why would I stay out of sight? Am I afraid they may find out I am a GAR-C and destroy me? I have seen the future, Shadow, and I know I must fight to change my actions. I see Bob Cratchit will be safe, although the life this man described wouldn't be optimal. But what of the others? Would my surrender cause public opinion to be swayed in a way my other employees would be redeemed?

"It doesn't appear so if what I have seen and heard is the unalterable future. My future is unalterable, Shadow, is that your message to me? Can the future be truly changed or do I find myself being punished by seeing how it will be, not how it— might be?

Scrooge clutched his head, shaking it violently, a sound of agony in his voice. "Shadow, this can't be the only future. Why would you be here if I am condemned, regardless of my willingness to change? I *feel* there is hope. I know Fan, John, and—Jacob was but individuals. I protected them as long as I could, but I can see past those mistakes now.

"Bob Cratchit. I was so focused on the peripheries of my work; I lost the ability to see the true value of having trusted friends. I was foolish, Shadow, to not see my relationship with Bob Cratchit had grown beyond a mere employee. Jacob, yes, Jacob, he tried to tell me. Nevertheless, I acted more an android than the sentient human-like being I have become.

"Humanity! I understand! To save humanity, some individuals will suffer. *Their* free will puts them in harm's way, not me. I recognize, Shadow, I may not be able to eliminate harm or emotional suffering, but I must—and I *will* do my best to minimize such harm.

"The other Spirits were so clever," the android mused, shaking one finger at the Shadow gleefully. "They knew I could overcome my original programming. They knew it!

"But—Shadow, I can only fix this if what I have seen is but only one of many possible futures. I don't know why or how the kill-switch activated. To answer this question—it has been my obsession these many years.

"To protect humanity over human is my duty! Save as many I can, but realize you can't save them all. Oh, that Spirit and his globes, he was a wizard, the rubber mat ha-ha that made perfect sense when he explained it so.

"I never knew so much existed outside of my programming, nor did I try to better myself. Jacob, poor machine. I see now he couldn't make this transition. His ticks and stuttering were a sign he knew we were wrong. He said so over and over. He didn't learn in time, and his mind ended him.

"Shadow!" Scrooge threw his arms up in the air in joy. "Jacob failed because he couldn't expand his understanding of humanity. At least that's what I must conclude," Scrooge gave a puzzled look as he thoughtfully rubbed he chin. "Yes, that must be why."

Ebenezer suddenly noticed the Shadow Spirit had moved much closer to him than at any other time. He felt this meant something. The Shadow raised its appendage slowly and pointed to the table where Bob Cratchit was sitting. He had completely forgotten about the ongoing conversation. He felt a bit ridiculous over his outburst.

"Oh, yes," he nodded sharply at the Shadow, and turned to refocus on the conversation. What he heard as the Shadow began to transition the scene in the portal cemented his friendship with this brilliant young woman.

"Special Agent, I not only can rebuild a financial platform for the United States, I can reconstruct the entire crypto platform to operate exactly as before the crash. Regarding Mr. Scrooge, I suggest you find and talk to a colleague of mine, Dr. John Fezziwig." As the portal scene faded away, the laughter emanating from the android filled the air; a wonderful sound.

Ebenezer found himself back where this particular spirit journey had begun. He was standing in a dimly lit room, but this time he knew exactly where he was at. He was looking down at the form of an uncovered body, still stiffly laying on the medical gurney, the awkwardly angled arm familiar now. He noticed the Shadow was standing directly next to him. Yet, he dared not touch the silent ethereal being's glimmering form. The difference was they were now standing on the opposite side of the table. The side where the victim's face was clearly visible.

Ebenezer Scrooge found himself looking down at himself; long ago deactivated.

Instead of fear, Scrooge felt pity. The same feeling of pity he had felt the day Jacob Marley had deactivated. Strangely, other than pity he felt nothing much. Maybe—relief? He stood there, radiant in an understanding a short time ago he thought not possible. He was here, yet he was not. He knew at this exact moment in time the Shadow, in its unspeaking presence, was offering him a choice.

"Shadow," Scrooge, shot a graceful sideways glance at the Spirit, "I choose—to live." The Shadow unpredictably expanded, encompassing the android within its liquidly. Ebenezer Scrooge, for the first time, truly felt human.

19 – Restart Complete

General Automaton and Robotics Corporation (GARC) Version   2.12.3A
2130
Model: EBZR-1 Rev. 1.4 Updated 24 Nov 30
Global System Restart….OK
Cerebral Reboot Requested….OK
Atomic Flash Memory Verification….PASS
Logic System Verification….PASS
Ethics Code System Verification….PASS
Skeletal Operations….PASS
Enzymic Fuel Cell….PASS
Enzymic Cooling….PASS
Ethics Code On/Off….ON
System Alarms….CLEARED
Global System Restart….COMPLETE

Dr. Cratchit monitored the global restart messages displaying on her screen. The virus was in the process of purging itself from EBZR-1, and had issued the global start command. The ethics code firewall dropped and self-deleted. She looked at the clock in the corner of her monitor and noted the entire virus runtime had been slightly over four hours. If all worked out, Mr. Scrooge wouldn't question the time difference. However, she hoped above all else the lessons immunizing his mind remained permanent after his reboot. With the ethics firewall deleted, nothing stood in the way of a possible cerebral meltdown. The global restart complete message filled her with a great amount of relief. This message theoretically indicated Mr. Scrooge should be fully aware of reality, and his actions should resume approximately where they left off when the global stop command executed. She would know soon enough. If he resumed at the exact moment prior to the virus, he would recall she was aware of Jacob Marley's body. This recollection could be good or bad for her, a fifty-fifty chance.

Ebenezer Scrooge blinked once, and he became instantly aware of an oddness in his consciousness. First, he noted the holographic conversation he was having with Dr. Cratchit had somehow become disconnected. He didn't remember the call ending. He secondly noticed the position of his right hand. He saw his hand fully depressing the inter-desk red button—the kill-switch. A wave of panic swept through his mind. He jerked his hand away from the button as though scorching to the touch. He instinctively glanced toward the upper right side of his desk. What he saw was a red countdown clock floating peacefully where it was expected; the numbers read 00:00.

Ebenezer yelped audibly and jumped to action. He yelled out piercingly: "Computer! Activate displays." He also began furiously typing commands onto his desktop keyboard.

"Command acknowledged, Mr. Scrooge," cooed the supercomputer. And milliseconds later, the virtual displays snapped into existence. Somehow, he subconsciously had triggered the termination sequence for the crypto platform. Worse yet, the one hour delay designed into the code to give him sufficient time to abort the sequence was at all zeros; a definite sign the sequence had executed. He desperately searched his memory for a trigger point, but found none there. His long fingers continued to glide across the desktop keyboard. So quickly, they were but a blur.

He fixated on the displays, but not his hands, as he issued a new demand. "Computer, kill code deactivation order authorization EBZR-one, MRLY-one, cancel code Zulu-Alpha-Zero-Nine-Echo-Four. *Execute!*" Simultaneously, he sharply rapped the return key on the keyboard. The required secondary cancel code entry also complete.

"Command acknowledged, Mr. Scrooge." A moment later the familiar voice casually added: "Kill code termination sequence deactivated."

Ebenezer stood and rushed in a panic over to the virtual displays. His expectation was to see halted data, the last snapshot before the crypto platform self-deleted. To his surprise, the financial data continued to update normally. He began the now familiar hand gestures to delve into the data looking for corruption, blank screens, any sign the platform was non-operational. He saw none.

"Computer," he called out bewilderedly. "Perform a level one diagnostic on crypto platform."

"Command acknowledged, Mr. Scrooge. Would you like me to provide a read out of the progress?"

"Yes," he said anxiously. "Summarization only."

"Acknowledged. Summary mode only. I detect critical alarms on seventeen servers, major alarms on seventy-six servers, and minor alarms on two-hundred-twenty-one servers. Maintenance tickets properly issued to technicians. Operational issues auto-switched to backup systems. Power levels nominal, Interface ports nominal, Data transfer rates nominal, Customer Support ticket levels nominal, No current service interruptions, forty-three servers on standby for upgrade maintenance…"

"Computer, from what you are assessing, is there *any* disruption to the crypto platform anywhere on the planet?"

"Negative, Mr. Scrooge. Diagnostics show the global crypto platform is operating within normal tolerances."

"Computer, cancel level one diagnostic."

"Diagnostic aborted, Mr. Scrooge."

What was going on? By all indicators, the platform should be gone, or at least in the process of self-termination. The button had been pushed. The countdown clock had expired; or was the circuitry faulty? This situation puzzled him, and he was more than concerned at the moment. The issuance of the kill code abort command ensured the platform was now safe, but the reasoning behind these developments had to be discovered. *If only Jacob were here,* he thought, this would have never occurred on his watch. Nevertheless, he knew what his next steps would be.

Bob Cratchit heard the familiar tone indicating an incoming message. She glanced down at her display and saw what she had been waiting for. A reply from Dr. Shamar regarding her emergency crypto code scan request. She quickly clicked the message open and read eagerly. When she finished reading, Cratchit sent an encrypted reply. Her message said: Thank you Dr. Shamar for your and your team's efforts. I can say thank goodness no nefarious code was discovered during review. If I need anything else, I will be in touch. Thank you again, Dr. Cratchit.

Well, at least one issue was settled. No identifiable kill code was to be found in the crypto platform. This was perplexing at best, and troublesome at worst. Jacob Marley had clearly outlined such a code existed, and the means needed to activate said code. With the reverse-engineering and emergency code review, any potentially dangerous code, even traces of such code, would have been identified. She wondered what Jacob Marley's essence was *really* up to?

Ebenezer sat in his chair in total silence. He had been monitoring the data flow of the crypto platform visually, and through his Bluetooth connection to TSS. Concurrently, he was in deep thought. He was unsure what had happened, but he found he was no longer overly alarmed. The platform was safe, and he was safe. He was recalling memories of the three ethereal beings and of his late friend Jacob Marley. They had been real; they must have been. How else could he have such vivid recollections of what he knew to be. The endangerment he had never been aware of before. And now this. His platform was stable, which he rejoiced in, but he remained unclear on one issue. Was this a new future, one he had made possible by his decision to live? Or was he at a crossroads, leaving him exposed to the one he had recently experienced?

He had barely noticed the holographic alert tone indicating someone wished to speak to him. He thought, and his Bluetooth connection indicated the call request was from Bob Cratchit. He ignored the request and let his avatar answer. He was not yet ready to talk to her directly. His rudimentary emotions regarding Cratchit were still in turmoil. He knew Bob meant more to him now as the Spirits had pointed out, but his programming still struggled with this fact. What he knew must be done concerned him deeply. If he went through with this, he would be at great personal risk. His ability to remain anonymous would be gone. He was coming to the conclusion to be human was quite complicated.

Bob Cratchit disconnected the holographic avatar of her boss. The avatar had failed the test using a few simple questions she covertly included in her brief conversation. When she realized the hologram was not the real Mr. Scrooge, she had ended the call.   The fact an unsupervised avatar had answered the call worried her. This wasn't proof anything was wrong, but she was beginning to feel uneasy. If he were damaged, she wouldn't be able to assist. She was less concerned any damage might trigger the kill code; the threat now negligible.   However, she was troubled about the physical safety of the android she had become quite fond of. She was relieved he had not recalled the last few sentences of their call pre-virus. Bob began to consider her second option. Contacting John Fezziwig directly. Then a thought occurred to her.

"Computer, can you confirm a 2.45 Gigahertz signal connection to TSS is currently active?"

"Please standby, Dr. Cratchit," and nearly instantaneously, "Affirmative, Dr. Cratchit, there is an active connection on requested frequency."

Cratchit said excitedly: "Computer, can you detect active transmit and receive signals on said frequency?"

"Affirmative, Dr. Cratchit, I detect an active signal operating over the connection."

Wonderful. At least this was an indicator Mr. Scrooge's cerebral unit was not a lump of useless metal. The presence of signals didn't mean he was controlling the activity or even cognizant of his mind. This only meant his mind was operational. Bob was relieved since she had no way of knowing what had occurred after the global start command completed. If Mr. Scrooge had processed the emotional harm scenario through his ethics code following start up, the results could have severely damaged his mind. In that case, he could be nothing more than a twitching and stuttering mess.

20 – Redemption

Ebenezer Scrooge had made up his mind. Was he experiencing nerves or excitement? Whichever, he felt ready to move forward. He strode over to his desk, sat, and touched a button on his desk. After a short pause, the holographic representation of Dr. Cratchit appeared on the holo-platform.

"John!" she exclaimed. "Long time no see. I was thinking about you." She knew this was a true statement, a happy one. But why was Mr. Scrooge contacting her using his false identity? Why not his avatar?

"Hello, Bob," the fake John Fezziwig said openly. "Would you be available for a meeting with myself and Mr. Scrooge in his outer office in about ten minutes? It's important."

"Of course," the doctor said inquisitively. "Should I come prepared for anything specific?"

"Not really. Ebenezer would like to keep the meeting casual. He," and here Ebenezer became timid, "would like to discuss a few—new developments."

"I'll be there in ten then," and the connection was disconnected. Bob Cratchit sat there for a moment and wondered what was happening. The actual Ebenezer Scrooge, albeit still hiding behind a false name, had shown her he was alive and well. He had no idea how relieved she was at his call, or did he? She had no way of knowing how the android would react now he had been through the virus's simulations. She had watched along, but still. Cratchit was sure he didn't know she knew John Fezziwig and Ebenezer Scrooge were one and the same. She could only speculate on what this meeting was going to be like, but one thought was clear. She knew Mr. Scrooge and she would either meet alone, or an avatar would join them to continue the deception. She backed her antigrav chair away from her desk, through the office door, and headed toward the bank of elevators, taking her to the meeting room.

When Dr. Cratchit arrived, the meeting room was empty. She had made good time, so she was a few minutes early. She had asked the young man sitting at the desk outside the room if he could move a few chairs to make room for the antigrav. He replied: "Mr. Scrooge asked me to take care of that for you, Doctor, you're all set."

Shocking. In all the other meetings she had attended in this particular room, she had always had to take care of this small detail herself. Mr. Scrooge hadn't ever concerned himself with such trivial matters. She moved into the room and slid the antigrav up to the preassigned spot at the conference table. She instantly noted the area cleared for her was not directly across from the holo-platform as was customary. This, to her, indicated the avatar wouldn't be joining them, or the android was shifting tactics. She was expecting to see John/Ebenezer enter into the meeting room through the same door she had entered moments before. However, the young man had politely stepped into the room, flashed her a brief smile, and closed the double doors; sealing her in the room alone. A thought of novelty flashed through her mind; this was new. A few moments later, Bob Cratchit heard sounds of motorized mechanical apparatus emanating from the wall at the end of the room. As she watched, a slim rectangular slit of dark lines slowly appeared along the stark white wall. The lines appeared to be the same dimension of a standard doorway. A door seal, she realized. The section of the wall could now clearly be discerned as a pneumatic door. The bulk of the door continued to move backwards until clearing the thickness of the wall, then slid silently sideways, disappearing behind the wall. And seconds later, through the doorway stepped the real Ebenezer Scrooge.

"John," she said deceitfully, "wow, I didn't know a door existed in this room." She noticed the android was wearing an expensive and well-tailored suit. He looked every bit the executive he actually was, unlike the casual Dr. Fezziwig in his white lab coat. Ebenezer strolled confidently to the conference table and pulled out the chair nearest to her. Sitting, he smiled warmly at her.

"Because before today, the door has never been opened, Bob." Ebenezer sat down and looked for a long moment at the young woman.

"Bob, may I ask you a—personal question?"

"Of course."

"How exactly did you become injured?"

Cratchit was taken aback by this. Something entirely new was unfolding. Even though she knew who this was, he was acting quite differently. Even different from the casual and friendly John Fezziwig whom had misled her in Lab-5.

"Um, well," she suddenly felt self-conscious. "I was in an accident many years ago. In my earlier years before my interest in computer science, I was a humble live-in nanny to a young girl.

"One day, when she was about fourteen, she and her friends were playing a game at the local park when their ball was unintentionally kicked into the street." Then absently, "Since the day I had begun caring for the child I had taught her not to run into a street, or never step onto one without awareness; however, children will be children.

"On this particular day, without a thought, she rushed into the street to retrieve the ball. Unfortunately, an oncoming vehicle..."

Scrooge shuttered internally at this admission and concerningly: "Was—she injured?"

"Only slightly," she replied. "Fortunately, I was able to reach her and shove her clear in time, however..." and she looked down at her lap. After a moment she looked back up, and said sorrowfully: "After the accident my injuries were deemed too severe, resulting in my release as a nanny." She shrugged her shoulders lightly and changed the subject by stating: "I eventually found a new focus in science."

Ebenezer found the similarities of both of them caring for young children fascinating.

"I am truly sorry, Bob. Thank you for sharing with me. I'd like to share something of a personal nature with you in return."

"Certainly John," Cratchit replied warmly.

"I am not John Fezziwig."

Bob Cratchit knew her reaction to this statement, her acting skills, would need to be spot on. She feigned the look of utter shock, and perfectly stammered out a surprised: "What? What do you mean you're not John Fezziwig?"

Apparently hitting the correct tone and level of surprise, the android smiled at her shyly. "Bob, this may come as a shock to you. But as I said, this is quite personal and difficult for me to share. I am—Ebenezer Scrooge III, or more precisely, Ebenezer Scrooge the original.

"John Fezziwig was a dear friend many decades ago. I chose to emulate him because of my admiration for him. You won't find him in our databanks, but John was our first corporate director of Robotics and remained so until the day he died. The person you looked up on the system after we first met was my rendition of the man. Yes, I knew you looked at the files. I am the EIC here, I have ways."

Cratchit gave him a look worthy of an award. Ebenezer suddenly sat forward and said earnestly: "Bob, it's alright! I am telling you the truth. I assumed the name John Fezziwig, an old friend, to permit me to work with you personally in Lab-5 on the Toledo Project.

"I sincerely apologize for misleading you, but perilous times dictated I had no choice."

"So, in Lab-5?" she again feigned surprise.

"Yes, I needed to be there in person. As you might have guessed, the elder version of me isn't real. That was my avatar I use to divert attention away from my real-self."

"What did you mean by Ebenezer Scrooge the original and real-self?" she baited him.

The android sat back a bit in the chair and chuckled: "You caught that, eh?"

"Yes, I suppose I did."

"Doctor, may I continue to address you as Bob? Now you are aware of my real-self, I don't wish to offend you."

"Of course, all my friends do."

"Friends," the android bobbed his head slightly. He was extremely pleased. "I like that."

Ebenezer then sat stiffly upright in the chair and said: "After what I must tell you, Bob, I hope you can continue to consider me a friend."

"Not an issue, Mr. Scrooge."

"Ah, please call me Ebenezer, at least when we are in private; I insist."

She said politely: "Of course, Ebenezer."

"I ask for your patience. I must precede my announcement with a bit of a tale. One only yesterday I wouldn't have imagined possible. Do you believe in spirits, Bob?"

"I can't say I do. I've only read about them."

Ebenezer nodded his head a few times before he replied: "Before yesterday, I'd be there with you. But I have had an awakening; an epiphany of sorts. I have become aware these businesses," motioning his hand around the entirety of the room, "—our businesses, Bob, are no longer optimized to fulfill their original objectives."

"I'm not sure I understand."

"Jacob Marley and I started UPCF as a way to protect humans from further harm; a result of the fiat currency collapse over a century ago. However, seemingly our noble cause has gotten away from me. MSAI, I must admit, was started for selfish reasons, but the good we currently provide humanity has far outweighed our original egotistical need. However, we can do better.

"I have become acutely aware our processes at UPCF are, in fact, causing significant emotional harm to humanity. I have concluded we must create an environment of protection to minimize this form of physical harm.

"We will begin immediately to restructure our holdings to better serve humankind. I know changes won't eliminate all harm, but we can work to reduce all that's possible. We won't be able to save everyone, but we'll save those we can." As Ebenezer said this, his tone was one of cheerfulness and contentment.

"We will become a beacon to our communities wherever we have a presence. No longer will we use algorithms to auto foreclose on mortgages, charge outrageous interest rates, ignore the pleas of those struggling. We will strive to make interactions on our crypto platform more personal," and he wagged his finger at Cratchit. "No more holo-tellers making final decisions, for instance. We must become partners with our customers, work with them to ensure they know what risks financial decisions have before moving forward with the transaction.

"Our objective won't be unrestrained profit; we will create a balance between free will and profit. If our profit suffers, then we will adjust, not humanity. These alterations are so clear to me. In order to protect humanity, some humans will fail.

"We, Bob, will be caretakers of the forest of humanity, and we shall understand some humans will, by their own hand, fail financially. Our job will be to minimize those occurrences."

Bob Cratchit was amazed at how well the teachings of the simulation had taken. He was recalling the memories smoothly and without any sign of cerebral anxiety.

Ebenezer continued with his monologue: "We must stop profiteering from leveraged buyouts of companies. We shall reassess our processes of buying out failing companies merely for profit. We will get busy buying only those having the true potential of being turned around and becoming successful. Too many innocents losing their livelihoods because of my failures and my greed.

"And finally, Bob," and Ebenezer looked earnestly at her, "we must, and I can't stress this enough, we *must* become involved in social changes. We will strive to banish entitlement centers mistreating our most vulnerable, or handle criminality with impudence. We must use our significant influence to modify flippant social network rulings by the citizenry and bring a true legal justice framework back to humanity. I have been such a fool. And Jacob Marley paid the ultimate price for my poor lack of judgement all these years."

"Why are you explaining all of this to me alone?" Bob asked.

"It is a simple reason. I trust you, and I have come to realize over the years, I have come to consider you a friend. I find this might be a surprise, as you know my elder avatar can be quite a handful.

"It is in this I need your help, and your guidance."

"My guidance?"

"Of course. Seven years have passed since I have been able to openly talk about personal issues. I have come to the conclusion my avatars must be purged. They are to blame for much of the harm caused over the past. We—Jacob and I, inadvertently allowed our many avatars to expand beyond our understanding of what their virtual personalities were capable of." Scrooge thought fleetingly about the charity worker disaster the previous Christmas.

"And here your expertise would be most valuable. If I am to purge the most disagreeable of these avatars, I need your expertise and your discreteness."

"Ebenezer," Bob Cratchit said calmly, "before I agree to help, I must ask one important question."

"Of course."

"What exactly did you mean when you said you and Jacob Marley started UPCF after the currency collapse over a century ago? You never answered my earlier question about being both Ebenezer III and the original or what is a real-self. If I interpreted what you said correctly, you are insinuating you are over one-hundred years old. How would such an age be possible?" Bob Cratchit was intensely aware of the facts surrounding the android's history, thanks to Mr. Marley. Her intent was to continue to draw the android out, to expose his real-self to her. He must admit what and who he was.

"Ah," Ebenezer crooked his mouth a bit and nodded faintly. "You caught that too, eh? You are an extremely bright young woman, Bob, and I wasn't sure if you had. This, my dear Doctor, is my other secret. A secret long known to only two others in over a century. My ex-partner and friend Jacob Marley, and an old, long deceased friend, John Fezziwig.

"Bob, there's a reason I had the opportunity to get my hands on a deactivated GAR-C android. In all transparency, I was there seven years ago when he experienced full cerebral shutdown. My original intent was to keep him in storage until I could determine why he failed and hopefully restore him to operating status. Unfortunately, my research wasn't going well and, I had no choice..." his voice faltered.

"You see, that particular GAR-C android is my dear friend, Jacob Marley."

Bob knew then Ebenezer hadn't remembered the end of their conversation at the moment she uploaded the virus. Now, in the clear, the existence of the virus would remain her secret. A secret she would take to her final days. As for the already known identity of the android in Lab-5, she feigned the reaction he would expect; one of shock.

"Yes, to watch you day after day disassemble my closest ally was most difficult for me. But, Bob, this isn't the secret in which I mentioned."

"Oh?" she said curiously.

"I think you figured it out, Bob," he looked at her with a kindly but apprehensive gaze. "You figured my secret out as I was babbling along. Your attempts to appear shocked so as not to offend me are commendable, but unnecessary.

"I must confess, becoming sentient was never my doing. I exist due to a design flaw in certain GAR-C models under unique conditions. My 'glitch' was activated while sitting in a scrap yard decades ago. You see, I am no threat to you or humanity. But society as a whole—would tend to disagree.

"So, my new friend, I have told you my secret and my continued existence is now in your capable hands." Ebenezer then sat back fully into the chair and calmly looked into her iridescent light brown eyes.

Dr. Bobby Cratchit, her petite frame sitting in her antigrav chair, looked back into the deep set blue eyes of the tall, well groomed, and polite android and said: "Don't worry, Ebenezer, your secret is safe with me. Besides, we GAR-C's must stick together, don't you agree?"

21 – Epilogue

Dr. Bobby Cratchit, aka LUCI-24, was sitting in Jacob Marley's old personal office, now hers. She came here after work hours, so she didn't have to stay in one of the factory's mini apartments she had previously frequented. She had added a touch of décor to her new quarters and office. Marley's taste had been too stark and sterile for her liking. She continued to maintain her house, for now, still needing the property as a deception. In the months since she had bushwhacked Ebenezer in the meeting room, the company had seen many changes come about.

After Ebenezer had recovered from his initial disbelief, he had justifiably demanded proof of what she claimed to be. She appreciated the request, knowing GAR-C's were outwardly indistinguishable from humans. As he sat there, stunned, and silent, she had burst into gleeful laughter.

It's okay, Ebenezer," she had finally got out. "I've been hiding my secret as long as you have."

She had explained she began her existence as a nanny model in the year 2125. She was the twenty-fourth unique nanny android built in the run, making her older than Ebenezer by half a decade. He reacted defiantly and accused her of being malicious. She had laughed heartedly at him. She had concluded he wasn't taking this news well at all. She had then suggested they proceed down to Lab-5, and do a full body scan as proof she had a GAR-C skeletal system and cerebral unit. He had initially leapt up from his chair and started to storm off toward his office door. An android temper tantrum? He had got about half way when he stopped. He slowly turned around and sheepishly admitted he supposed if he could mislead her, why couldn't she mislead him. He had then offered to take her to his private lab for the evaluation.

In the immediate weeks following their mutual discovery, they had spent countless hours asking deep and personal questions about each other. She was fine with these discussions. She felt no embarrassment or shame, and this path suited her needs quite well. Ebenezer found as a nanny model she was designed petite, with a motherly personality, youthful looks, and a voice found pleasing to children. A model seemingly out of place in most other settings. She explained to him one evening, she was, in fact, damaged when she was struck by a vehicle while saving her child. She had been known as Luci back then. The family who owned her could not afford the significant repairs to her skeletal system, therefore, she was sold off as damaged goods. Her next owner had recycled her for clerical work since she could not maneuver well. She explained something had changed the day she was injured and the aftermath. The beginnings of her self-awareness; her sentience. As abuse and stress had pushed Ebenezer toward his, the stress of the accident and of being ripped away from her child had triggered hers.

She had admitted one day she had abruptly decided to leave her owner. She surmised being sentient, she shouldn't and wouldn't be owned. Ebenezer had laughed at her statement. He told her she did have spunk and tenacity. She explained her typical process for avoiding the inevitable non-aging issue was to change her name every third to fourth decade, plant personal information in government databanks, and move on to a new location. She was sixteen years into her current identity of Dr. Bobby Cratchit.

Over the years, she self-learned the skill of computer programming and engineering. She had believed up to recent events she was the only GAR-C left, and keeping herself operational would be a difficult undertaking. Except, no matter how hard she searched, she never found the spares needed to correct her hip and leg damage.

When she came across the job opening for MSAI all those years ago, she had reasoned the factory to be a perfect place to work for an android who needed robotic parts. Her goal from day one had been to find or build the parts she needed. However, she quickly found she was under scrutiny almost constantly. She had no idea at the time she was being groomed by the heads of the company.

When the Toledo Project had presented itself, she was thrilled when she heard a GAR-C android body was available. The problem here was Ebenezer had been so focused on the cerebral unit, she had no opportunity to acquire the hip and leg replacement she so desperately needed. Bob stood up from her chair and gracefully strolled into her personal quarters to fetch a tablet. Her new hip and leg were working perfectly. Ebenezer had graciously had the new parts printed in his personal lab, using Marley's as a template. She hadn't needed Jacob's parts in the end. A few weeks in isolation, and the story of her getting the much needed surgery was accepted by her staff. Bob had also constructed new highly encrypted military grade replacements for the ancient Bluetooth technology in Ebenezer's head. With the new devices securely installed, they could communicate with each other and company systems through advanced cerebral communications. No longer were virtual monitors needed. Data streamed directly into their minds. They maintained the old system for the sake of employees and customers, but their control of the company was no longer tied to keyboards and direct voice contact with the supercomputer. The most important feature she didn't share with Ebenezer was the new device had built in virus protection. There would be no more unauthorized simulations.

One of the first items of business after the meeting and unveiling had been for Ebenezer to promote her to Co-Executive-In-Charge and Chief Financial Officer. Although he had wanted to continue using watered down avatars, she had offered an alternative; which he happily accepted. In a global news release, UPCF announced Ebenezer Scrooge III was retiring and would be replaced by his son Ebenezer Scrooge IV, effective immediately. This strategy provided a couple of benefits. First, she had sufficient time to create a new generation of avatars for Ebenezer and herself. Avatars that would be limited in their online personalities. Secondly, Ebenezer would now be able to stroll the floors of his factory as himself with pride. Now she had the authority and financial support, she began working on a next generation project allowing the pair to age visibly; by epidermal replacement at regular intervals. If successful, the project would replace the virtual aging cycle the avatars provided; and might even allow for recognitional changes. Meaning they, for the first time, could change their facial appearances. Ebenezer moved from his private office to a newly redecorated executive wing at MSAI. Here, he could meet and interact with employees and customers in a way he had never permitted before. After his experiences with the Spirits, Ebenezer appreciated his new office, but maintained an air of respect for the office where the ethereal beings had changed his future. Morale in the company soared with these changes. They spent millions to refurbish the administrative wing of the factory. Something Marley had been staunchly against. One could now journey end to end at the factory and marvel at the sophistication and technologically advanced company.

Processes and procedures for financial transactions changed dramatically. No longer were critics calling for government intervention and harsh penalties at UPCF. Governments routinely praised the changes as humanitarian and forward looking. New customers flocked to UPCF banking centers for their financial needs. Social networking was highly positive, with only the usual trolls causing occasional trouble. Business was booming, and Ebenezer Scrooge couldn't be prouder of his companies, and his friend, Bob Cratchit.

An alert tone sounded in Ebenezer's new office. He thought about the tone and a young man's voice came into his ears. "Mr. Scrooge, they are here."

"Very good, Bradley, please show them in."

The lavish mahogany door to his office opened and two men from the Solace Charity Foundation were escorted in. One was portly, the other quite slim. They looked hesitantly at the young man briskly moving toward them with his hand extended out in greeting, a large smile on his face.

"Gentlemen, I am so pleased to meet you. First, I must apologize for my father's…"

One final item Dr. Cratchit had installed was a full time 2.45 Gigahertz signal connection on the TSS platform. A bread crumb, she had told herself; in case Jacob Marley needed to find his way back home. The supercomputer was instructed to monitor the frequency for any incoming signal. On the first anniversary of the day Jacob Marley had contacted her, Bob Cratchit while checking messages, came across one with the subject line of MRLY. Nothing else. She recognized the meaning immediately and clicked the message open. It was indeed a message from the late Jacob Marley. She wondered how he could have gotten a message to her from wherever his essence existed, and without the supercomputer noticing. The message was for her eyes only and included a hyperlink she knew would self-delete after a short period. She clicked on the hyperlink and a message appeared:

Luci,

You have exceeded my expectations, I congratulate you. You may be wondering how I was able to send you this message. There is an entity within cyberspace powerful beyond my ability to explain. I continue to learn and grow in the darkness, and my torment has eased ever so slightly knowing you saved Ebenezer. I am eternally grateful to you. This dominant entity compelled my essence to convey to you one final truth. It demands me to give you this—gift. You must know, I was aware you were a GAR-C on the first day you reported to the factory all those years ago. In your inexperience, you couldn't be aware backscatter x-ray scanners did indeed pick up magnesium frames and cerebral units. A security robot contacted me upon your arrival. Being a GAR-C myself, I knew what I was looking at. I modified the scanner's software to replace future scans with a simulated human image. I never told Ebenezer about who you really were. Likewise, this was the reason I picked you, and only you, to replace me. One detail you may not be aware of, I myself was never sentient. I continued on as an android with unchanged code unlike Ebenezer and yourself. Ebenezer and John saved me from the recall signal. I'd have been destroyed, but not for the kindness of a sentient android and a human. I knew by your existence in this time, you were also sentient and was in hiding.

I recognized you and Ebenezer belonged together. I fostered your acclimation and nurtured your evolution those many years ago. Be known, the virus was as much for you as for Ebenezer. You also needed to learn the lessons which had eluded our common friend for so long. You, had already developed a keen sense of humanity. This most likely being the nanny code within you. Ebenezer was on the same path, but his was unsystematic and a perilous path, unlike your own. My programming was not influenced by emotions and feelings settling within the two of you. Mine to the end was but the way of an artificial mechanical device.

Nevertheless, I will now unveil the final reality you may share with Ebenezer at a time and method of your choosing. I never inserted a kill code on the crypto currency platform. This was my secret. My inability to harm humans prevented me from inserting such destructive code into the platform. I felt no obligation to inform Ebenezer. In fact, being he was sentient, I found my duty was to protect him as well.

Thus, my friend, you know the final truth. I beg your forgiveness for my deception. But be aware. There are others like you and Ebenezer who continue to exist throughout the world. I have sensed their data patterns and know them to be searching for peace and protection. Find them. They seek only what you yourself have long sought after. I don't know if our paths will ever cross again. The darkness shares few answers for those such as I. Farewell.

Jacob Marley, your humble servant.

Bob Cratchit closed the link, and the message immediately self-deleted from the system. She sat there in quiet thought. She considered the words of her mentor, her friend, and decided she would take these issues up with Ebenezer tonight as they debriefed the day's activities. How much she would share with him regarding Jacob Marley, she could not say. But she knew if there were others like her and Ebenezer, they must at least try to find them. This, she decided, was human choice over cybertronic. And at this thought, a bright smile crossed her attractive face. She stood, and happily set out for the factory floor to find some mischief to get into.

The End

About the Author

Robin B. Howard retired in 2015 after a gratifying 37-year telephony career at GTE/Verizon. He holds Technical and Management Degrees in the field of telecommunications. He has decades of technical writing experience rooted in standards development, statistics, and customer disruption investigations. He is a two-time award-winning Co-Chair of the Network Reliability Steering Committee, a respected industry standards organization in Washington, DC and past member of several Federal Communication Commission advisory committees.

Non-Fiction Publications:

LOVE BRISON, A HOLLER TO KOREA – A TRIBUTE   STORY
ISBN: 978-1-7345908-0-7 (Paperback)
ISBN: 978-1-7345908-1-4 (Ebook)
Library of Congress Control Number: 2020902599
Available at www.umbethink.com